THE MAYHEM SISTERS

A SISTER WITCHES MYSTERY

LAUREN QUICK

1

G LITTERING STARS FILLED THE VELVETY sky. A spark of uncertainty sailed on the wind, a mood that anything could happen. October was an unpredictable month. The steamy summer had finally died off, and the crisp fall days were piling up like heaps of autumn leaves. The night air was cool in her throat as if Vivian Mayhem had gulped a cold glass of water. She loved nights like this, and any other time would stop to soak up some moonbeams and revel in the ambiance, but after devouring a roast chicken with potatoes, polishing off a bottle of red wine, and having a marathon chat-fest with her sister, she was ready to curl up in her comfy bed and sleep like the dead.

Her feet were quick on the well-worn path that led from Clover's house to the closest portal gate. Traveling in the modern witching world of Everland would have been simple if Vivi were a natural-born flyer like her other sister Honora. If she were in town, she could hop on the Silver Train that zipped across the land, connecting Stargazer City to the multitude of villages and hamlets, but Clover lived out in the Meadowlands, a far cry from the bustling city, and the fastest way to Vivi's village of Willow Realm was by the lone portal gate near her sister's house.

The closer Vivi got to the portal, the more her nose twitched. There was a thick, heady scent in the air that made her cautious. She wrapped her favorite knit sweater coat tighter around her middle to ward off the chill and quickened her pace. Relief washed over her when the huge centuries-old oak came into view, the portal gate, a rounded door with a thick frame, carved into its knobby side.

Vivi was only a few yards away when she heard a twig snap. Leaves rustled. The light of the moon cast the path in misshapen shadows. Orbs of illuma light were stationed a few feet apart to keep travelers from falling on their faces, but not much else. Her senses went on high alert. The hairs on the back of her neck prickled. Someone was lurking in the woods just outside of her sight.

Vivi scanned the dark forest. She held up her right hand, focusing an antique ring with a chunk of moonstone embedded in the silver setting toward the woods. She whispered, "Illuminus." The enchanted stone burst to life and a halo of white light brightened her surroundings.

A lone woman dressed in a frayed black gown glided out of the forest and across the path like a shadow startled to life. Her gaunt frame was as skeletal as the tree limbs. Long black hair trailed down her back in curly tangles. Her skin was milky pale, her cheeks hollow. Bare feet poked out of the bottom of her dress. Vivi sucked in a gasp of recognition, for she knew the woman from her childhood. She hadn't seen her for years, not since high school. Esmeralda had been a beautiful, vibrant, and powerful witch once, the envy of all, but now she looked withered.

Everland was brimming with magic. All witches had some degree of magical potential. During their Haven Academy days, young witches and wizards learned the fundamentals of spellcasting, potions, charms, earth magic, and wandwork. But what really made a witch special was her *persuasion*—the magical power she was born with.

Esmeralda was no exception. Unfortunately, she had been born with a difficult *persuasion*, causing her to practically disappear from the witching community. She was a seer, and her intuitive powers of premonition were unmatched in the witching world. However, the *persuasion* forced her to live with one foot in the present and one in the future. Most witches with the seer's eye went mad, losing themselves in the visions that cluttered their minds, becoming outcasts, unable to maintain productive, stable lives.

She didn't look hurt, so Vivi wondered what she was doing all the way out here, wandering the woods alone late at night. Her brow pinched suddenly at a sharp pain. Her headaches were back in full force. She needed to navigate around the witch and make a quick getaway through the portal gate without disturbing her.

Esmeralda stopped on the path, blocking her way.

Vivi jerked back. The last thing she wanted was a confrontation with the seer. She pulled her golden portal key from the chain around her neck and clenched it in her hand like a talisman. Just a few steps and she would be home free.

Esmeralda muttered to herself, shoulders rocking back and forth, completely oblivious to Vivi's presence. Her gaze was far off, watching another time play out. Was that what *seeing* looked like? The witch was totally out of it. Esmeralda stirred strange feelings in her—pity laced with fear.

Approaching as quietly as her leather boots

would allow, Vivi eased by the other witch. Once clear, she felt a well of relief, but it lasted for only a second, as suddenly the crazed witch's wiry fingers snaked out, grabbed her arm, and pulled her backward, away from the portal gate. Vivi gasped and struggled under the older witch's tight grasp. Esmeralda was much stronger than she looked. The witch slipped her bony arm around Vivi's waist, pulling her into an uncomfortable nearness.

"Trouble, sister!" Her cracked lips were inches from Vivi's ear. Her breath was a hot breeze, sending a shiver down her spine. "There's trouble coming. Can't you feel it?"

Vivi recoiled and broke free from the witch's hold. "No! I can't!" Her voice was too harsh, defensive. She rubbed her wrist where the witch had grabbed her.

"Yes, you can." Esmeralda's eyes filled with pity. Lines crisscrossed her soft cheeks. Her teeth were cracked, and dark under-eye circles marred her pale face. "I've seen you."

"You knew me as a child." Vivi took a step backwards, but it did little good. Esmeralda was not about to let her go so easily.

"I've seen you in the future," Esmeralda said. "You have a secret that you're desperate to keep."

Vivi's stomach churned. *How did she know? She's a seer, that's how.* "Don't we all?" Vivi asked, trying to make light of the situation.

She wasn't in the mood for fortune-telling.

"I've seen terrible events on the horizon of time," the witch continued. "You'll see them, too. You'll try to save her, but *he* is stronger than anyone realizes. I've seen you caught in a witch's snare." She winced, the word a burr on her tongue.

"Stop it. This isn't funny." Vivi eyed the portal. She had had enough of bad fortunes. "I don't know what you're talking about, but it's late. I've got to go home." *Time to bolt.* Vivi pushed by the witch on the path.

But Esmeralda wasn't finished. "You'll see into the darkness and all will be clear. You'll feel it on your skin, in your heart, in your mind." The witch's strange words trailed behind her.

Vivi swallowed hard and made a beeline for the portal. The pain between her brows sharpened into a tiny dagger, causing her to grit her teeth. Damn headache.

Esmeralda continued with a throaty laugh. "You know all about trouble. You're a Mayhem sister."

The statement stopped Vivi in her tracks.

Thanks to her great-great-grandmother Rosemary's feud with a disreputable trader of witches' familiars, she had grown up as a Mayhem. Rosemary had freed the animals from the terrible conditions on the trader's farm and turned him into the police. The animals were safe, but before the trader was sent to prison, he laid a curse on Rosemary and her descendants—a curse of mayhem—and it had meant pure trouble for generations.

Rosemary had wanted to give the trader less satisfaction from his black magic, so she took the curse as her name to claim it, forcing the majority of the mayhem on herself in hopes that life would grow easier for her descendants. The curse lessened with each generation, but Vivi and her sisters always knew that mayhem was just a whisper away.

"Yes, I'm a Mayhem sister," Vivi said. Why had this broken witch crossed her path? Esmeralda was a reminder of everything Vivi was trying to hide, push down inside of herself. Seeing the future was the real curse, one she refused to acknowledge. "What do you want from me?"

Esmeralda's face filled with concern. "Nothing. I follow the visions to wherever they lead me, and tonight I came here. It was you, Mayhem sister, who crossed my path."

"You're alone in the woods in the middle of the night because people avoid you." The words stung, but she couldn't help it. "They fear the things you tell them."

"Just remember to follow the visions wherever they take you."

A knot twisted in Vivi's stomach. It was as if Esmeralda could see right through her, knew her secrets, recognized her lies. She sniffed the air and grimaced. The wind had turned.

"You smell it, too," she said. "There's blood in the air."

Vivi's nerves were shot. She was done listening to ramblings. The bark of the old oak tree was rough and sturdy beneath her fingertips. A cold metal plate was embedded in the side of the wooden door. Vivi slipped her key inside the lock and gave it a quick turn. A warm glow lit up the side of the tree, transforming the portal gate into a swirling surface. She closed her eyes and let the warmth of the magic wash over her. Within seconds she would be back in her village and close to home.

Before walking through the portal, Vivi gave one last glance over her shoulder.

Esmeralda held up her hand in goodbye. "You'll see."

"Willow Realm," Vivi said into the oak's magical surface and stepped through, but she couldn't help but twitch her nose. She had smelled it, too. Blood was in the air. Trouble was not far behind, but what had she expected from October? Unpredictable as ever, her luck could go either way.

2

A GLOSSY BLACK RAVEN TAPPED ON the glass of Vivi's bedroom window with his sharp beak. He peered into her room like an avian voyeur, eyeing her disapprovingly as she lay sprawled in a tangle of blankets. He had been out all night, perched in the tree outside of her window, standing guard like an armored sentry. Vivi pitied anyone who tried to break into her shop, or the apartment above it where she lived, when Rumor was on duty.

Every witch and wizard had at least one familiar during his or her life, forming a close bond, an intuitive understanding, and providing companionship. Rumor had been her familiar for years, and he always knew when she wasn't feeling like herself. Out on the ledge, he puffed up his feathers and gave them a ruffled shake, doing his little raven shimmy. A smile bloomed across Vivi's face. Cheering up a bad mood was Rumor's specialty. She couldn't get anything by him. Besides her sisters, that bird was her best friend.

Vivi stared at the ceiling for a few seconds, realizing that she couldn't snuggle in bed all day. Time to get to work. She threw back the covers, slid into a pair of fuzzy slippers, and opened the window. With an extension of his black wings, Rumor launched himself into the room and found his perch of elaborately carved wood in the corner. He gave a squawk of greeting and nodded his beak up and down, giving her the once-over.

"I know," Vivi said, the dull throb in her head still there. "I feel as bad as I must look."

After her run-in with Esmeralda last night, Vivi had barely slept. She'd tossed and turned all night, her dreams crowded with shadows and voices. Seeing the witch had dredged up old feelings that she was trying to ignore. Vivi had been doing a superb job of living in denial for years now, and she wasn't going to let Esmeralda and her visions spook her into questioning her judgment on how to live her life. Her feet were firmly planted in the present. The future could wait its turn.

Wanting to get moving with her day, she peeled out of her pajamas and took a quick shower. Next, she slid on a pair of worn jeans and a loose peasant top, draped some strands of beads over her neck, pulled a row of silver bangles up her wrist, tapped powder on her nose and a sweep of blush across her cheeks to finish the "alive and well" look, and she was ready to go.

One of the best things about owning her own shop was that she didn't have to dress up in ankle-breaking high heels or stuffy business suits. She brewed a cup of fragrant black tea in a ceramic mug and gingerly carried it out the door. Work had always been the cure to her woes, her refuge in life, and she headed down the back stairs of her apartment to her shop, her euphoria, The Potion Garden.

Vivi unlocked the back door, whispered the basic spell to unlock the security ward, and stepped inside. Every time she opened the door, her heart leapt a little when she inhaled the exotic fragrance of herbs and spices that formed the base for her potions. She had launched the shop three years ago, and it had been growing ever since, making her feel both giddy and secure. She loved every little glass vial and corked bottle brimming with magic. It was her home base.

By trade Vivi was a potion master, a brewer of elixirs, and a conjurer of the kettle, but she had a secret—a true *persuasion* that she pushed deep down inside her, and *that* magic was beginning to stir, whether she liked it or not.

As far as the Mayhem witches went, Vivian was the middle sister. She always felt a little like she was occupying the space between two extremes. She wasn't strong and powerful, driven to solve twisted mysteries like her private investigator baby sister, Honora, nor was she voluptuous and curvy, a creative wunderkind weaving magical stories for adoring fans like her older sister, Clover. She always thought of herself as the sensible sister—the rock of the family. But when she stepped into her shop, she stepped into a special place that defined her—a growing, glittery business she had brewed up with an old copper pot and a little magic.

Everland was a haven for witches. A thousand years ago, the Witch Council was formed when witches rose out of earth's dark ages, banded together in a coven of one, and created a parallel world exclusively for themselves. Many fabled creatures existed outside of the witching world and lived in the Otherworld: fairies, nymphs, sprites, and creatures of night and shadows like vampires, ghouls, goblins, and werewolves, not to mention the magical beasts of the forest, desert, air, and sea. There were also the humans.

At one time the witches coexisted with the others, crossing over the barrier, learning and developing, as the Otherworld did, but not anymore. It was too dangerous. Many humans had accepted, even welcomed, magical ways, but most were suspicious of things they couldn't explain. So witches chose a world of their own kind, mostly to avoid being burned at the stake or hung by the neck, self-preservation being highly valued.

Vivi inhaled the rich scents that mingled in the air. The shop was stocked with beautiful hand-blown glass bottles filled with potions and elixirs. Potions for headaches and heartaches sat next to potions for laughter and levitation. Bath salts sat on a shelf next to circle-casting salt. A discerning witch could find a potion for more wrinkles or fewer wrinkles, depending on whom she wanted to impress, or a potion for a mood mender and daily happiness drops. Vivi could whip up a potion to cure the driest of skin or rekindle the stalest of romances. She brewed balms for chapped lips and sore souls. An elixir could cause a spark or soothe an ache, depending on how she made the magic work.

The best thing for business was that potions weren't permanent. They were a quick fix, a burst of magic. Love potions never lasted long and crow's feet always came marching back.

Vivi scanned her daily to-do list. She pulled the cash box out from the safe in the back room and slipped it under the front counter. Though bartering still happened, gold was the currency of Everland. She unlocked the box and fingered a few dozen coins. In Willow Realm, her customers still tended to use real gold, but wanting to stay on the cutting edge, she had invested in a shiny, new card reader, since the gold card was becoming more and more popular for modern witches who didn't want to lug around a bag of gold in their purses.

After setting out a stack of blank receipts and refilling the stock, Vivi decided to brew a new potion to raise her spirits, maybe one for wishful thinking or a pleasant surprise. She kicked off her shoes and wiggled her toes on the hard pine floor in the back room of her shop. Some witches tucked their wands behind their ears when they worked, but not Vivi. She tended to stick sprigs of rosemary or stalks of larkspur behind her ear or in her hair. Within a few minutes of brainstorming, she had so many pieces of dried flowers poking out of her mass of pinned-up hair that it felt like a bird had taken roost.

Concocting was one of Vivi's favorite things to do, brewing up new formulas to sell to her ever-demanding clients. She quickly fell into a rhythm of chopping herbs and adding flower essences to the brew bubbling in a giant copper cauldron. With a wooden spoon, she stirred the thickening mixture as steam rose off the surface like fog on a cold lake.

She leaned over the pot, a loose strand of her curly brown hair falling across her forehead as warm air drifted over her face. *Best steamy facial ever,* she thought.

The jingle of the doorbell caught her attention.

Vivi's spunky young assistant, Pepper Rue, bounced through the door, her auburn bobbed hair swinging. She wore a pair of funky green glasses perched on the tip of her pert nose and hurried into the back room from the front of the shop.

"Hey, boss." Pepper stuffed her gigantic leather satchel under the counter. "Did you have fun at Clover's house last night?" With her lithe frame, she easily hopped up onto the smooth wooden work surface to have a morning chat. She was in her mid-twenties and had graduated from Haven Academy at the top of her class.

"It was fine," Vivi said, not showing any expression or emotion. She didn't want to talk about what happened with Esmeralda, and she knew what Pepper *really* wanted to talk about. "Nothing exciting."

Vivi was driving Pepper crazy by withholding details of her dinner date with her sister. Clover was a word witch, her *persuasion* being storytelling, and she wrote the hottest magical romance novels in Everland's history. "*Spellbinders*" was a phenomenal bestselling series, filled with steamy love-laced magical romps that were highly addictive. The only caveat was that Clover wrote under the pseudonym of Cassandra Reason, and only a handful of witches knew her real identity and what she did for a living, Vivi's details-hungry assistant being one of them.

Feigning concentration, Vivi hummed and stared intently into the pot.

"Oh, please! Spill it, you sinister witch." Pepper jumped off the counter and fell to her knees. "I'm begging."

"Spill what?" Vivi tried to hide a smile. "You mean the sordid details of the fantastic new book?" Her eyes rolled back. "It's sooooo good. You won't believe what happens. It's hot and has a ton of surprises you won't see coming."

Pepper dramatically clutched at her boss's leg. "Does Adeline lose her power? Does Jacob still love her, even though her family shunned her? Please, I can't take waiting." Her voice rose to a high-pitched squeal.

"My lips are sealed." Vivi turned down the heat under the pot to let the mixture simmer.

Pepper's shoulders slumped as she got to her feet. "I'll work every Friday and Saturday until the winter solstice. Just a little hint," she pleaded.

"No, really, my lips are sealed. Clover made me drink one of my own secret-keeping potions so I wouldn't be strong-armed by any crazy *Spellbinder* fans, namely *you*, into spilling her plot before the launch tomorrow." Vivi shrugged. "You'll have to wait."

"That's pretty clever, actually." Pepper tied an embroidered apron around her waist. In a moment of sheer dedication, she had sewn the shop's logo of snaking vines and flowers onto the crisp green fabric.

"I can tell you that the book will drive you wild. It's the best one yet." Vivi's eyes widened. She was proud of her big sister.

Pepper gave a little clap of her hands in joyful anticipation. "Waiting's all part of the fun. Your sister really knows how to punch up the anticipation," she said and then nosed over the pot, inhaling the scent. "Whatcha making?"

"Just a little wishful thinking," Vivi said. "I wanted to create a potion that grants one simple wish. Nothing crazy, like the man of your dreams or a giant sack of gold or anything over the top—just a little wish, like a sale on shoes, or a tasting of hot baked scones at Nocturnes."

"Sounds fun." Pepper headed up front to open the shop for the day. "I would wish for a ton of happy customers."

Vivi smiled. Pepper was the best assistant she could ever want. Her positive attitude was infectious. She discovered early on that Pepper's *persuasion* was in potions, and no matter how hard Vivi tried, she never came close to her assistant in whipping up the perfect brew.

A tiny spark crackled on Vivi's fingertips when she reached for the lavender. She crushed the purple buds in her hands, and suddenly something tripped a switch in her brain, sending a jolt of pain through her temples. Stupid headaches. She swayed on her feet and grabbed the counter for support. It wasn't just a headache that was forcing its way into her mind's eye, and she knew it.

The vision overwhelmed her thoughts. It was much stronger than the flashes of images she had seen and repressed in the past. Maybe it was the perfume of the crushed flower, the smell triggering the sight. Vivi sunk down to the floor, her feet sliding out from under her. The feeling was sharp, as if a giant hook pierced her stomach and pulled her right out of her shop and into an ethereal future world.

"Everything okay in there?" Pepper asked, but Vivi wasn't listening.

Shrouded in misty fog, the Dire Woods—the infamous blackened forest—refuge to dark sorcerers and their ilk, surrounded her on all sides. She tried to tell herself that it wasn't real, that she was back in her warm shop, safe and sound, but the cold air clung to her arms and legs, sending a cascade of shivers through her. She was far from safe and sound.

No one went to the Dire Woods unless desperate or dragged. The woods permeated with the stench of black magic—brimstone, sulfur, rotten eggs, and burning wood, the dregs of dark sorcery. The sound of scurrying claws clutching the bark of trees filled the air. Vivi spun in circles, her eyes wide, searching the dense black forest for lurking predators, because suddenly, even in the ethereal vision, she felt like prey.

Tangled wiry branches snagged her top. Fear pulsed through her as Vivi stumbled backwards into the rough trunk of a tree. Her bare feet scrambled on the cold hard ground when she tried to push away from the bark. She was trapped. There was no way out of the vision. All she could do was watch, a witness to a strange scene playing out in front of her. Vivi realized with a flash of relief that she was hidden in plain sight from danger. She slowed her breathing, and her nerves calmed.

A rustling noise echoed in the distance. Someone was coming. She crouched down. A wizard dressed entirely in black burst through the underbrush, forcing a path through the woods. His panic flowed out of him and into her with a jolt of emotion. The visions were brutal that way, giving her more information than she could ever want. Deception flowed from him, and Vivi knew instinctively he was on the run, trying to hide, to escape. He had stolen something, but what, she couldn't tell. His long black coat slapped at the trees as he circled the small clearing. He reeked of smoke and carried a black sack thrown over his shoulder that weighed heavily on him, causing Vivi's shoulder to ache.

Something moved inside, wiggling under the fabric. It cried, a pitiful whimpering. He set the bag down on the ground with a thud and another whimper escaped from beneath the thin fabric, but this time the sound was a sharp cry of pain and fear. He picked at the knotted closure with his ragged and blackened fingertips that looked like they had been dipped in ink or ash.

What rotten wizardry had he been practicing?

Vivi had grown up hearing the tales of witches and wizards who had gone bad. Their teeth rotted and their fingertips split and blistered from the rancid deeds of black magic. Did a horrid creature lay trapped under the cloth?

The form moved, shifting Vivi's attention. The bag was much larger than she had originally realized. The knot loosened and the fabric pooled open to reveal the contents. Huddled on the ground, wearing a thin blouse and skirt, frail as a butterfly caught in a net, was a young witch.

The wizard had kidnapped a witch.

Her make-up was smeared, her face streaked with grime. Her bottom lip was split and wet with berry-red blood. Her eyes were moist wide pools, overflowing with tears. "Please, don't hurt me," she pleaded.

Too late, Vivi thought.

Her attention jerked toward the wizard. She wanted to get a good look at him, but even though she was so close, she could barely see him, his features blurring in and out of focus, his face obscured by his collar and a hood.

He laughed and circled the shivering witch. "You are my greatest prize." His voice was thick and deep. He grabbed her hair and pulled her close. "I will never let you go." The wizard projected a cold void of emotion. A sickening sense of power surged through Vivi's body.

Panic and tears welled in the young witch's desperate green eyes. She gasped, struggling to get away from him. "Help me! Please, someone, please! I don't want to die!" But, besides the dark wizard, Vivi was the only one to hear.

The vision began to shift and melt away. Vivi screamed, "No!" trying to hold on to the scene with her mind, not wanting to lose the witch. She charged forward, pushing herself between the wizard and the young witch, ready to fight, scratch, and claw, but they were gone.

The woods faded into the background, the vision changed, and the girl re-emerged.

This time she was being held in a cramped, dark place, but exactly where, Vivi couldn't tell. Her delicate clothes were torn and dirty, and her long strawberry blonde hair hung in greasy hanks, as if she hadn't bathed in weeks. Her bare arms were covered in scratches from the thorn bushes and prickly brambles that thrived in the Dire Woods. The skin on her wrists was raw and broken. She was trembling so hard that Vivi grabbed her own arms to still the shaking.

He was there, too, skimming the shadows. Vivi narrowed her eyes and focused all her attention on him; a sharp pain seared her mind, but she kept watching as if peering through a keyhole into his dark world. He had a purpose for the young witch. A deep voice of knowing told her that he had kidnapped her, kept her hidden, and was using her in magical experiments.

The wizard pulled three pouches from the folds of his coat and approached the trembling girl to prepare for the ritual. From one, he poured red salt in a circle around her. A staple of the black magic spell box, red salt, also called blood salt, was made from salted blood. From the next pouch, he poured black ash. Vivi's heart raced. Black ash had been brought from the Otherworld and the times of witch burnings. The ash was collected from the burned bodies and the stakes the witches were bound to when lit on fire. It was also collected from the hanging trees that were burned down after the bodies were taken and buried at a crossroad. It, too, was a powerful tool used in conjuring dark forces. The last pouch was filled with broken things—shards of glass, shattered bits of bone, and chipped teeth. Vivi's stomach rolled over. *He's going to kill her.*

Vivi could barely watch, but the reek of burning ash filled her nose. The magic pierced her skin like a hot needle pricking, pulling burning blackness through the thread of her soul. The witch's eyes had gone vacant like a doll face with black buttons sewed on, as if the fear had drained her of fight. He was erasing the best part of her, and Vivi didn't know how to make it stop.

She tried to scream. A hot tear slid down her cheek. *This can't be happening. The visions aren't real. Please let this be a mistake.* But she knew it wasn't. She had been lying to herself for a long time now, pretending to be something she wasn't, and now she couldn't turn away.

The dark wizard advanced from the shadows with a wand of twisted black walnut clutched in his hand, a wicked spell pouring from his lips. Every witch knew defensive spells as well as some basic fighting magic taught for protection, but the young witch just shrunk as his figure towered over her and whispered wickedness that knocked the wind out of her, leaving her gasping on the ground. Her green eyes rolled back in her head, and that was when Vivi realized that the witch had nothing left to fight with. Her magic had been drained. She twitched uncontrollably, collapsing in a heap.

Vivi could barely hold on to the scene. The edges of the vision shrank. The witch was slipping from her mental grasp. She focused all her attention on the sight. She was losing her. "No! Wait!" Vivi tasted blood in her mouth. Her eyes burned. The smell of ash and brimstone choked her nose and throat.

The vision changed again. The woods were still. The wizard was gone. Vivi stood in a clearing. Ahead of her in the woods, she saw a familiar face.

Sheriff Gardener was standing over the witch's body, a magical crime scene ward glowing red, illuminating the woods where her body had been discarded like a paper cup. It was too late. She was dead. That was her fate. But the future was not carved in stone or made of soot and ash. It was yet to be lived. The future was a thing made of potential and purpose. Vivi clung to the hope that the future could be changed.

3

VIVI WOKE DRENCHED IN SWEAT. As the fog of the vision lifted, she realized she was lying legs sprawled, body limp, on the floor of the back room. Pepper, with a look of concern on her face, pressed a wet washcloth to her forehead. Vivi leaned up and grabbed her pounding head while trying to regain an ounce of self-respect and process what had just happened. Her assistant leapt into action, quickly uncorked a tiny potion bottle and poured the contents down her throat. One of their most popular revival potions, the minty lemongrass mixture went to work within seconds, warming her body and refreshing her mind. Her headache receded.

Vivi eased to her feet.

"Take it slow. Here, sit down." Pepper guided her to the table and chairs they'd arranged in the back room for a quiet place to sit and eat lunch.

"I'm sorry." Embarrassment mixed with anguish washed over her. She rested her head in her hands. "I must have fainted."

"Fainted?" Pepper released a long exasperated sigh. She brushed a sweaty clump of hair out of Vivi's face. "I've known you for three years, since you opened the shop, right?"

She placed a hand on Pepper's arm. "Since *we* opened the shop."

"Then why do you keep hiding the truth from me? I thought we were friends."

"We're more than friends. We're family." But the truth was, Vivi didn't want anyone to know. She suspected that Honora and Clover had their suspicions, but they never said anything, waiting for her to confess, she guessed, but Vivi never did.

"I know about the visions." Pepper stared Vivi in the eye. "I know about your *persuasion*."

The words hung in the air between them. Her secret was finally out.

"How'd you know?"

"Little things. Once, I saw you up front when no one was around and you got a far off gaze on your face and suddenly your body jerked and you grabbed your head in your hands. Plus, you knew about the birthday surprise I arranged last year. When I took you to a play in Stargazer City. You weren't *really* shocked, even though the show had been sold out for months." Pepper shrugged. "You take more headache potions than any witch I've ever met. I figured something serious was up, so I did a little digging."

"You're right about my birthday. I'd seen a flash of us sitting in the dark, staring at a stage. I tried to pretend I didn't know. I guess I'm a bad actress." Vivi blinked back tears.

"Why are you fighting your gift?" Pepper asked, pulling up a chair and sitting next to her. Her voice was soft as down.

"Because it isn't a gift. It'll ruin my life, everything I've built."

"You'll always have the shop. That won't change."

"Pepper, don't be naïve. You know what happens to seers. They start to go a little loopy and end up shunned and isolated. I don't want to be alone." Vivi's voice caught in her throat. The raw memory of the kidnapped witch's anguish twisted her gut. How could she be so selfish? How could she turn away when the witch she had seen in her vision was in so much pain?

"Seeing is one of the most powerful *persuasions*." Pepper snorted. "I should've known you weren't just a potion maker. Mayhem sisters have some serious power. You can't deny that."

"Can't I? I've been doing a good job of it for years." Vivi had been hiding her visions since she was a teenager, too afraid to admit to possessing the powerful gift. She'd always seen harmless events, even happy flashes—a wedding bouquet flying through the air, a baby wiggling in his mother's arms, a necklace under shiny wrapping paper. She thought she could keep these flashes to herself, even repress them. But now this dark vision had come, and it had brought pain and fear with it, shattering her plan to keep her power a secret.

"*Persuasions* can't be denied. Look what just happened to you. And I doubt this was the first time." Pepper gave her a narrow glance.

In the past, whenever a strong vision had tried to emerge, she pushed the images deep inside her brain, and for a long time it had worked. The snippets of future events became fewer and far between, but lately the headaches had come, and her ability to repress her sight was ending. Pepper was right. Vivi had tried to fight her *persuasion,* but the visions returned, stronger and stronger as if trying to be born from her, fighting to be seen.

"I guess I can't even have one secret from you," Vivi said.

"Well, we do have a potion for keeping a secret, but it doesn't last that long. Secrets are powerful. They're hard to keep hidden, even by the toughest witches."

"I don't want anyone to know. I want things to stay the same." Even as she said the words, Vivi knew that things would never be the same again, especially after what she had seen. She couldn't ignore the young witch and her desperate plea.

The time for pretending was over.

"Oh, honey. It'll be okay. I'm here and so are your sisters." Pepper threw her thin arms around Vivi's shoulders in a light hug.

"Pepper, it was really bad. It was like no other vision I've ever had." Vivi swallowed hard. She shook her head.

"Do you want to talk about it?"

If she opened up now, there was no turning back. Her biggest fear was coming true. Her real *persuasion* made people cross the street when they saw a witch with the terrible gift. Maybe this was part of the Mayhem curse, her fate—to be shunned, avoided, and whispered about.

If she didn't face it, things would only get worse.

Vivi had no choice. She had to report the crime. The young witch was in serious trouble, and if someone didn't help her, she would be dead soon. She told Pepper everything she could remember about the vision, the images and senses pouring out of her, and a huge weight lifted from her shoulders when she was done.

"What are you going to do now?" Pepper asked.

"The only thing I can. Pay a visit to Sheriff Gardener. I'm going to report what I saw and get help for that witch."

Before leaving the shop, Vivi dug around on the shelves in the back room and found a small blank notebook with a smooth felt cover she had bought for jotting down potion recipes, and she transcribed the details from her vision, leaving nothing out. No image or sense was too small, no matter how uncertain she was about the way they all connected, and then she was ready.

The village of Willow Realm held onto many traditional magical practices and was a special place to live. The town was the perfect size, not too big or too small. It had one police station and one sheriff with a slew of deputies to keep the witches and wizards of the realm safe. Walking into the police station was one of the hardest things she had done in her entire life. Vivi steeled her nerves and pushed open the front door. The vestibule hummed with the energy of protective magical wards that were both intimidating and reassuring.

Her mouth was dry as dust when she approached the receptionist's desk. Honey Hardburn had worked for the sheriff for about three hundred years, give or take, and since witches lived for over five hundred years, she was still spry. A pair of cat's eye glasses sat perched on her sharp nose. Her jet-black hair was piled on top of her head in the largest beehive hairstyle Vivi had ever seen.

"Sign in," Honey said, pushing a thick ledger across the desk. "What do you want?" She wasn't one for small talk.

"I need to speak with the sheriff," Vivi said, dipping a quill into a bottle of ink and scratching her name across the creamy parchment.

"About what?" Honey tapped her pointy enameled fingernails on the desk. *She must sharpen those talons nightly*, Vivi thought.

Vivi lowered her voice. "It's business."

"Something happen at your shop?" Honey pried. "Someone steal one of those pretty potions? You put them in such nice little bottles. I wouldn't be surprised."

"No, nothing like that." Vivi unzipped her handbag.

"If I were going to steal a potion from your shop, it would be something good like that potion that makes your hair sparkle." She patted the side of her towering do. "I think I would look good with a hint of magenta. Don't you think?" Her eyes gleamed hopefully.

"Yes, pink does suit your complexion, but lapis lazuli is all the rage." Vivi pulled a glittery blue bottle out of her handbag and set it on the desk. She knew that Honey loved any and all potions that altered her appearance, especially her pride and joy hair. The receptionist was very experimental, and Vivi had come prepared.

Honey's eyes widened and she slipped the tiny bottle into her desk drawer. "You really are my favorite Mayhem sister. Not bossy like the flyer or aloof like the other one. I'll send a finch back to his office right away to let Sheriff Gardener know he has an appointment."

A giant gilded cage, filled with the tiny chirping birds, sat next to her desk. Honey flicked open the gate with one of her long nails and released a fluttering finch into the room. It hovered for a moment as the receptionist whispered instructions, and then flew off, expertly navigating the many hallways.

Vivi paced for a few minutes before sitting on a hard wooden bench, waiting for her chance to speak with the sheriff. *Persuasions* came in all types. Some were service- oriented, like law enforcement, and were considered trade *persuasions*. As the sheriff, Lance Gardener's name suited him perfectly. He was a straight arrow, honest to a fault, and he tended to Willow Realm with the heart and soul of a gardener nurturing his precious plants. A *persuasion* like Sheriff Gardener's gave him an overwhelming need to seek justice, to protect and to serve, and he had been taking care of their little nook of the witching world for the past ten years.

The sheriff often passed by Vivi's shop on his way to grab a cup of coffee at Nocturnes, and she couldn't help but stop whatever she was doing and watch him amble by. He had broad shoulders and wore a simple yet beautiful cherry wood wand secured to his belt loop as the only weapon against crime. Never rushing or raising his voice, he was a pool of calm, and was always around when anyone needed him. She was counting on that now.

Finally, Juniper White, one of the sheriff's deputies, appeared in the waiting area, pulling Vivi out of her head, reminding her why she had come. She tucked a strand of her short blond hair behind her ear as she approached. Technically, Juniper was an assistant deputy, but her work ethic and dedication were legendary around town.

"Come on back, Vivi."

The Willow Realm Police Station was a labyrinth of oddly shaped rooms, twisted staircases, and angled hallways, which helped to break up any unexpected onslaught of attack magic, and the station was prepared for the worst. Vivi couldn't decide if it was paranoia or precaution. The witching world had experienced troubled times marred with dark sorcery that left a bloody scar across its history, but that was in the past. Wasn't it?

Vivi never thought anything bad would happen in her village, but times changed, sometimes for the better and sometimes for the worse.

Juniper led Vivi into a square interview room with a circular wooden table in the center. Engraved in the wood grain surface was the Witch Council motto: *The blood of our sisters and brothers binds us as a coven of one.* Vivi took a deep breath and thought about what the motto meant. The Witch Council had been established after the witches and wizards decided to leave the Otherworld behind and form Everland. It had been a tumultuous time and the idea of the coven of one stood for strength and unity. No witch or wizard was ever alone. Vivi was among her kind. They would help her.

Sheriff Gardener stepped into the room and shut the door. He had wavy blond hair, and his strong jaw was smooth as a baby's bottom, without a hint of stubble. He was even more handsome now than he was back at Haven Academy, where they had been in the same class. She flushed at a memory of the crush she had on him back when they stole glances of each other between classes. She could have sworn she caught a flash of excitement in his golden-brown eyes when he saw her, too.

"Good to see you." He shook her hand, holding it tightly for a moment. His eyes locked with hers, a smile turning up one corner of his mouth.

"You, too." In the years since high school, Vivi had often caught herself daydreaming about the two of them reconnecting, enjoying a romantic dinner, walking hand in hand through the park, followed by a long warm embrace. Never, though, had she imagined their reunion would be in the police station and under terrible circumstances.

"I hear this isn't a social call, so let's get down to business. Juniper will be recording your visit and taking some notes for the record." He pulled out a chair for her to sit and then joined her on the opposite side of the table.

Juniper straightened a stack of parchment and held a thin reed pen on the table in front of her.

"The record," Vivi said. There was no tension in the room, but there was an air of official business.

"I like to go by the book. It's a bit formal, but keeps things in order. Less mistakes that way. I see you brought some notes. That's a good sign." He reached over and tapped the cover of her journal in a casual way.

"Formal," Vivi repeated. A lump caught in her throat. She sounded like a parrot. Formal was not the way she wanted to go. She was hoping to do a quick drop-off of information and put the sheriff into motion, get him to investigate the witch, make sure she was all right, so she could stop having visions about her.

The sheriff smiled. "I like to follow protocol. Record all complaints officially."

Vivi's pulse quickened. The last thing she wanted was to be recorded, officially or otherwise. "Well, you see, Sheriff, I was hoping to keep this matter as quiet as possible. I'm here to do my duty and hopefully help a witch in trouble."

"Really?" His eyebrow raised, his curiosity piqued. "Why don't you tell me everything and we'll go from there?"

"I saw something," Vivi began. *Just tell the truth*, she thought.

Growing up had been rough. Not many kids wanted to be friends with a witch with the last name of Mayhem, but Lance had always been kind to her and her sisters, never taunted or ridiculed or shied away, but treated them like they were just like everyone else. If anyone would believe her, it would be Lance.

"You witnessed a crime?" he asked. Concern welled in his golden-brown eyes.

"Yes. Well, no. I mean, yes." Vivi stumbled on her words.

"Don't be nervous." He reached out and

put a warm steady hand on her arm. There was something magical and reassuring in the gesture, a strong kindness.

Vivi began again. "I witnessed a kidnapping. A young witch taken by a dark wizard. She's in terrible danger." Her words came out quick and sharp. "You have to help her."

Juniper glanced up from her notes.

"Slow down and tell me everything you saw," Sheriff Gardener said.

"He carried her in a sack through the Dire Woods. I don't know exactly where he's holding her now. I just know he's going to hurt her." Vivi touched her forehead as the memory of the vision flooded back. "I felt it. She's weakening, and she's so cold and alone." Vivi felt clammy as if the room had grown hotter, and the sheriff must have sensed it.

"Keep going. You're doing fine," he said, encouragingly.

"She's in a tight dark space. It's cold and dank." She rubbed her arms without thinking. "The sorcerer's performing terrible magic. I don't know what he's using her for, but it's the blackest magic I've ever sensed. You must hurry, before it's too late."

"Too late?" The sheriff's strong gaze held her steady.

"I think he's going to kill her." Vivi swallowed. She didn't want to tell him that she also saw him standing over the witch's dead body in the woods. Not yet.

Juniper let out a small gasp.

"Keep writing," he said to her. Juniper's pen flicked fast across the page.

"Can you identify him? Tell me everything you can about these two."

Vivi continued, "He was wearing a hood. It was too blurry to see his face." Her brow furrowed in concentration. She focused her attention on the grain in the wood table and tried to recall exactly what she had seen, hoping any detail would help with the investigation. "It kept shifting. I couldn't see where he was holding her." She let out an exasperated sigh.

"Wait, I thought you said the girl was in the Dire Woods?" The sheriff propped his chin in his hand, a slight frown forming on his face.

"She was at first. That was where he went after he captured her. I just don't know where he took her. It's not a big help, but I think he's keeping her in a tight cold space. You should check out the woods first, maybe look for caves or abandoned tunnels or an old well." Vivi thumbed the pages of her journal, scanning her notes while trying to gage their reactions.

Juniper stopped writing. She and the sheriff exchanged a widened look of disbelief, coupled with a barely disguised eye-roll on Juniper's part. He tilted his head and readdressed Vivi with a kinder tone.

"When exactly did this happen?" His brow arched inquisitively, and under other circumstances she would have considered it sexy, but now she was in the uncomfortable position of having to reveal parts of herself to him that she hadn't even faced herself.

"That's the thing that I wanted to keep just between us."

"You can tell us in full confidence." He gave Juniper a narrowed glance, and she nodded. "Nothing leaves this room."

"I saw it happen this morning, but I can't tell you exactly when she was taken or where. I believe she's already been kidnapped, but is still alive. That's why we have to hurry." Vivi watched Sheriff Gardener's face for a hint of expression. A muscle flinched in his neck. His jaw tensed.

"Are you saying what I think you're saying?" he asked.

"Well, um, if you think I had a premonition, then yes." Premonitions were not as strong as visions; in fact, most witches got premonitions all the time, but Vivi wasn't ready to totally come clean, even with the sheriff.

"Vivi, this sounds a lot more complicated than a premonition." He sat up straighter in his chair.

"It sounds like a full psychic vision," Juniper blurted out. "Did you have a vision?"

The tone of her question was curious, almost fascinated.

Obviously, Vivi wasn't fooling them with her subtlety. She had expected the sheriff would need a little convincing, but she thought once he heard her story, he would take action, search for the kidnapped witch, and she could fade into the background.

"We should be focusing on who this witch is and what's going to happen if we don't find her. We have to help her. I won't let her die out there alone in the woods." Vivi's attempt to ride the fence on her *persuasion* was shot. Time to admit what little she knew about her magic. "The one thing I know for certain about my visions is that the clearer the image, the closer in time. The scene in the Dire Woods was sharp, almost entirely in focus, which means it either just happened or is about to."

"That's good to know," Juniper said. "Helps with a timeline."

"The consecutive visions became fuzzier, meaning they happened later in time, and they were progressing." She flipped through the pages of her notebook, checking what she had written down, trying to make sense of her *persuasion*.

"Vivian Mayhem." Sheriff Gardener shook his head. His gaze was sympathetic, but his stance was firm. "You aren't a registered prophetic seer. You're not even a clairvoyant that I know of. No one in your family is. So how are you seeing future events all of a sudden?" He gave her a stern, yet slightly bewildered look. "I thought your *persuasion* was potions."

"I know I'm not officially a psychic witch, but you have to help me. I can't walk away from this and pretend it didn't happen." She had to convince him. Lance was her best chance. "Please, I know what I saw."

"Who's this witch? Do you even know her name?" he asked.

"No, but that shouldn't matter. She's a witch. She's one of us." Vivi ran her fingers over the engraved words in the wooden table—*coven of one*. "It's your job to protect our realm. You have to help her."

"I know what my job is, and I also know that at this sheriff's department we only use the word of registered seers, and you're not one of them. I can't go chasing this." He stood. His chair legs scraped against the floor.

"You would risk a witch's life?" she asked. Panic bloomed inside her chest.

"She has a point," Juniper said.

"Am I the only one who realizes that we have no proof the mysterious witch has been kidnapped yet? I understand your concern, but you think you saw something, in what may or may not be a vision." His brow was pinched. "I can't send out a team to check this on your hunch."

Vivi stood too quickly, her chair slamming to the ground. "It's not a hunch. I saw him using blood salt and black ash. I felt her fear and emptiness. I smelled the soot in the air, and the skin on her wrists was broken. He's hurting her, yesterday or now or in an hour." A searing pain shot through her head that made her wince.

"Calm down." He tried to reach out to her, but she pulled back before he could touch her. There was something soothing in his touch, and the last thing she wanted in that moment was to relax. "I want to help you. I do. It just sounds so strange. Perhaps the vision was a bad dream." He slipped his hands in his pockets and rocked back on his heels.

She bit the inside of her cheek. *Bad dream? Try nightmare.* "I guess that's the problem with prophecies. They appear as blurred images with flashes of emotion. I felt another witch's choking fear, but I don't know her name. The black magic terrified me to my core, but I can't identify the wizard casting the spell." Vivi had come this far. She couldn't back down now.

The sheriff took a deep breath and let it out slowly in a controlled exhalation, as if the long exhale gave him pause to think. *Not a good sign,* she thought.

"No rule book or procedure for you to follow either," Vivi said. She grabbed her purse, seeing how this was going.

"Why didn't you tell anyone that you could *see*?" he asked. His voice lost its edge and was more curious than accusatory.

"For the exact reason that you're staring at me right now. You think I'm crazy, or worse, you think I'm wrong. And you know what? I might be. I could be totally wrong, but I have a feeling deep in my bones that I'm not." In the time she had been in the office, Vivi's confidence had grown, or perhaps she just didn't care about appearances anymore.

"I don't know if I can help you, but there might be someone here who can," he said, seeming to relent.

"Thank you." She wondered who he was talking about—a special deputy, maybe.

"Don't thank me yet. In fact, I was a little surprised when I saw you today." The sheriff motioned over his shoulder for Vivi to follow him.

"Why's that?" she asked. They made their way down a hallway that veered to the left. He stood aside, gestured to a small waiting area.

Sitting in a chair, clad in worn leather and flying gear, mud-splattered boots propped up on a desk, was one tough-looking witch. She glanced up, a devilish grin spread across her face. "What are you doing here? Have you been a *bad* little witch?" Her voice was smoky with a cool edge, like a jazz singer's.

Relief flooded over Vivi. Finally, she had caught a break, and had never been happier to see her little sis, Honora. If she had to choose anyone to be by her side in that moment, it would be her no-nonsense, driven sister.

"Two Mayhem Sisters in my office in one day," the sheriff said. "What are the odds?"

"Why do I have the feeling we're going to get really busy really fast?" Juniper asked, striding over to her desk.

4

E VEN THOUGH HONORA WAS THE baby of the three sisters, she was the toughest— lean and mean, the tallest by at least three inches. She had long obsidian-black hair that she wore with blunt bangs and tied in an elaborately woven braid to keep it from tangling when she flew. Her flying goggles, flecked with insects, dangled around her neck. Her jacket was casually thrown over the arm of a chair.

Flying was one of the witching world's most coveted *persuasions*, and her sister was a gifted fly-witch who made her magical talents appear effortless. Honora was physically stronger than other witches, since a flyer's bones and muscles were built to withstand the force of being airborne. They were also mentally tougher, had faster reflexes, and were utterly fearless. Having these qualities often led flyers to take up dangerous occupations, and Honora was no exception, running her own private investigation company.

Vivi's eyes must have been as wide as two full moons.

"You okay?" Honora asked, her boots thudding to the floor as she sat up in her chair upon seeing her sister.

"Not really," Vivi said. "What are you doing all the way out here in Willow Realm? Not exactly your stomping grounds."

Honora lived in the glittery cosmopolitan mecca of Stargazer City and, unless she was visiting her sisters or working a case, rarely ventured this far from her beloved urban domain.

"Got a job. I'm looking for someone."

Goosebumps prickled Vivi's skin. Could they be searching for the same witch? "Is she in her early twenties? Does she have long strawberry-blonde hair? Pretty? Very thin?" the words spilled from Vivi's mouth in a desperate flood.

Worry spread across Honora's face. "No. Vivi, sit down. What's going on? What are you doing in the sheriff's station?"

Vivi sunk into the chair next to her sister. "I saw something," she whispered. "Something really bad. Honora, I had a vision."

Honora closed her eyes for a brief second,

as if gathering her thoughts, and shook her head. "Damn. We should have said something sooner. Clover and I both wondered if there wasn't more to your *persuasion*, but we thought you would tell us when you were ready. I had no idea it was this serious."

"It's not your fault. I should have said something, but I didn't want to deal with it, and now I'm here."

Honora gave her sister a knowing nod. "Well, it must have been pretty bad for you to come to the police. Like, criminal bad." Honora glanced over at Sheriff Gardener. "What are you going to do about this, Sheriff?" she asked.

"Me? I was hoping to hand the problem over to you." He raised his eyebrows and gave them both an affable shrug. "This isn't an official case. Vivian isn't a registered seer. She's a potion maker as far as I'm concerned." He shifted nervously under Honora's penetrating gaze. "A very fine potion maker, I might add."

"Oh, please. Don't give me that." Honora glided over so she was face to face with the sheriff. Dressed in her dark brown leathers, she was almost as tall as he was, with broad shoulders and an athletic build. Imposing was an understatement when it came to Honora. She was strong and smart, and she knew it. Confidence danced off her skin like a spark.

"My sister came to you for help. I'm

guessing she already told you all about her vision. The question now is are you going to help us or not?" Honora had a way of getting right to the point, which she liked to sharpen.

Vivi let out a long breath that she had been holding in her chest. Her sister's determination was infectious. All she needed was for one person to believe her.

"I'll help," Juniper said, stepping forward from behind her desk. "Whatever I can do. Organize a search party, call in the dogs."

"Hold on there, go-getter," Sheriff Gardener said to his eager deputy assistant. "No, you won't."

"How am I supposed to prove myself if you never let me do anything?" Juniper pleaded her case. She was wiry, her crisp uniform gaping around her thin arms.

"This isn't about you, Juniper. It's about Ms. Mayhem." The sheriff crossed his muscled forearms over his chest and addressed Honora with an annoyed glance. "I'm not your whipping boy. We follow the rules in this town. From your reputation, I realize you like to make your own rules, but you can't come in here and just boss us around."

"I think I just did," Honora said.

Juniper made a little squeak noise.

Sheriff Gardener didn't even flinch but moved within inches of Honora's face.

"I've known the Mayhem sisters a long

time. I'm not afraid to say no to you. I thought you could help your sister. Don't know why she came to me in the first place."

"Looks like she made a mistake, putting her faith in the wrong wizard," Honora jabbed. Vivi wedged her way between the two before a fight broke out. "Stop. Please, I don't want to make things worse."

Juniper took a tentative step toward her boss. "We can sense for a magical signature. See if there's anything out there worth investigating. The black magic Vivi described in her vision would definitely leave a stain," Juniper said. "Then if we find anything, we can head out. With Honora in the air and the three of us on foot, we can at least make a pass of a small area."

"The voice of reason," Honora said and gave Juniper a little bow.

"That's all I'm asking for." Vivi held the sheriff's attention, his warm gaze softening toward her.

He didn't look away. His shoulders relaxed and he paused, considering the suggestion. "The Dire Woods isn't a picnic spot. The forest is wide and deep. One flyer, a wizard, and two witches aren't going to be able to cover it on foot without a detection spell done first. We'll try to identify trace magic, and if we find something, I'll order a small controlled search."

Vivi wanted to hug him. "Thank you, Sheriff. You won't regret this."

"Don't thank me yet." He turned to Honora. "You sure her vision doesn't have anything to do with the job you're on?"

"I'm looking for a guy named Maynard Luck. He's a really nice wizard, part of a flying club I used to belong to. He went missing a few weeks ago. So, at first glance, no, but you never know in the private investigation business," Honora said. "I came to check your files. He has a small cottage out here in Willow Realm where he does a lot of practice flights. Since I was here, I wanted to see if you had anything on him."

"Let's get moving then and fire up the detection spell with the dragon glass. Hope it shows us some magic out in the woods," he said, giving Vivi a reassuring nod.

Witches were not impossible to locate. Magical devices like scrying mirrors and locator spells made finding someone pretty routine for a witch with magic detection skills. Hiding took talent, cloaking was a tough spell to master, and any magical object that could hide a witch left an energy signature. Because Vivi didn't know who the kidnapped witch was, the only thing they could use to identify a location was magical residue left from sorcery. If the witch was being held against her will, then cloaking her took layered spellcraft. Vivi hoped the sorcery she saw in her vision was enough to leave a glaring magical signature that would lead them right to her.

While the preparations were being made for the detection spell, Vivi filled Honora in on details of her vision. "What if we don't find anything?" She shifted nervously from foot to foot. "What if I'm wrong?"

"We'll deal with that later. Hold off your worrying until after we learn the results," Honora whispered.

"It's my fault. I've been ignoring my *persuasion* for so long, I don't even know my own power. The vision was a series of images and emotion. I couldn't give the sheriff a solid timeline of events. We could be too late to detect any magic."

"You know what they say, timing is everything." Honora rubbed Vivi's shoulder. "If the magic is as black as you say, he probably has a taste for it. He's practiced, Vivi. We're going to catch him."

Her sister was so certain. It was exactly the kind of pep talk she needed. "I'm glad you're here."

Juniper guided Honora and Vivi into the room the sheriff's department had dedicated to surveillance, location, and scrying. Illuma light glowed from the wall sconces. Vivi rubbed her arms against the chill as they all gathered around the edges of the room. Once they were settled, Sheriff Gardener released a lever in the wall, lowering a heavy glass table from the ceiling by three thick ropes. A map of Everland was etched into the opaque and milky surface that was warped and uneven. The history books revealed that the magical substance called dragon's glass had been forged by the fiery breath of the deadly mythical beasts, at the edge of the witching world where the land met the sea. The ancient history of the fabled world never ceased to amaze Vivi with its misty seaside and fiery magical creatures. But dragons hadn't been seen for centuries, and all that was left of them were mysterious tales and chunks of magical glass.

The sheriff took a bottle from a shelf and pulled the cork. He poured a mixture directly onto the center of the table. The fluid pooled like liquid silver, metallic and reflective, that beaded and flowed across the glass surface. Next, he waved his wand over the silvery pool and spoke the activation spell. The mixture acted like a homing beacon, seeking out and locating magical traces in the woods, trying to find a clue that would lead them to the missing witch.

Sheriff Gardener continued with the spell and the liquid trembled and swirled around the glass surface as if alive. When he reached the part of the spell narrowing down the location to a specific region of Everland, they all joined in and whispered, "Dire Woods, Dire Woods, Dire Woods!" A chill went through the room.

The silver surface undulated with the voices of the witches, and at their command, stretched itself thin over the table into a wiry snake that rolled over the surface of the glass map, searching for a signature of dark magic. When working perfectly, the metallic liquid beaded up like mercury, circling an area on the map, then pooling open so the center of the circle revealed a location, but in this case, the liquid kept moving, seeking.

"Let's see if we have a sign." The sheriff leaned over the table, his gaze trained on the silver orb.

They watched and waited.

Nothing happened.

The room grew awkwardly silent.

"Try the spell again," Honora said. "You could have uttered the incantation wrong."

"I've never had a problem before." He narrowed his eyes at her, but relented with a shrug and went through the spell again.

The second time, they still got nothing. They waited a few more minutes, but as the stillness grew it seemed pointless. Nothing showed up on the glass. No black magic had been detected. Vivi felt defeated. She had been so sure. Juniper began packing up.

"We can't stop now. There has to be

something else we can try," Vivi said.

Juniper opened her mouth to speak, but the sheriff nudged her with his elbow before his assistant could get any words out. "There isn't anything we can do."

He cleared his throat, causing Juniper to twist up her mouth in repressed silence. "We tried. I'm really sorry. I know it doesn't seem that way now, but I am." He turned his broad back on Vivi, avoiding her gaze for the first time.

That was strange, she thought. Something was up with him.

Honora pulled her shoulders back in defiance. "We'll do the search on our own. I'll help you."

Vivi could tell by his reaction to Juniper that the sheriff was hiding something, and she wasn't about to leave without finding out what. "Can you two give us a moment alone?"

Juniper and Honora filed out of the room.

"Can I ask you a question?" Vivi asked.

"Sure." He tucked his hands in his pockets and rocked back on his heels.

"Why aren't you doing everything you can to locate the witch?" It was her turn to be direct.

He raised his brow. "Here, I thought I was doing you a favor." He snorted. "I can assure you, I take my job seriously. We used the glass, didn't we?"

"You're going through the motions, so if that's a favor, then yes, you're doing the bare minimum. But you can do more. I know there's something you're holding back."

He crossed his arms over his chest, creating a barrier between them. "You don't understand."

"Then make me." Talking to him was like trying to pry open a clam.

"My job isn't as simple as it may seem. And what you're asking me to do would violate protocol." He cleared his throat.

She didn't remember Lance being so uptight and by the book back at Haven Academy. "What protocol? What are you talking about?"

He hesitated, standing firm. *Stubborn wizard.*

"I can stand here all day, and I'm not leaving without an answer." She crossed her arms loosely over her chest, matching his stance, and realizing they both needed to work on their trust issues.

His gazed shifted to the floor, unable to keep eye contact with her. "Let's just say I'm under certain rules and restrictions by the council." His voice lowered to practically a whisper.

"What does that mean?" Why would the council care about Willow Realm? They were small potatoes in the witching world, unless it wasn't them they were worried about. "It's the Dire Woods. That's what you're avoiding?"

"I'm not avoiding, just following the rules concerning magical monitoring of the woods." He rolled his eyes as if she had just pried some precious secret from him. "See, I shouldn't have told you that."

Vivi's brow knitted. She considered what he had said. "You're saying we aren't allowed to know what's going on in the Dire Woods? You aren't allowed to monitor magic?" *That was interesting and a little scary.*

"Pretty much. Searching those woods is advised against. It's frowned upon, if you know what I mean. There are things going on in Everland that the council doesn't want the general public knowing about."

"Then we have to do it. Don't you see? The fact the council doesn't want us poking around is practically proof that something's going on out there."

"Vivi, a lot of bad stuff, suspect magic, and downright weirdness goes on out there all the time. The council advises law enforcement to stay out of it and let their team, the Hex Division, handle things, and I'm inclined to agree."

Hex Division was an elite police force that worked directly under council orders and handled the most dangerous cases.

"We need to act now." The image of the bound witch flashed in her mind's eye. "She won't last long. I don't know how I know this, I just do." Vivi brushed her hair out of her face. "I've made mistakes in the past, but this can't be one of them. I can't wait. If you won't help me, then Honora and I will go out there totally blind and alone."

He rubbed his chin thoughtfully. "There is something. The Dire Woods has been neutral territory for a while now, and much of what goes on of a questionable nature is overlooked for political purposes, but I never liked *not knowing*."

"You have a way around it, don't you?" She eyed him shrewdly. Lance was a smart wizard.

"Yes, I do." He broke into a smile under her unrelenting stare.

"Good, then we take another look. This time we might find something."

"Vivi, I hope you realize this could cost me my job. The council keeps things from us for a good reason. If they find out, I'll be in a lot of trouble."

Admitting to seeing visions was hard enough, but now she had to convince the sheriff to take a chance on her and potentially risk his job when even she wasn't entirely certain. "I don't have a right to ask you to trust me, but I am. Saving a witch from harm is worth it. And if we don't find anything, I'll take the blame."

They all filed back into the room. The

sheriff retrieved an old black bottle shrouded with dust from a back corner of his shelf and pulled the old cork stopper free from the metal-ringed lip. A sharp acrid smell hit Vivi's nostrils, causing her to cough, as the fumes instantly filled the room once the sheriff poured the pungent liquid onto the dragon's glass. He spoke a different spell, one she had never heard, the words rolling off his tongue in the thick old-world language. Unlike the liquid from the first attempt, this liquid oozed like tar, slow and steady, following the command of his voice. It bubbled up, hissed, and popped, and then congealed into a slithering black snake, searching every crevice and corner of the map, probing until it slowly, finally encircled one area.

"There it is!" Vivi yelled and pointed to the stain on the glass. It resembled a burn mark, a smudge of black that crackled. "The edges are blood red. There's a lot of it." Her stomach twisted, for she was both relieved and repulsed by what the sign meant. She might be right.

"Is that the location in the Dire Woods I think it is?" Juniper asked. Her hand nervously tapped on the wand she wore strapped to her belt.

"North quadrant. That's deep in the woods and not a nice neighborhood. We'll need to ride out." He scrubbed his hands over his face. "Magic that dark deserves an initial investigation. I don't know if this has anything to do with the missing witch you saw, but we can follow up."

Suddenly, the black tar-like substance shattered, causing Vivi to jump. The black snake that encircled the area on the map dissolved into a pile of ash.

"That's a good sign," Juniper said. "It means the black magic was recent. We're going to find something out there."

"Looks like I owe you two a search," the sheriff said, his shoulders tensed. Silence filled the room, but only for a fleeting moment.

"The north quadrant of the Dire Woods is where the Darklander lives. That's his territory," Honora said with a furrowed brow. "What have you gotten yourself into, sister?"

Vivi didn't have an answer, but she had a bad feeling it was the reason the council didn't want anyone poking around in the woods.

5

THE POTION GARDEN WAS QUIET when Vivi
returned to check on Pepper and
fill her in on the *interesting* events
that had transpired at the sheriff's station.
Sunlight spilled through the shop windows,
reflecting off the bottles and creating a
kaleidoscope of color across the thick maple
countertop, reminding Vivi the world was still
an enchanting place, despite recent events.
Pepper's gaze was intent. Her lips twisted
into a tight bud as she sat perched on a
stool in rapt attention, hanging on her boss's
every word.

While recapping the events, Vivi got an
idea, sending her digging through a cluttered
cabinet where she had stored miscellaneous
and *eccentric* items she had traded for over
the years. Her moonstone ring glowed into

the dusty abyss. Finally finding what she was looking for, she pulled out a cloth-wrapped package and placed it on the counter. Her eyes widened as she peeled back the fabric, revealing a gorgeous bandolier that a witch with some serious leather-crafting skills had made for her in exchange for a broken heart salve. Never in a million years had she imagined she would strap on the two crisscrossing bands of leather, until today.

"Wow!" Pepper said, wiggling her eyebrows. "That's amazing. You could hold about a dozen potion vials at one time."

The pliable leather felt strong, yet supple, between her fingers. "That's the plan."

She ungracefully wrangled the bandolier over her head, awkwardly maneuvering through the armholes, and finally fitting the device snuggly across her chest. "Whoa," she huffed, a light sweat forming on her brow. "This thing is worse than a corset."

"Some wizards might find it sexy," Pepper said, motioning to the design.

A series of loops ran down the leather straps and were meant to hold potion vials, giving her easy access to her magical arsenal. She tightened the ends of the bandolier, pulling it securely around her. It had been custom-made, and it felt right.

No. It felt good. She wasn't about to go strolling into a dangerous forest without a little protection. No matter what she encountered in the woods, she planned on being prepared. Never one to master wandwork, Vivi preferred her potions, and even though they might not be as dramatic as spellcasting, they worked some powerful magic in their own right.

"Technically, the Dire Woods is a sanctuary for magical outcasts, not *really* dire." Pepper adjusted her glasses. Logic was a mental tonic to her. "It's not that dangerous, right?"

"No, not at all. It's fine," Vivi lied, but what was she supposed to tell her young assistant who looked as worried as a mother hen? The reality was the Dire Woods had earned its name, and danger came with the territory.

Pepper hopped off her stool and restlessly stocked the shelves with fresh potion bottles. "I'll just keep telling myself that until you come back in one piece."

Vivi hurried around the shop, snatching up every imaginable potion she might need from finding-and-seeking potions to a tonic to cure snakebites and loaded them gingerly into the leather bandolier. "Will you close up for me today?" she asked, glancing at her assistant.

"Of course, you don't even have to ask," Pepper said. "Here, take this one." She handed Vivi a tiny vial filled with swirling amber liquid. "It's a protective ward."

"Honora said the area we're going to is Darklander territory." Vivi took the bottle, hoping she would never need to use it.

"You don't think that outcast scumbag wizard is involved, do you?" Pepper asked, pulling her long sleeves down over her hands and visibly shuddering.

"I honestly don't know. I didn't sense anyone as powerful as him, but the wizard in the vision could have been anyone. I'm guessing there's a lot we don't know about what goes on out there." The dark wizard was a stain on the witching world, but like it or not, he wasn't going away.

Magic was all about energy and intention. It could be used for good or bad. In the worst cases, magic could be twisted like a thorny vine, forced to grow in devious ways. Some witches wanted a quick fix and didn't want to follow any rules of conduct. Some became obsessed with power and controlling others. If the will of the witch was rotten, the magic turned black and could be used to hurt, deceive, bind, and curse.

Consisting of twelve well-respected elders, the Witch Council was the governing body that made the rules, held the society of witches and wizards to high standards of conduct, and brought peace and prosperity to the magical world. Mostly, anyway. There were a few exceptions, the Darklander being one of the more nasty.

The Darklander had once been one of

the most revered wizards of Everland, but his hunger for supremacy drove him to experiment with blood magic and twisted sorcery. His insatiable desire for powerful dark magic grew, and after more than a few terrible crimes were linked to him, though never proven due to disappearing evidence and recanted testimony, he was banished from witch society by the council and was allowed to make his home in the Dire Woods. From what Vivi had heard, he had built a stone fortress to house his followers; rumors spread that the woods were filled with a slowly growing society of witches and wizards who practiced dark magic, seeking power through blood, sacrifice, pain, and even death.

Her vision was leading her to the razor's edge of a dark world, one she hardly recognized or understood. But wasn't that what Esmeralda had told her? *"Follow the visions wherever they take you."* The Dire Woods was her only real link to the missing witch being carried in a black bag like a small scared animal. Perhaps Vivi was being foolish, but she hoped they would travel into the Dire Woods, find the young witch alive, scoop her up, and bring her home, but with a sinking feeling, she knew there was little chance of that happening.

They met at the edge of Willow Realm, where the village bordered the forest. A thick line of pine trees fringed a sloping meadow. Vivi kicked through the clearing, the edge of her canvas coat brushing against the long grass. All witches had an enchanted traveling coat that was worn when going long distances and might encounter offensive magic. The witching world was an unpredictable place, and the coats, spelled with magic deflectors, offered additional protection from the elements and dangerous witchcraft.

Sheriff Gardener and Juniper were already at the location when Vivi and her familiar arrived. She had decided at the last minute that Rumor's keen eye would be useful, plus it was always good to have a sharp-clawed, overprotective raven watching her back.

The sheriff nodded when he saw Vivi, his gaze lingering on the bandolier strapped over her chest. "You came prepared," he said, admiring her potion ammo.

"See anything you like?" Vivi asked in a moment of spontaneous flirting, causing a wide smile to brighten his face.

"No comment, for now. But catch me on my day off, and I might say otherwise." He slowly put on his leather gloves and regained a professional demeanor, but the smile remained on his lips.

Within seconds, Honora dropped to the

ground light as a feather, her goggles flecked with dirt and a few insect wings.

Both the sheriff and Juniper had a sleek metal and chrome hover bike. The Dire Woods was too dense with trees to take a hovercraft. They needed speed and maneuverability. Broomsticks, though nostalgic, were a thing of the past, impractical in the modern witching world, and really uncomfortable. Who wanted to sit sidesaddle on a stick for any length of time? The sleek bikes were nothing like the bicycle with a woven basket tied to the front that Clover puttered around on. These bikes were magical speedsters powered by a levitation spell and a magical mechanical control system for steering. No pedaling required.

"Where did you get the slick ride?" Honora asked, clearly impressed.

"He's totally hooked up," Juniper said, right in front of her boss. "Don't tell him I told you, but he has connections."

The sheriff shot his deputy assistant a stern glance. "Juni, how many times do I have to tell you, sucking up isn't going to work? I need you focused, riding point, and staying alert to dangers," he said.

"What dangers, specifically?" Juniper asked, clutching at the wand that hung on her belt loop. Her expression turned serious. "You know, so I can be ready."

"The Darklander and his minions, for a start," Honora said, hands on her slender waist. "I hear he's built quite a fortress."

"This isn't about the Darklander," Vivi said, hip cocked.

"How can you be so sure?" Honora asked. Along with her goggles, she wore a leather cap. "The dark wizard you saw *could* be the Darklander, especially if you saw him using blood salt and black ash."

That was what Vivi was afraid of, but she reasoned, "No, I would have sensed him." *Wouldn't I?*

"We've had word from our scouts that his followers camp in the woods with their weird familiars—bizarre creatures. They conjure up animalus with horns, wings, and claws from ancient texts," the sheriff said. "Many of the Dire Woods legends used to scare people from going into the forest aren't just stories."

"Maybe we'll see a ghoul, too." Honora was clearly joking. This was not the time to go on a mission to search and identify foul creatures of the Dire Woods.

"We need to stay focused, stay on task, and make this quick," the sheriff said.

"When we arrive, I want to try and sense the witch," Vivi said.

The sheriff nodded and pulled a roll of thick parchment from a compartment under the seat of his bike. With Juniper's help, he unrolled a map of the woods and spread it out for them to see. "The locator spell gives us a five-mile radius of the magical signature. We located the center of the area, which is here." He pointed to a marked location on the map. "We meet up there, and then proceed with a search. Keep alert. Be prepared for anything."

"I came prepared." Honora tapped a baton of wood about two feet long that she had strapped to her back. Thicker than a wand, but not as unwieldy as a staff, the baton channeled magical energy or, in a worst-case scenario, doubled as a club.

Sheriff Gardener raised his brow. "Let's not get overzealous, Honora."

Vivi watched as her sister lifted up off the ground in a graceful movement. Her arms were outstretched, commanding the air, and within seconds she was high above them and out of sight.

With a sly grin, he tossed Vivi a helmet. "You've ridden before, right?"

"Of course." Vivi didn't mention that the only time she had ridden a hover bike was when she'd been fifteen at Haven Academy and sneaked out late one night with a hot young wizard she was dating. She drank too much kindle brew, got a little tipsy, and experienced an ugly bout of motion sickness. The date had not ended well.

Vivi quickly suppressed the memory. If she

was going to go into the Dire Woods, she was going to have to ride with the handsome sheriff.

Juniper slipped on a sleek red helmet and mounted her bike.

Vivi straddled the bike, positioning herself behind the sheriff, and wrapped her arms around his rock-hard middle. He definitely worked out. Her heart raced. She tried not to be too handsy, but once settled, she couldn't resist tightening her grip and resting her check against his back.

"Don't worry. We'll do our best to find her. I promise." He squeezed her hand, reassuringly.

Vivi felt a sensation of calm. What was up with that? She had felt the same calm soothing sensation back at the station when the sheriff had touched her arm. His magic was definitely powerful, but there was something special about it, too. She wondered if he wasn't keeping a few secrets of his own.

"Thank you, Sheriff."

"You can call me Lance when it's just us. I like to keep things professional around my deputies, but I realize it must be weird calling me sheriff. We've known each other a long time."

"We've been around." *Been around.* Really, that was the best thing she could come up with to say? Her conversation skills with handsome men were sorely lacking.

He nodded, adjusted the visor of his helmet

and sped off into the woods. The speed took her breath away. He maneuvered the bike effortlessly over the rough terrain and glided through a gauntlet of trees and debris. It was still afternoon, but the forest was shrouded in a cool dusky haze, lending an unmistakable allure. The fog-shrouded trees stood like sentries defending a dark and foreboding magical presence.

The woods were nothing like the lush forests that surrounded Vivi's village or the Meadowlands near Clover's house. What foliage did grow here was thorny and blackened as if black magic had seeped right into the roots and the trees had adapted to the dark world. The bark was thick and gnarled, the leaves waxy as if dipped in tar. The woods were steeped in brimstone, soot, and ash. The name Dire suited them, for Vivi couldn't help but be overwhelmed by the sense of dread that soaked down to her bones.

Once they got moving and the air washed over her face, she started to relax. She closed her eyes and pictured the young witch in her mind's eye—tangled strawberry blond hair, skinny build, haunting doe eyes that were dazzling green, gazing out of the darkness. Her trembling lips had pleaded for help. The pain of the vision had shot through them both and had been too real, almost too much to bear.

Vivi focused on her fear, pictured the witch's desperate eyes. As the bike raced forward, she was drawn deeper into her subconscious. The images blended with emotion and suddenly a picture appeared in her mind—a forked tree. It was a huge old growth tree and appeared to have been sliced in half by a bolt of lightning, creating the shape of a Y. There were few discerning landmarks around the forked tree in her vision, just more spindly trees.

Her eyes snapped open. She scanned the woods, searching for the needle in the forest, the one tree split down the middle. She couldn't find it in the blur of trees racing by the hover bike. Her stomach clenched. There had been no sign of the missing witch. She had sensed and seen nothing and now had no idea which way to go.

The bike slowed. Lance pulled up next to a clump of trees, deactivated the levitation spell, and released the stand.

With his haunting black wingspan, Rumor glided down from above, coasted to a tree branch near Vivi, and gave her a reassuring caw.

Within minutes, Juniper and Honora joined them in the woods. On foot, they circled the immediate area the sheriff had pinpointed on the map, where the magic stain had been discovered, but there was nothing—no remnants of soot or blood salt, no scorched circle, no sign of anyone.

Lance spread the map out in front of Vivi. "Any ideas?"

Her confidence shaken but not discouraged, she searched for a solution. She would have to find the witch the old-fashioned way and do a little detecting of her own. "I haven't gotten any sense of her. We'll have to do a foot search of the area."

The sheriff drew his finger across the rough surface of the map. "We have a five-mile circumference radiating outward from where the magic was detected, so we need to split up to cover the most ground. Honora can explore to the east by air. Vivi can go north. Juniper and I can investigate west and south. This is a 'search and report back.' If you find anything, don't touch it."

Vivi pulled a chunk of quartz from her pocket and rolled it around in her hand to help her focus. Rumor cawed from his perch up in the trees to let everyone know he was there. She glanced up. "The raven can alert us if we find something or if anything goes wrong."

"Sounds good. Let's get moving. We head out, and no matter what, we circle back and meet up again in two hours," Lance said, and the group dispersed.

The forest floor was littered with blackened logs and jagged stones, some as large as boulders, protruding dangerously from the ground. Vivi walked for a few miles, switching back and forth in long lines to cover the most ground. The only sound was her leather boots tromping through the leaf debris. Sweat beaded on her forehead. Frustration filled her. She tugged a thin vial from the bandolier of potions strapped to her chest, pulled out the cork, and poured the liquid onto the ground where it evaporated. A pungent scent of sandalwood rose up in a cloud of amber smoke.

The potion was a simple one, used for finding lost objects. The smoke was supposed to indicate the direction to whatever she was looking for, or at least it always had when she was searching for her keys. The smoke withered and dissipated, being swallowed by the Dire Woods. She got nothing—no indication or impression. She felt foolish. One tiny potion was not going to find a kidnapped witch.

Vivi focused, drawing on her *persuasion* to guide her. Her head ached. It felt like she was digging for something crammed into the back of a drawer, something lost and forgotten. She tried to call her magic forward, to draw it upward from the base of her spine. She pulled and pushed, focused and begged. She pleaded with the small spark of magic, but it was like yelling into a dark and distant place and no one answering.

What had she expected? That she was

going to pull up a vision from the dark pit of her subconscious and dazzle everyone with her wise foresight?

Vivi had neglected her *persuasion* for so long, how could she expect it to respond now, on command, when she needed it most? Magic didn't work that way. Performing magic demanded practice, patience, and daily work. No flick of the wand or whisper of spells made it jump to life unless the witch had trained. That was why it was called witchcraft, because magic needed to be honed like art, respected as a gift, and nurtured like a child. It was special and would not respond to idle commands, no matter how good the intentions.

Her magic abandoned her, just like she had abandoned it.

Vivi sat on a large boulder and ran her hand through her hair. Defeat was not a state she was comfortable with. She got up and walked on with a mixture of sadness touched with shame welling in her heart, because now an innocent witch would pay for the fear and neglect she had for her *persuasion*. She had been afraid to see, and now her intuition was blind.

Rumor cawed. Her familiar circled above her head, his wings ruffling in the wind.

Staring into the distance, Vivi saw the cleaved tree.

She stopped dead, assessing what stood in

the clearing ahead of her. She felt a flicker of hope.

It was a sign; she was close.

Vivi eased forward, scanning the woods. A scuffing sound came from the distance, pulling her forward. Then the scent of brimstone and burnt ash hit her in the face. Through the trees she saw a figure moving, stumbling, hunched and swaying. It had to be the witch from her vision. She quickened her pace, her stomach lurching.

"Rumor! Get the sheriff!"

The bird flew off in the opposite direction. Vivi's heart pounded in her chest. She had found her! Vivi ran as fast as she could across the uneven ground. "Hey! Over here! I'm coming!"

The closer she got to the Y-shaped tree, the stranger the figure looked. Viewed from behind, the witch's long tangled hair was darkened with sweat and mud, but it wasn't blonde. It was shot through with gray. Vivi squinted and brushed the sweat from her brow. She ran to the witch's side and clutched her thin body in her arms, and as she stared into her face, she realized immediately that the witch wasn't young. Her eyes weren't green but faded blue, and her smooth skin was creased with wrinkles. Vivi held a witch hunched, not from exhaustion, but from time. She wasn't young at all, but an old woman, and she definitely *wasn't* the witch from her vision.

The witch cradled in her arms was a complete stranger.

Vivi spoke with a calm soothing voice. "Can you hear me?" There was no response. She gently eased the old witch to the ground. "I'm not going to hurt you. You're safe now."

The witch gave no indication that she heard Vivi or even knew she was there. Vivi stroked the woman's long matted hair and tried to comfort her. Two deep red grooves encircled her wrists, similar to the marks on the witch from her vision. She winced at the sight of torn red skin, indicating the poor witch had been bound.

"Can you hear me? Were you alone? Was there another witch with you?" Vivi pleaded, searching the woman's eyes for answers, a sign she understood, but the witch said nothing. She was so thin and frail Vivi thought if she squeezed too hard, she might break, but she held her in her arms and tried to comfort her. Her body trembled. She was wearing only a shredded gown that looked like it came from a healer's ward. Vivi slipped her coat off and wrapped it around the witch's body to try and warm her up a little until help arrived.

With a terrible realization, Vivi sensed the witch was empty, void of the energetic spark all witches carried inside of them, as if her magic had been drained. It was another thing she and the witch from her vision had in common. The idea of losing her magic turned Vivi's stomach, both angering and sickening her. Who could do this? A lump formed in her throat. Sorrow and disappointment filled her, but her feelings were trivial compared to what this witch must have gone through.

Time seemed suspended before Sheriff Gardener and Juniper arrived. Luckily for Vivi, Lance took control of the situation and immediately sent Juniper for a hover-transport to come and take the injured witch to the nearest healer ward. His swift, decisive actions were those of an experienced officer. Vivi sat on a boulder off to the side while he worked, putting up a barrier spell that acted as magical crime tape. Two more deputies arrived shortly after and began an investigation of the area.

The sheriff handed out orders and then joined her. "So any idea who the witch is?" he asked.

"No. I'm sorry, I don't." Vivi shook her head. "She's not the one I saw in my vision."

"Well, there isn't much more you can do here. For now this area is considered a crime scene, and it goes in one big circle." He motioned a giant arc with his arm, pointing out the large scorch mark on the ground caused from burned ash and brimstone.

"That's the black magic that was detected back at the station," Vivi said.

"You got that part right, at least," he said with a shrug.

Vivi knew he didn't mean to sound harsh, but the words stung. She had to face the fact that her information wasn't entirely accurate. That was probably why the sheriff only used *registered* seers. They didn't screw up the details they reported to the police. She felt like a young witch, playing at magic.

"We rescued a witch in desperate need of help. That's important," he said, reassuring her. "Why don't you head home? Not much more you can do here. Get a good night's rest, and we'll catch up later." He gave her a professional nod and returned to his work.

Her sister dropped to the ground next to her after making another pass of the area. "You saved that witch," Honora said, easing down next to her. "You should be proud."

"I know, but this isn't over. I have to find the witch I came for." She was determined to push on, no matter how disappointed. This wasn't over.

"Let me know if you need help." Honora gave her a sympathetic nod.

Vivi rubbed her hands over her face. "I let it go for so long, Honora. I was so afraid of what I might see that I avoided my magic. I was ashamed of what people might say and think—of what they still might say. Except now my problem is that no one will believe me. My credibility just went out the window."

"No one will believe you because *you* don't believe," Honora said. "You have to start trusting yourself and working on your *persuasion*. It's not going to just come to you. You think flying came naturally to me?"

"Yes! You fly like a hawk, a sparrow, and a hummingbird all rolled into one. You are the strongest and most graceful flyer in all of Everland." Vivi smiled. "You make it look easy."

"It wasn't. I trained constantly. I'm not going to tell you how many buildings and trees I crashed into during the learning curve. It takes time. And sometimes you make a fool out of yourself and it hurts."

"Thanks. I guess I just needed to hear it." Vivi was glad to have her sister by her side. Honora understood. She was equal parts encouragement and butt-kicking.

"Come on, I'll give you a lift back. Lance said I could borrow a hover bike. We can hit Nocturnes. I'll buy you a cup of tea."

"I'm going to need a really strong cup."

About two hundred yards off in the distance, Vivi noticed a shining obsidian rock face rising out of the ground that she hadn't seen before. Honora caught her stare. "That's the Darklander's fortress."

"It's awfully close to the crime scene," Vivi said.

"Yeah, we noticed. The sheriff doesn't seem too happy about it."

"It's gorgeous," Vivi said, admiring the sleek stone and the towering walls with sharp jagged edges. The building was a mix of dull gray stone, but the façade was pure glossy black rock with a giant wooded door studded with huge nail heads.

Honora arched her eyebrow. "Not thinking of going to the dark side, are you, sister?"

"No, but you have to admit that the place is pretty in an evil overlord kind of way."

Honora put her arm around her sister. "We need to get you out of here." She shook her head and grinned. "The brimstone stench on the air is starting to get to you."

6

THE VILLAGE OF WILLOW REALM was a tight-knit community held together by a bustling main street with curious shops and restaurants to tempt even the most discerning witch and wizard. Vivi's shop was located down one of the cobblestone side streets, so she quickly ducked inside to check on Pepper while Honora returned the hover bike to the police station. Pepper was getting ready to close for the night following a day of steady customers. After performing a few helpful sweeping and tidying spells and activating the security ward, Vivi headed over to meet up with her sister at one of their favorite haunts—Nocturnes.

Loath to rise early, witches were nocturnal by nature. Nighttime was when witches kicked back and had their fun as their senses heightened and the spark of the natural world nipped at their heels. Nocturnes was a cozy restaurant where witches could relax and feel at home. Sophisticated and social, the owner Arnica Delacqua served countless blends of exotic teas and roasted coffees, delectable soups and buttery scones, cakes and pies, and sandwiches and stews, but what she really served up best was comfort and community, making Nocturnes' customers feel like they were with family.

A long counter lined with bar stools and café tables filled the front of the shop, and in the back a huge stone fireplace anchored a cozy dining and sitting room packed with overstuffed sofas and chairs covered in velvet pillows. A fire crackled warmly on the hearth. Vivi found her favorite nook in a discreet corner with three red velvet wingback chairs surrounding a tufted leather ottoman and surrendered into the soft cushions.

She listened to the rhythmic clicking of knitting needles as a gaggle of witches chatted over a steamy pot of tea and finger sandwiches. Gossip was practically a sport in the witching world, and the group of knitters was trading off turns talking and giggling, their needles moving quick and nimble, eating up strands of yarn and spitting out colorful scarves.

Just another night at Nocturnes, she thought.

Vivi groaned with delight when she saw Arnica heading over with a full tray. Arnica had owned the shop for decades and was a fixture in the town. Her black hair was pinned up in a pile of curls. Her laid-back demeanor personified warmth and comfort, and her smile could turn around anyone's bad day, even Vivi's. Arnica's *persuasion* was hospitality through and through. Plus, she wasn't too shabby with baking spells, either.

"Good evening, little Mayhem witch. Here comes a pick-me-up hot from the kitchen." She set the tray, holding two bowls brimming with rich meaty stew, some warm sourdough bread, two ceramic mugs of hot chocolate, and a plate heaped with her famous shortbread for dessert, on the ottoman.

"You're too good to me," Vivi said, raising the cup of hot chocolate up to her nose and inhaling the rich scent of deliciousness.

"I just know my customers, and you looked like you needed sustenance, and quickly." She gave Vivi a wink and headed back to the counter. Honora passed her on the way in and dropped down in the chair next to Vivi. The third chair was where Clover usually sat when they had a sisterly get-together, but tonight her seat was left empty, since the talented word witch was preparing for the launch of her latest novel.

Honora settled in and snatched up some

bread, dunking it in her bowl of stew. "Let's cut to the chase and talk *persuasions*, shall we?" she mumbled through a mouthful.

She arched a perfectly shaped brow at Vivi, who buried her face in the billow of steam that rose up from her cup before taking a sip. The hot liquid slid down her throat and seeped into her veins. There was a low note of a deep dark spice, cinnamon or cardamom. She wasn't sure what Arnica put in the hot chocolate, but whatever it was, it unwound her slowly. She could already tell she was going to sleep like a corpse.

After the day she'd had, Vivi decided not to fight it and told her sister everything about the vision, about hiding her true *persuasion* all these years, her fears and regrets flooding out of her in a whoosh of words. This was the first time Vivi had spoken to anyone about her *persuasion* in any great detail, and it felt good to unload.

"The greater a witch's *strength*, the heavier her burden," Honora said, biting into a hunk of bread after repeating the old Haven Academy mantra. The two sisters laughed together, letting the stress of the day fall away.

Honora flashed a wolfish smile at her sister. "You want me to give you a piece of advice?" She pulled a thin, ivory-handled blade out of a sheath concealed in her boot and used it to cut a loose thread on her shirt.

"No. But I have a feeling you're going to anyway, so go ahead."

"Your problem is that you think you're ordinary, simple, but *we* aren't. We were born different with special *persuasions*. It wasn't just the curse that our ancestors gave us. They gave us power. So think differently. Think brilliant, think stellar, think big. I know I do." Her fingertip tapped at the tip of her knife.

"Let's just say I'm still adjusting to finding that out. I was good with being normal," Vivi said. "Normal," however, was not acceptable in the Mayhem household, and she had been hiding in the comfortable role of middle sister for a long time—too long, she was realizing.

"We will never be normal, so stop trying so hard to be something you're not."

"What am I supposed to do now? I just can't leave it. The witch from my vision is out there and I have to help her."

"The first thing you need to do is practice your *persuasion*. You can't keep repressing it. Are you prepared to accept it?" Honora asked.

Vivi hesitated. "I think so."

"That doesn't sound convincing." Honora held a heaping spoonful of stew up to her lips and blew.

"Yes, I will. I have to. It's just..." Vivi bit into a hunk of bread. The heady sourdough satisfied her hunger, filling her up.

"Just what? Come on, spill it."

Vivi swallowed and cleared her throat. She didn't want to think about the dark wizard, or about how clueless she was to her *persuasion*. "Honora, I'm afraid of this guy. What if his magic is too strong?"

"You can't worry about the future right now." Honora swallowed a spoonful of stew and then pointed at Vivi with her spoon for emphasis. "You have to focus on what's important in this moment and act on that."

"You're right." In reality, though, Vivi wanted to do more. She didn't have time to wait for her *persuasion* to catch up. She fished around in her purse and pulled out her notebook and reed pen. Flipping to a blank page, she said, "So, Miss Private Investigator, tell me. I'm not having any luck finding the missing witch, so how do I find the wizard who took her?" She cocked her head, listening with pen held over the paper, ready to take notes.

Honora snorted and smiled. "First, ask yourself what he needs the witches for and what he's doing with them."

"He's experimenting. He wants their magic, and he's desperate. I could feel it." Vivi wrote her thoughts down in her notebook.

"That's a start. Now ask why. What motivates him?"

"Good question. I hadn't considered that." She tapped the pen against her cheek. "I'll have to think more about it. Get inside of this wizard's head."

"Keep questioning, always. Never be satisfied. Just remember all magic is done for a reason, even dark magic. You'll figure this out."

They finished eating, and even though the mood of the night was bleak, Vivi felt a spark of hope. She was more determined than ever to find this witch, no matter where she had to look.

"Let's go," Honora said. "I'll walk you home."

The streets of Willow Realm were bustling with activity. Vivi loved her little village. There was a line out the door as witches and wizards waited for a table at The Brewery Tavern. Illuma lights glowed brightly in the window of Goodspells Grimoire. The bookstore was packed with an all-night vigil party as eager fans camped out for the next *Spellbinder* novel to come out tomorrow. Honora and Vivi smiled, both thinking of Clover, and continued up the street, strolling past The Charmery and Wildwoods Wands and Woodcrafts, which like The Potion Garden were already closed up tight for the evening.

Rumor was perched up in his tree, waiting for Vivi when she got home. Her sister zipped up her jacket, slipped on her leather hood, and adjusted her goggles before saying goodnight and disappearing into the starry sky like a beautiful night bird.

Vivi climbed the stairs up to her apartment and slipped inside, happy to finally be home after such a long day. Her place was the perfect size for her and her familiar. At the top of the stairs was a cozy nook for a bookshelf and an oversized chair where she liked to curl up and read, the high windows of the old building letting in shafts of sunlight. There was also a nice-sized living room and a kitchen with a built-in banquette and table. A bathroom and bedroom made up the rest of the apartment.

Her style was eclectic. She collected most of her furniture from antique shops or local artists selling handcrafted furniture, glass-covered illuma lights, iron candleholders, woven wool rugs, and gorgeous paintings of the magical world. Colorful scarves and knitted throws were scattered on armrests and sofa backs. And, for her familiar roommate, there were plenty of handcrafted wooden perches positioned around the apartment.

Rumor gave her a welcoming caw when she opened the window and he joined her. Vivi shook a paper sack filled with seeds and dried berries and smiled. She filled a small dish at the base of his perch with the mixture as a little treat. Mostly, Rumor dined al fresco, catching prey or snacking on what he could find in the wild. Ravens were omnivores and ate an array of tidbits including insects, seeds, berries, meat, and carrion, the dead flesh of animals, which made her cringe. Sometimes Vivi thought that Rumor would eat anything. Live and let live. As long as he didn't bring his dinner home with him, she was fine with his wild appetite.

Vivi stroked the top of Rumor's glossy black head. He tolerated a stroke or two, but he was not the touchy-feely type of guy. Her thoughts returned to the bike ride out to the Dire Woods and wrapping her arms around the rock-hard body of Lance Gardener. She sighed, wondering if the sheriff had a girlfriend, if he had someone to go home to at night, or was single like she was. Maybe one day she would put the time in to have a real relationship, instead of working all the time in her shop. A date wouldn't kill her; it might even lead to something more romantic.

One day, she thought. *Just not today.*

She should meditate and think about her *persuasion*, but she didn't have the energy. What she really *needed* was a good long soak. Her claw-foot porcelain tub was calling to her. She poured herself a glass of wine and snatched up a jar of new bath salts she had imbibed with a muscle-easing potion which made her whole body feel like it was being submerged in a warm, pillowy ooze.

Within minutes, Vivi was immersed in a wickedly hot bath, surrounded by twinkling candlelight, and sipping on a dry white. Since seeing Esmeralda on the path last night, she felt as if events were spiraling out of her control. The seer had predicted things that she didn't want to face, and then Vivi had experienced a vision so powerful, even she, in her perpetual state of denial, couldn't ignore. None of it made sense. Had she been wrong? Did the young witch even exist? Doubt gnawed at her insides, but she brushed it away, for she needed to focus on finding out what motivated this dark wizard and why he was hurting witches.

Vivi set the glass on the edge of the tub and closed her eyes for just a second. The warm water eased her mind, pulling her down into the shadowy land between sleep and wakefulness where visions stirred.

Tiny claws scratched at the windowpane. Tapped on the glass. Tap tap tap. Scurrying sounds pierced the silence, scratching at the wooden frame, trying to get inside, wanting to tell a terrible secret. Voices whispered, pleaded, cried out in gravely voices. Vivi tossed and turned in a tight space, her wrists burning and bound.

He was there, on the edge of her sight, thin as smoke drifting under the bathroom door, then rising and taking shape—the dark wizard had come for her. "He is stronger than anyone realizes," Esmeralda's voice whispered in Vivi's ear. He crossed the room in a dark blur and poured a jar of blood salt into the bath, staining the water with crimson swirls. A black cloth smothered her face, pushing her down farther and farther into darkness. A burning sensation exploded in her throat and neck, making it impossible to breathe. Her limbs grew heavy and weak.

Vivi jerked awake. Freezing cold water sloshed over the side of the tub in the darkness. She panicked, jerked up, and knocked the wine glass to the floor, shattering it into a million tiny shards. She clutched at her neck, recalling the strangling nightmare. Slowly her body calmed and her senses returned. She had fallen asleep in the tub. The candles had long since burned out. Illuma light glowed from the living room, but otherwise her apartment was shrouded in darkness.

There was no one there. She was alone.

She climbed out of the tub and wrapped herself in a towel. Tiptoeing through the minefield of broken glass that covered the bathroom floor, she realized it was the perfect metaphor for how she felt—one misstep and she would slice open a gash in her foot and bleed, but the glass was nearly invisible, impossible to see.

Sick and tired of being at the mercy of her *persuasion*, Vivi couldn't go on like this. Something was pounding on the door of her intuition, wanting to get in, calling for her to listen. She needed to figure out how to harness her *persuasion* and make it work for her. If she didn't find this girl, she would never forgive herself, and from her latest vision, it was becoming clear that the wizard responsible for her suffering was involved in a dangerous magic and would haunt her dreams if she didn't do something. Now.

Vivi woke early, threw on a sweater and a jacket, and headed out, but before leaving, she popped out back and gathered a small bouquet from the flower garden that grew in her yard. The shop didn't open until ten, giving her about an hour to pay a visit to the old witch in the healer ward. She knew it was a long shot the woman would be able to help her, but she had to start somewhere. The healer ward was on the other side of town, so she took the closest portal gate, which dropped her off a block away.

The ward was quiet when she entered. She approached the receptionist's desk and asked to speak to the healer in charge, hoping to check on the witch and express her sympathies. A gentle-looking witch dressed in a simple tunic and slacks led her into a waiting room. Vivi explained that she had been working with the sheriff and found the witch yesterday in the woods. The healer nodded and gave her a kind smile. "Yes, Sheriff Gardener was in last night with her and gave you all the credit for finding the poor dear. You should be proud."

Really? That was nice of him. "Is she speaking? Do you know who she is?" Vivi asked.

"She hasn't said a word. We did a blood test and looked her up in the Everland registry. That's how we got her name and address. She lives alone on the edge of Willow Realm near the Meadowlands and has no family. We're still searching. So far we haven't found anyone."

All witches and wizards were recorded in the public registry when they were born, and it contained a birth certificate and known addresses, although it wasn't always kept up to date with witches moving from place to place. They were lucky to have found her current residence.

"How's she doing, if you don't mind my asking?"

"Not bad for the state she was in last night. She's suffering from dehydration, exhaustion, and is very weak. I shouldn't say more about what was done to her." Her brow furrowed. "What she endured was terrible."

Vivi nodded. "I understand. May I sit with her for a few minutes? I won't disturb her. I just wanted to bring her these and make sure she was okay." She held out the small bouquet.

"I don't see why not. There's been a healer with her all night, who's with her now. Normally, we wouldn't let anyone see a patient, but the poor woman has no one."

"May I ask her name?"

"Sure, it's Clarissa Taylor. Right this way." The healer showed her to a small room with a bed surrounded by curtains. Another healer stood and nodded to Vivi. She walked quietly out of the room, only to return a few seconds later with a small glass vase for the flowers.

"We'll be right outside if you need us."

"One more thing. Did the registry happen to mention what her *persuasion* is?"

"Yes, it did. Fascinatingly enough, the witch is an empath. But I guess it didn't help her stop whoever did this."

Vivi sat in a chair next to the bed. The witch lay on white sheets and was propped up on pillows, her long gray hair fanned out around her shoulders. Her skin was papery and had a gray tinge. Both of her wrists were covered in gauze.

This was a talented witch with a strong *persuasion*. Empaths intuitively felt another witch's or wizard's true feelings and emotions. While she sat with the witch, Vivi pulled out her notebook and recorded the details of what she had just learned. Having no family and living in an isolated area of town made the witch a perfect target, but it was strange that she had been unable to sense deception from her attacker, especially being empathic. The attacker must have hid his true nature well, and that didn't bode well for her catching him.

A FTER HER EARLY VISIT TO the healer ward, a mix of feelings battled inside her—sadness, anger, and frustration. But a new desire was rising to the top of the heap of emotions: resolve. She wanted to get this guy. Vivi opened the shop on time and enjoyed an onslaught of eager customers before Pepper arrived after taking a well-deserved morning off.

Once her assistant was settled, Vivi darted out for her lunch break, but she had no intention of eating. Having not gathered much information from the injured witch, save her name and *persuasion*, Vivi realized her vision was the key, and the only other witch who could help her was Esmeralda. Now all she had to do was find the elusive seer, and she knew just where to go—The Evil Queen.

Technically, the owner of the clairvoyant shop, Scarlet Card, wasn't evil, nor was she a queen, but the name she chose suited her perfectly. Crisp leaves skidded across the sidewalk as Vivi hurried down Main Street and cut across to a narrow alley. The rich smoky scent of autumn hung in the air. This was usually her favorite time of year—the harvest time, a time for reaping what had been sown all summer, a time of reward and relaxation.

Not this year.

Vivi pushed open the door to The Evil Queen and was immediately enveloped into a lush room filled with flickering candles. Velvet fabrics draped every surface, pillows crowded chaise lounges, and spicy-scented incense curled upward, pooling on the ceiling in smoky wafts. Wooden shelves were filled with worn-edged tarot decks hundreds of years old, crystal balls of all sizes, and stacks of porcelain teacups littered every nook and cranny. Vivi got a little shiver of excitement, seeing all the traditional tools of the fortune-telling trade displayed in the shop.

A striking woman with a long sheet of cherry red hair that hung past her waist pushed through a beaded curtain from the back room. "I knew you would come see me sooner or later," Scarlet said, slinking up to the counter like a lynx. Dark kohl rimmed her almond-shaped eyes.

Vivi should have told Honora before coming here, but she needed help fast and didn't have time to be picky. Scarlet and Honora had been best friends all through Haven Academy. They had been like sisters, sharing every secret, dreaming of their futures, before their wild ways got them into trouble and their friendship ended in a full-blown fight. Over the years, Vivi had seen less and less of Scarlet, who'd once been a fixture in their house, glued to Honora's hip.

Since Scarlet opened her shop, Vivi saw her in town occasionally, but had never taken the time to stop in and look around. She gave Scarlet a warm smile, hoping she would help her for old times' sake.

"Looks like sooner." Vivi leaned against the glass counter and admired an antique crystal ball on a carved silver pedestal displayed inside. "How've you been, Scarlet?"

"Better than you." The sultry witch eyed Vivi up and down. "Your aura is cloudy, kind of murky around the edges. I'm guessing you aren't sleeping much. You've been having bad dreams. Headaches, too. Am I right?"

Great, her troubles were so transparent it was as if she were wearing them around like a gaudy cloak. "I was hoping you could help me find Esmeralda Westbourne? I ran into her two nights ago out by the Meadowland old oak portal. She said a few things that I need clarified, to say the least."

"Sure, I've seen Esmeralda."

"Great." *Now I'm getting somewhere.* "Where can I reach her? It's really important."

"Well, then, you're out of luck. She's gone, and from what she told me, she'll be gone for a long time. She's headed out on a retreat. Needed to get away and do some meditating, releasing."

Panic sparked in Vivi. "But where? I have to find her."

"Sorry, she didn't tell me."

Scarlet motioned to a low table surrounded by cushions. "Maybe I can help you. Sit. We'll have a look, shall we?" A thumbed, worn stack of tarot cards rested on the table. Scarlet scooped them up and shuffled them lazily with her long fingers.

"I just wanted to talk to her."

Scarlet smirked. "I hear that lie every day of my life. Everyone says they just want to talk. Does anyone saunter up to a bar to chitchat with the bartender? No, paying customers want a drink. And since I'm not selling cocktails, the only reason anyone walks through my door is to see the future and get some answers. Just like you." She wore a blouse of black lace and a necklace of twisted metal and leather around her slender neck. She reminded Vivi of her sister—tough, beautiful, and brutally honest.

Scarlet's *persuasion* was a seer, but her *persuasion* wasn't strong and she used magical tools like tarot cards, tea leaves, auras, and palm reading to get a better bead on the future. She also turned her talent into a lucrative business. Scarlet's mother had been a powerful psychic, not unlike Esmeralda, but Scarlet hadn't inherit her mother's power, so she dabbled at the edge of dark magic, pushing her talents to the limits, earning her a slightly shady reputation within the witching community. Prissy witches loved to gossip about Scarlet, who relished giving them juicy stories to cluck about. But it had also isolated her; witches and wizards of their small town feared she was a dark witch.

Vivi refused to believe Scarlet had gone bad. She sat on one of the cushions and crossed her legs. "I do want to talk. I need your help with something I've been struggling with." Might as well get right to the point.

"Finally, the great and powerful Mayhem sister has decided to come out of the closet." Scarlet set the deck of cards down in front of Vivi. "You should never have been ashamed of being an oracle girl."

"I don't know what I am. That's the problem. How did you know?" Vivi's stomach jumped. Obviously, she had not been as subtle as she thought. "And don't say it's because you're psychic or you saw it in the cards."

"My mom told me. She knew it way back when we were kids. Don't be angry with her. She didn't mean to tell me. It just slipped out one night when she was in a trance. I never told anyone. I've kept your secret all these years."

"How's your mom doing?" Last Vivi had heard, Scarlet's mother was living alone somewhere in the Meadowlands.

"She's managing it. But I am guessing from your visit to little old me, you aren't handling it as well." Scarlet fanned the cards out onto the table.

"No, I'm not. I've pretty much ignored my *persuasion,* and now I don't know how to handle it. I'm overwhelmed with images and dreams, and I don't know what they mean. Where do I start?"

"Asking for help is a good first step," Scarlet said. "Since you haven't been using your magic, images have been building up and are leaking into your consciousness. Your *persuasion* isn't going to go away. It'll come out whether you like it or not."

"Leaking. That's an interesting way to put it. I'll have to bottle it up," Vivi said with levity, but Scarlet didn't smile.

"I'm guessing something really powerful has happened and the magic wants to be seen. You're a conduit." The red-headed witch ran a long nail across the surface of the card deck.

"But why me? Why not you or some other witch who wants to see the future and help people? I don't want it." Vivi put her elbow on the table and rested her forehead against her hand.

Scarlet frowned. "You Mayhem sisters have always taken the huge gifts you were given for granted. Witches don't get to pick and choose their *persuasions*. Magic chooses the witch. The gift picked you and you scoff at it." She scooped up the cards in one swift motion and stood. "You don't deserve the power you've been given. I would do anything to have your talent." She shook her head in disgust. "I can't help you." Scarlet swept past Vivi and disappeared into the back room.

"No, wait. Please, Scarlet. With Esmeralda gone, you're the only witch I can turn to who understands." Vivi parted the glass bead curtain and followed her. The back room was even nicer than the front. Scarlet nodded to two young witches and they gathered up a pair of teacups and went to the front of the shop. "You're right. I have taken my *persuasion* for granted. But I realize that now, and I'm asking for help. You've dealt with seeing and made a real life for yourself."

"You mean not gone crazy." Scarlet eased down in a low chair with a high back, looking regal, ready to judge Vivi for herself.

"Yes. I guess." Vivi plopped down on a

golden velvet chaise lounge. She fingered the fringe of a throw pillow. "I'm scared. I've seen terrible things and I don't know what they mean. I'm in trouble."

Scarlet stared at her, considering something, but Vivi didn't know what. "If I help you, then you have to do what I say, no questioning. And it's going to cost you. I don't hand out professional advice for free." She seemed to think for a moment. "I get my pick of potions."

"Deal. I'm in as long as the magic isn't black," Vivi said. "I'm not doing anything with blood or sacrifice."

Scarlet rolled her dark brown eyes. "No kidding. Of all the Mayhem sisters, you're the squeaky-clean one. I wouldn't dream of dirtying your hands."

"What? I can be *edgy*."

Scarlet threw her head back and laughed. The sound was relaxed and encouraging, the sharpness in her voice dissolving, and for a second Vivi saw the young Scarlet she remembered. "Honey, edgy just isn't your style."

"You'll help?"

"For starters, you need to tell me everything that's happened. We'll go from there."

Over the next two hours, Vivi told Scarlet everything, and in return Scarlet bestowed her soothsaying wisdom. She taught her how to focus her thoughts and how to create a mental trigger for accessing her sight. She also showed her some quick meditation techniques to drop down fast into a quiet state. Vivi learned more in the short time with Scarlet than she had from any other teacher.

"You're really good at this."

"Thanks. I have to practice a lot. My gift demands study, practice, and a ton of patience, and I'm probably half as talented as you. You're a natural." Scarlet's lip curled up in an envious smirk.

"A natural at seeing terrible things." Vivi felt a pang of guilt.

"The things you see won't *all* be terrible. You just haven't given yourself the chance to see the good stuff, the bad stuff, and the simple, everyday life stuff, too, so then you can control your magic and only the most powerful and profound visions come through."

"I hope you're right. I couldn't handle seeing this kind of thing all the time." Vivi thumbed the edge of a tarot card.

"That's why you need to learn to control it, so you see when you want to see and don't end up sprawled on your back-room floor, though I don't make any promises."

"Can you help me try and find the witch? I need to see what happened, get some clue as to who she is and how I can find her." Vivi eyed Scarlet as she glanced at her delicate jeweled watch.

"I have a client coming in twenty minutes. Maybe come back tomorrow."

Vivi panicked. After the vision she'd had about *him*, she couldn't wait another day. Desperately, she latched onto Scarlet's arm. "Please. Just one try. I need a clue, something to go on."

Scarlet pulled away. "You Mayhem sisters are so pushy." She drummed the table with her long nails. "Fine, but we make it quick. I have a feeling I'm going to regret this. Close your eyes and sink deep, like I taught you."

Vivi focused easily enough, but nothing came. She quieted her racing thoughts and meditated. Her mind's eye sifted through a fog layer. Scarlet's voice sounded far away as if Vivi were submerged in water, the sounds muffled. She couldn't get a clear vision of the kidnapped witch no matter how hard she tried, and when she felt an image approaching, it drifted out of sight.

Finally, one image flashed before her—two flat black birds that looked like they had been cut out of black paper were positioned over an arrow. She tried again and again, but the image of the birds kept flashing in her head, hard and sharp, as if pecking at her attention. When she focused on a feeling, she felt someone sewing, which made even less sense. Her head ached. All she saw were those black birds, constantly rising to the surface of her mind, an arrow, and sewing. Weird.

What kind of bird was flat?

She opened her eyes, but no one was there. The room was empty. She got up from her cross-legged position on the floor, wincing from her tight muscles. The sharp sensation of pins and needles raced down her legs, and she hobbled through the bead curtain to the front room, trying to circulate the blood.

"Finally awake, I see?" Scarlet said, standing behind the counter. A group of young witches sheathed in black stared curiously at Vivi as they gathered up their bags and left the shop.

"What do you mean?" Vivi asked, checking her watch. "That can't be right."

"You've been back there for over an hour. My client has come and gone. Did you get anything on the witch? Any new clue?" Scarlet asked.

"Yes, but it's stupid. It doesn't mean anything."

"Nothing's stupid or meaningless. Sometimes visions come in symbols. Maybe you need help interpreting what you saw." Scarlet dropped a few gold coins in the cash box that she stashed under the counter. Vivi definitely owed her a couple of potions in trade for the witch's time.

"I saw two flat black birds and a thin sharp

arrow. Oh, and I got a weird feeling about someone sewing, but that can't be right." Vivi cringed, her vision sounded childish. "That's it." She shrugged. "Basically, I got nothing."

"Two flat birds with an arrow, huh?" Scarlet drummed her fingers on the glass countertop. "Are you sure?"

"I saw them over and over. They looked strange, not like real feathery birds. Flat as pancakes. Totally lame. What could flat birds mean? Are they dead?" Vivi couldn't think of any meaning or how it could be connected.

"Don't worry. I'll figure this out. There are other uses for symbols." Scarlet turned around and dug through an old armoire for a few minutes.

"What're you looking for?" Vivi asked.

"One second, impatient one." Scarlet pulled out an old scroll of parchment and stretched it out on the counter. "Did the birds look like this?" She tapped a long red nail on an image stamped on the page.

Two black birds in silhouette. "That's it! Those are the birds I saw in my mind. I thought of the witch and envisioned her in the dank cell with the scumbag lurking in the shadows like a coward, and that's the image I got." A rush of excitement filled her. Maybe she could make her *persuasion* work after all. "This is awesome. It worked."

"Don't get too excited," Scarlet said, raising

her brow.

"Why? What's the image? It looks a little familiar now that you show it to me on paper." Had she seen the image before?

"You really don't get out much, do you?" Scarlet asked, the corner of her lip upturned.

"What's that supposed to mean?"

"It's a corporate logo for a company in Stargazer City." Scarlet prompted. "Care to take a wild guess?"

"I don't get to the city much." Vivi's stomach did a little flip. She was getting a bad feeling about this.

"It's Dax's company—Mender Corp." Scarlet rolled up the parchment and tucked it away. "It wasn't sewing, but mending. The word is a take on healing and medicine. Dax recently invested with them. But that's all I know."

"You're kidding. Dax? Honora's Dax?" Vivi was mortified. Dax was her sister's first love, a cherished boyfriend and family friend for years."

"You mean *my* Dax, right?" Scarlet's stare turned glacial. Dax was the reason for her and Honora's falling-out. He had come between them and destroyed their friendship, and now Vivi had seen the logo of his company when she tried to locate the missing witch. To Vivi's knowledge neither witch was seeing Dax anymore, but it was still a touchy subject.

Talk about awkward.

"What does it mean?" Vivi tried to navigate around the issue. "Probably nothing. He couldn't be involved."

"I don't know. You said you saw the logo. You can't pretend you didn't just because you don't like what it stands for." Scarlet put her hands up in surrender. "But remember, this is all on you. It's your vision, not mine. Honora isn't going to be happy."

"It's one clue. It might not mean anything."

"Or it could mean everything."

That's what Vivi was afraid of. Honora was really going to kill her now. She had enlisted the help of her sister's best friend turned nemesis, who sort of helped her implicate her ex-boyfriend's company as the only clue she had to finding a missing witch. On the bright side, at least she was one step closer.

8

THE DOOR SHUT BEHIND HER as Vivi hurried out of The Evil Queen and headed back to The Potion Garden. She slipped into her shop and took a deep breath. Scents of sandalwood and lemongrass wafted on the air. She hadn't meant to spend so much time with Scarlet, but time had slipped away from her. Truth be told, she'd had a great afternoon. Even with struggling to get a handle on her magic, she was doing something important, trying to figure out how to navigate her *persuasion*. For the first time, she felt in control.

Unfortunately, her time in training with Scarlet did not come without consequences. The one big clue to finding the missing witch happened to be the corporation invested in by one of Everland's most successful, brilliant, and devilishly handsome businessmen,

Honora's ex-boyfriend, Dax Cross. She would have to handle that bit of news later. Time to get to work.

"How's it going?" Vivi asked Pepper, shoving her purse under the counter. A few customers mingled around the shop.

"Great. You just missed the rush. The wishful-thinking potion you whipped up is selling like crazy. We'll probably need another batch." Pepper handled the afternoon crowd like a pro.

Vivi tied an apron around her waist. "You're a lifesaver." She gave Pepper a little squeeze. "Thanks for taking care of things around here the past two days. I don't know where I'd be without you."

"No problem. We're a team." Pepper giggled and a tiny furry head poked out of her shirt pocket. A little black nose sniffed the air, whiskers twitching. It was Teeny, Pepper's chipmunk familiar. He often hitched a ride in her pocket while she worked. The curious, hyper little guy was a good match for her active assistant. They both had the same speedy temperament.

"Looks like your little boy's helping out." Vivi smiled.

"Not really. He just likes to run around and find little hidey-holes behind the potion bottles. He practically scared Lavender to death."

"How's she doing? I hardly ever get to see her anymore, now that her shop's going gangbusters."

Lavender Blue ran The Charmery, the hot new shop on Main Street.

"Great. She's a workaholic like you. She was in shopping for a calming balm. After the big charm gala last week, business boomed, so she needed a potion to help her relax."

"That was the best party ever. She had dozens of gorgeous metal charms and even introduced a jewelry line of cool necklaces and bracelets. I wanted them all." Vivi twisted up her lips in concentration. "I was thinking we could try something similar with a few popular potions."

"Like how?" Pepper asked, feeding Teeny a piece of popcorn.

"By using those extra-small vials we thought would never work for resale."

"Right. The ones the glassblower made way too small and we got stuck with three full boxes."

"What if we strung the tiny vials on necklaces using leather or silk cords? See how it works. Then, if they sell, we could upgrade to silver and gold chains."

"That's a great idea. Wearable potions. You're a genius." Pepper beamed.

"Not really. Just trying to keep up with the times."

Vivi headed into the back and grabbed her old trusty copper pot. Time to brew some more potions to keep the shelves filled, especially the new wishful-thinking potion that was a surprise hit. Brewing gave her time to think and time to relax. It also brought back memories of her childhood, when she'd learned how to conjure magic in the kitchen of their little cottage in the woods.

When Vivi was little, she used to curl up at her mother's feet as she bustled around in the kitchen, wearing a long soft apron that had been washed so often if felt like a lamb's ear rubbing against Vivi's cheek. Always baking up something special for her girls, Elspeth never scatted Vivi away when she played underfoot, but would sprinkle cinnamon or crystalized sugar down from above for her to catch on her tongue like delicious snowflakes. Vivi would hold her own little ceramic bowl in her lap, filled with pulverized wildflowers and a few unfortunate beetles that had clung to her mother's rose bushes and ended up as part of a make-believe magic potion she stirred up while her mother hummed a tune.

Elspeth always encouraged her to experiment, to take chances and mix many a strange and wonderful potion. Vivi had poured the powdery concoctions into tiny leather bags she kept in her pocket or tied to her belt. She knew the potions didn't work. She hadn't learned how to imbibe the ingredients with magic, but they made her feel better. Even as a child, Vivi realized potions fixed things.

Now in her back-room kitchen, she took a moment to think about everything that happened and how she fit into the world. Her shop was her anchor. Jars of honey sat next to bottles of melted mountain snow. Dried newt rested next to spiky cattails. Canisters of marigolds, lavender, toadstools, and poppies, vials of seeds, and jars of sap crowded her shelves. She collected the essence of the forest and the seas to make elixirs, tonics, potions, and salves.

Her life was sweet and sour, harsh as rain-swept wind. It ached and squeezed, loved and laughed. Life was supposed to be filled with good and bad. A tune her mother used to sing came back to her.

Sulfur, brimstone, soot and ash. Posies, roses, sugar, salt.

Life breaks the skin, the bone, the heart.

The potion maker steals the sun, the moon, the rain.

Bottling a better brew to ease the pain.

The memory of her mother was bittersweet, but it always grounded her, made her realize the one thing in her life she never questioned. Potions mended, healed, and hid the pain of life with a jolt of laughter, a wish whispered to the universe, a deep breath, or a moment of lightness.

These were the things of her shop: her pretend, her make-believe, made real.

Vivi didn't want to lose it. She didn't want to be alone like Esmeralda—a shunned seer. But what was done was done. Every step she took was taking her deeper into a mystery she wasn't sure she was prepared to solve, and now she had to face the things she saw and follow the visions where they took her. She shuddered, remembering what Esmeralda had told her that night in the woods.

Follow the visions wherever they take you.

That was her problem.

"Hey, Vivi," Pepper called from the front of the shop. "A giant owl just arrived." Her voice was stern. She was probably keeping a strong eye on the predator and making sure he steered clear of her meal-sized familiar. There was a strict no-eating policy in the shop, especially when it came to beloved chipmunks.

Vivi hurried to the front to see a huge brownish-gray barred owl perched on Rumor's stand. The owl gave a hoot when he saw her. Rumor was not in the shop, but he wouldn't mind sharing his perch with Honora's familiar, Barnaby. There was a tiny capsule attached to his leg. Vivi and Honora often exchanged messages through their familiars. She took the capsule and unrolled a tiny bit of parchment sealed inside.

The note read: *Dinner tonight at Clover's. See you there. H.*

Vivi loved it when her sisters got together to hang out, cook, eat, and talk. Any other night she would have been elated to see them, but now that she had seen the logo she would have to talk to Honora. No avoiding it. She knew if she wanted to follow her vision and get into Mender Corp, she would need her sister's advice. No one knew Dax Cross better.

Pepper tapped her foot, hands on hips. "I hope you haven't forgotten something."

"Never. A promise is a promise," Vivi said. Time she had a little fun with her assistant and pay a visit to the most famous word witch in Everland.

The local bookstore, Goodspells Grimoire, was packed with witches and wizards desperate to get a copy of the latest *Spellbinder* novel. The place hummed with excitement. Vivi had promised Pepper, who clutched the newly purchased novel to her chest as her gaze roved the bookshop, they could close up the shop for the afternoon and head over to the signing. They were crammed in with what looked like the entire town. An elbow jabbed Vivi in the ribcage. A witch wearing a long blue cape and a platinum waist-length wig stepped on her foot. Many of the witches jostling for position were dressed up as characters from the books.

A hushed silence filled the room as the famous Cassandra Reason passed through a silk curtain and made her way onto the stage. A cascade of rich brown curls cradled her shoulders. Wearing a long black dress with gathers in all the right places to show off her hourglass figure, Cassandra took her seat. Her nails were black enamel, and her lush lips were stained the color of blood. Crystal-blue eyes stared out from a gorgeous face with a delicate brow and high cheekbones. She oozed sultry with a splash of deviant goddess. Cassandra was creative and brilliant—a gifted word witch—and yet she remained humble and kind in the spotlight's bright glare.

She was also completely fictional.

Clover Mayhem had invented the fictitious witch to be her stand-in because she couldn't handle all the attention. She hated the spotlight that her *persuasion* as a wildly successful word witch had bestowed on her. She was much more comfortable camped out in her old-world-style house with a pitched roof and writing turret, devouring cupcakes, drinking wine, and writing stories than hanging out with throngs of adoring fans. But to be a successful novelist, she had to work the circuit and make public appearances.

So, to fix the problem, Clover devised the

bombshell—a dynamic, charismatic pseudo-witch to absorb the spotlight for her—and Vivi had been happy to conjure up the potion that, for four hours at a time, allowed her sister to magically transform into Cassandra Reason. Once the time elapse was up, she turned back into herself, or she could take a reversal potion, if she didn't want to wait.

The disguise worked like a charm. The Cassandra Reason series of romance mysteries had crowded the top of the best-seller list for the past five years. Clover stayed relatively anonymous, and the witches of Everland lapped up the show like cold cream with a coarse cat tongue.

From the length of the line, Vivi figured it would take a least an hour to get Pepper's book signed, and that gave her an idea. "Would you mind if I checked out the archives on the second floor while you're waiting?" Vivi asked.

"Not at all. I'm not going to be good company anyway. The potion you made for you-know-who is flawless. I want to take a good look, to study it."

"For professional potion-making research, of course." Vivi nudged her assistant with her elbow. "I'll be back soon."

On her way to the staircase that led upstairs, she waved down a flustered wizard with a barrel chest and a full brown beard. Bear Griswold hurried around the store, handing out books and answering questions, but when he caught Vivi's eye he joined her at the foot of the stairs in a flash.

"Thought I'd head up and check out some materials from the archives," Vivi said with a wink.

"Go on. In fact, lead the way. I could use a few minutes' break." Bear wiped the sweat from his forehead with a handkerchief and waved to his wife, Priscilla, motioning to where he was going, before following Vivi up the creaking stairs to the second floor.

Unlike Vivi, who had constructed an apartment on the second floor of her shop, Bear had built a space to store the town archives and back issues of *Witch World Daily*. It was a treasure trove of information on all things Everland. Bear was a lover of stories, and not only the fictional. He loved the stories of real witches and wizards who made up the community, so keeping the town records, newspapers, and catalogues was a labor of love. Plus, it saved the town from having to hire a curator.

The room was filled with shelves packed with huge ledgers and rolls of parchments containing back issues of the paper. Vivi was slightly overwhelmed and her wide-eyed expression made the wizard chuckle.

"What are you looking for? Maybe I can steer you in the right direction."

"I'm searching for information on a medical company in Stargazer City called Mender Corp, plus whatever we can dig up on the owners and Dax Cross."

Bear raised his brow and motioned for her to follow him down one of the aisles. "This area's where I like to keep the public records, licenses, and tax information on business establishments. Anything the company makes public. Not the originals, mind you, which are kept in the city of record, but I like to have copies for our local records."

"Wow, you've collected an impressive amount of data." Vivi brightened with admiration for the details-loving wizard.

"It's my passion, or as my wife would say, my obsession. I like to think of it as a tapestry of the *persuasions* of industry and progress." He waved his wand and muttered a spell that caused a number of books and scrolls on the shelves to shift and slide a few inches forward. "A sorting and searching spell I've been working on," he said for explanation and went to retrieve the materials.

"Great spell. It would have taken me hours to find this stuff."

He smiled. "Here you go. Feel free to look through them and others if you wish. There's paper and writing materials if you need to take notes. None of the books or parchments can leave the archives, I'm afraid, but you're welcome to stay as long as you like."

Vivi pulled out a chair as Bear set the materials down on the table. "Thanks. This is great." She spent the next hour gleaning the records for information on Dax and his new company. Mender Corp had been up and running for many years, Dax joining the company in the last year, and not surprisingly, business had jumped considerably under his guidance. They specialized in healing potions, capsules, and mass production of medicines, which were once only available from local healers. But Everland was moving into the modern world of medicine and demand for easy access to healing remedies was on the rise.

Most of the information on Dax she already knew, but the details on the founders of Mender Corp were enlightening. The company was the brainchild of twins—Mitchell and Miranda Mender. They were prodigies in the *persuasion* of healing, groomed at a young age to excel in medicine. Vivi scanned the company's public relations biography of the twins, which listed their extensive academy training and accolades, but it was an old news clipping that really got her attention. The story told the tragic tale of an accident at a laboratory, an explosion that killed the twins' parents, leaving them alone in the world with no other family. The photo depicted two pale, dazed children peeking sadly out from under mops of black hair. Orphans. Geniuses. Rising out of despair to form one of the most successful companies in Everland. Fascinating.

Next, Vivi discovered an article in the newspaper on Mender Corp by a witch who had taken a company tour of the healing facility that caused Vivi's senses to perk up. A tour was exactly what she needed. She selected a sheet of paper and a reed pen and composed a letter to old family friend Dax Cross, hoping he could get her a spot on one of the behind-the-scenes tours. *Couldn't hurt to ask*, she thought. After writing the note and sealing it up, she put all the books back on the shelves and headed back downstairs to see how the author signing was going.

Luckily, Pepper was close to the front of the line, so Vivi made her way to the table and stood off to the side, waiting for her assistant.

A wizard in his mid-twenties fumbled with a pile of hardbacks he was holding to get signed and dropped them on the floor at Cassandra's feet. He scrambled to gather up the books. Vivi couldn't see his face, but he gave her a weird sensation. She hopped out of line and went up to give him a hand. "Need some help?" she asked as she picked up a book that had fallen a few feet away.

"I got it," he said.

His face was gaunt and a line of acne scars lined his strong jaw, making him look more rugged than his tall, wiry frame would suggest. His hair was freshly washed and still wet, slicked back, showing off his hollow cheeks, beakish nose, and stiff grin. His face turned beet red. Cassandra had that effect on wizards, especially fans meeting her for the first time. When he took the book from her, Vivi noticed that he was wearing leather gloves.

"Thanks," he said, and turned his back on her.

Even though she wanted the nervous fanboy to hurry up, Vivi couldn't shake the strange feeling she got from him. She joined Pepper as the line advanced.

"I know how he feels," Pepper whispered, shifting from foot to foot. "I was a ball of nerves the first time I met Cassandra."

Finally, the next few people got their books signed and Vivi and Pepper approached the signing table.

"Now's your chance," Vivi nudged Pepper as their turn arrived.

Pepper giggled and set her book down in front of her literary idol, Cassandra Reason. "I love your work. It's brilliant," she gushed. "Please don't ever stop writing."

"You're so sweet, Pepper. And very perceptive." Cassandra arched a perfectly sculpted eyebrow at the two of them.

Vivi winked at her sister and made room for the next fan by standing off to the side.

After the book signing, they stopped off at the post office so Vivi could send the letter to Dax. The post was the main source of communication in Everland, and couriers went out numerous times day and night, delivering correspondence. Vivi was lucky, for when she walked in, an enthusiastic young witch with a messenger bag slung over her shoulder was about to leave with the next delivery, assuring the letter would reach Stargazer City later in the afternoon.

Having some time to kill, Vivi and Pepper stopped in the Brewery Tavern for a mug of kindle brew and some snacks before heading back to the shop to meet up with Clover. Two hours later the door swung open and a pretty woman with a pert nose and long curly blonde hair strolled into The Potion Garden. She was wearing a trailing skirt that skimmed the floor, an empire-waist blouse, and a wide-brimmed hat with flowers from her garden pinned to it.

Pepper raced over and gave Vivi's sister a big hug. "I'm so excited for you and the new book."

"Thanks, kitten. I'm glad you like it." She pulled off her hat and used it to fan herself. "Is it hot in here or is it just me?"

"It's you," Vivi said. "All that adoration has got you overheated." She laughed. "I'm just glad I don't have to keep my mouth shut about the book anymore now that it's out."

"Since the book is finally available for the masses, I might be in a little late tomorrow. I plan on staying up to read every word. I can't make any promises on my punctuality." Pepper clutched her package in her arms.

"No problem. You can take the late shift tomorrow. Now hurry home and get reading," Vivi said, but her assistant was already out the front door.

With the shop closed for the night, the two sisters sauntered into the back room. Clover made herself comfortable, brewing up a pot of tea for them while Vivi poured cooled potion mixtures, which she had brewed earlier that day, into bottles. She filled Clover in on the events of the past two days.

"I can't believe Esmeralda was wandering the woods near my house. That's a little sad and creepy," Clover said, sipping her tea.

"I'll say."

"What are you going to do now?" Clover asked.

"From what I can gather there's really only one thing I can do: check out Mender Corp. I sent a letter to Dax."

Clover practically choked on her tea. "Are you serious?" She cleared her throat.

"After my day with Scarlet, I really don't think I have a choice. I have to follow up on this lead and my gut."

"Does Honora know what you are planning

on doing?"

"If you mean does she know that I sought out council from her arch-rival, nemesis, and sworn enemy till death, then no. And she won't until I find a way of breaking it to her tonight at dinner, so mum's the word." Vivi eyed her sister. "Got it?"

"My lips are sealed. In fact, I'm going to put a spell on myself so I don't tell." Clover dramatically dug around in her bag. "Where did I put that lip-sealer potion?"

They both laughed. "You used it all up on me, remember? So I wouldn't spill any secrets from your new book."

"I wish there was something I could do to help," Clover said, pouring Vivi another cup of steaming tea.

"I've been avoiding the whole thing for too long. Scarlet really woke me up today about my *persuasion*. We have a lot in common. She made me realize that I can't keep wasting my magic." Vivi drizzled wax over the top of the corked bottles to seal them tight.

Clover didn't say anything, but her silence was loaded.

"What?" Vivi asked. She hated it when Clover got quiet.

"Be careful with her. Scarlet serves herself. She was into some dark stuff back in school." Clover ran her finger over the delicate edge of her cup. Being the eldest sister, she was the most protective by nature.

"That was a long time ago. Witches change. I'm keeping an open mind." Vivi put the hot copper pot down, careful not to burn herself.

Clover shook her head. "What's she up to these days?"

"She has a fortune-telling shop off Main Street." Vivi smiled and shrugged. "It's called The Evil Queen."

"Ha! Told you. I need to come into town more often. I'm missing all the fun."

9

VIVI STAYED IN TOWN TO freshen up before heading out to the Meadowlands to meet her sisters for dinner. Clover lived in a huge old-world-style house the color of a ripe pumpkin with white trim and black shutters and door to match. Everyone called it the pumpkin house because of the orange siding. The eccentric-looking house fit her sister's quirky personality perfectly, and gave off an air of perpetual Halloween. Both Clover and Honora were lounging in two wicker armchairs on the covered porch when Vivi arrived with her arms loaded down with groceries.

"Can I get some help with these?" Vivi yelled to them as she juggled the bags up the pathway to the house.

"Finally, the food has arrived." Clover

jumped to her feet and raced to help her with the goodies. She was infamous for her disasters in the kitchen, so Vivi and Honora did most of the cooking.

Nosy as a starving badger, Clover dug through the bag and latched onto a baguette, sliding it free. "Come to mama," she said, sniffing the golden-brown bread.

Honora grabbed a bag out of Vivi's arms but gave Clover a look of mock concern. "When you start to snuggle up with a loaf of bread, it's an emergency sign you need a date," Honora said, traipsing into the kitchen and unloading the food. "When was the last time you went out with a man? A *real* man, not an imaginary one you made up."

Clover twisted up her mouth in thought. "Two novels ago. Randal, remember?"

"Who was he again?" Honora asked as the three navigated their way around the huge kitchen.

"The librarian," Vivi yelped, pouring herself a glass of Clover's famous wine and fruit sangria, which had a serious kick. "The strong silent type. A bookworm."

"He was very, very sweet. And nice." Clover tossed a head of lettuce onto the counter and held up a cluster of tomatoes still dangling on the vine.

"Too nice from what I recall." Honora turned up the flame on the stove and warmed a pot of water.

"Isn't that always the problem? Wizards are either hard as nails or soft as a marshmallow. I'd like to meet one right in the middle," Clover said, starting to chop the vegetables for the salad.

"You need to whip us up a hot wizard potion, Vivi." Honora stirred the bubbling red sauce she had made earlier that day, warming it up.

"You both know that love potions never work for very long. You can't fake love." Vivi sliced the loaf of bread in half and slathered it with a butter and garlic mixture.

"Who was talking love?" Honora asked. "We just want a warm body with thick hair. He doesn't even have to talk. Just be gorgeous, sexy, and do whatever I tell him to do." She wiggled her eyebrows.

"And gives good back rubs, likes to read, and knows some basic cleaning spells," Clover chimed in, wielding her knife. She was not known for her neatness; in fact, she was a bit of a pack rat.

"I want a wizard who's a good kisser, not too gorgeous, more on the casual, lived-in handsome side, a jeans and T-shirt kind of guy with a good stable job and a dog," Vivi fantasized out loud.

"He sounds perfect for you." Clover mixed up the greens in a large wooden bowl and drizzled oil and vinegar over them.

Honora snorted. "Sounds like the sheriff."

Vivi opened the oven and slid the butter-slathered loaf inside, avoiding her sister's gaze. "Well, with all this garlic and onions, we're going to need a breath-freshening potion to go with our man potion because no one would kiss us after we ate this dinner."

The sisters settled into the comfortable rhythm of talking, laughing, and eating. They sat around Clover's old farm table with bowls of pasta drenched in sauce, salad, garlic bread, and a bottle of wine. Candles twinkled. Vivi leaned back in a padded high-backed chair and sighed. All the tension of the past few days had melted away. Dinner was perfect. She felt safe and at home with her sisters. Maybe the night wasn't going to be that bad. Surely Honora would understand what she had done.

"Speaking of eligible," Vivi said, awkwardly trying to transition the conversation to Honora's old flame. "When was the last time you saw Dax?"

"It's been a while." Her sister's body tensed and she sat up in her chair. "Almost a year. Why?" Honora gave Vivi and Clover a suspicious glare.

"I've been doing some digging about the case since the last time I saw you." Vivi dipped a chunk of bread into the sauce on her plate and stuffed it into her mouth. "And I was curious about Dax's company, so I did a little research in the town archives."

"Which one? He's diversified these last few years. He still owns the majority holding in the Silver Train, and last I heard he had invested in a medical company started by two weird genius twins." Honora pushed her chair back and propped her feet up on an old wooden crate.

Vivi pictured the two flat birds of the logo and the haunting photo of the orphan twins. "Mender Corp."

Clover returned to the table with a fresh bottle and poured a glug of wine into her glass. "Mitchell and Miranda. They're two talented witches. The healing *persuasion* techniques they have developed are phenomenal."

"Dax's all business these days. He always knew a good deal when he saw one, and he jumped at the chance to work with the twins," Honora said.

"Look how the Silver Train took off." Clover hiccupped. "You should give him a call. He's so hot, and his muscles have muscles. And he has thick hair. I love a man with a good head of hair." She ran her hands through her own hair, getting one of her rings caught.

"Down, girl," Honora said, helping get Clover's ring untangled. "You're going to hurt yourself."

"I never realized he was interested in healing," Vivi said.

"Dax's interested in maximizing profit. Why so curious, sister?" Honora was like a dog with a bone ever since she started her private investigation company.

"I hope you don't mind, but I sent him a letter today. I would love to get a tour of his new company and see how the healing potions are made." Vivi sipped her wine, Honora's gaze clinging to her like a shadow. She hopped up and dug through Clover's kitchen cabinets. "Do you have anything sweet? I need dessert."

"Cupcakes, second cabinet from the left," Clover said. "Get me one, too. Oh, heck, bring them all."

Vivi returned to the table with a bakery box filled with chocolate cupcakes. She handed one of the giant buttercream-frosted delicacies to Honora, hoping to divert her sister's attention.

"Wait a minute. Back up. Vivi, why would you want to go into the city and see Dax and his new company?" Honora swiped her finger across the rich icing and licked it off, watching her sister. "Does this have anything to do with your visions?"

"I focused on my *persuasion* like you suggested, and while in a trance I saw the logo for Mender Corp. I think it's a clue to the missing witch." She was planning to avoid mentioning Scarlet for as long as she could. Why bring her involvement up if she didn't have to?

"That's great. That's a strong clue, Vivi," Honora said, jerking up in her seat. "Maybe now you can figure out who this witch is and find her. Why didn't you just tell me? I don't mind if you go and see Dax."

"Well, I know things didn't go as planned with him. I didn't want to bring up bad memories." Or make her mad, especially if she knew that her nemesis had helped her channel her vision.

After the fallout with Scarlet, Dax and Honora had tried to keep up the steamy relationship but had hit a rough patch. Since then, they dated on and off for years. Currently it was off.

Honora sighed. "No problem. It's over. And if my connection with Dax can help, then I want to do what I can. You don't think he's involved?"

"Probably not. Like I said, I just got the image of the logo, so it really could mean anything. That's why I was hoping to get a peek at the inside. Do a little investigating."

"I'm sure he'll respond." Honora smiled. "He always liked you and Clover."

Vivi was relieved, but there was more to her story, and deep down, she knew she had to tell her sister everything. "There's something else."

"Wow, we're going to go there already," Clover said, eyes going wide. "I'll need another glass of wine."

"What is it? You can tell me anything."

"Since I decided to take my *persuasion* seriously, I'm training and studying with someone, and this witch really helped me to learn new meditation techniques."

"Oh, yeah? Who is this great teacher?" Honora asked.

"Spill it, Vivi," Clover said. *Easy for her to say,* Vivi thought.

"It's Scarlet," Vivi blurted out. "I went to see her to get help. She's the only witch I know who understands what I'm dealing with. I was desperate. You don't know what it's been like." All of the relaxation of the night had evaporated in an instant. The room was now practically crackling with tension. A log popped in the fireplace, sending sparks flying.

"You what?" Honora leapt to her feet and began to pace the way she did when she was angry. "I can't believe you would go behind my back and talk to her!"

"I didn't have a choice. I don't have anyone to help me." Vivi bit her bottom lip.

"We could help you," Clover said, trying to be helpful.

"You two are the only other witches I know who are busier than I am. You have great careers and lives of your own. You don't have time to hold my hand through this, especially since I don't even know what I need help with."

"You come to family first," Honora said.

"Scarlet understands how visions work." Vivi twisted up her napkin and tossed it on the table. "She's a good teacher."

"A good teacher? We should be helping you. Not her." Honora pointed to herself and Clover, who stuffed the rest of her cupcake into her mouth, wisely deciding to keep out of the quickly escalating argument.

"I need someone else. Someone who knows my *persuasion*." Vivi's shoulders tensed.

"Scarlet's a hack with barely any magic. And she hates me. Or did you forget that part while you were hanging out with my ex-best friend?" Honora's cheeks reddened.

"I know you two have had disagreements in the past, but I thought it was smoothed over enough. I hoped you would understand." Vivi gulped down the last of her wine.

"Seriously? You know that information about Dax is probably no good," Honora said, her hands on her hips.

"What do you mean? A minute ago you thought my information was fine and were willing to help me." Vivi gritted her teeth. She needed Honora's help, not her skepticism.

"That was before I found out where you got your information from. Now that I know it was

Scarlet, I know it's unreliable."

"I know what I saw, and it was the Mender Corp logo." Vivi clenched her jaw. Her face was getting warm, and it wasn't from the wine.

"I'm sorry, Vivi, but Scarlet is setting you up. She probably planted some idea or image in your head. She's still mad because Dax picked me over her, so she's trying to set him up or implicate him in something. She wants us to look like fools and she's using you."

"That's ridiculous. I went to her for help. She had no idea what was going on before I walked into her shop. And not everything in the world is about *you*!" Vivi snapped. She'd known Honora was going to be a *little* upset about her visit to Scarlet, but her sister was totally overreacting.

"You two need to calm down. It's not worth fighting over." Clover tried to interrupt them.

Honora leaned against the kitchen doorframe with her arms crossed over her chest. "You went to Scarlet for help and she saw her chance and grabbed it. You don't realize it because you don't want to. You feel guilty about what you saw and are desperate to find this girl. That's it. She took advantage of your weak magic."

Clover gasped. "Honora, that's not a nice thing to say. Vivi's not weak."

Honora held her ground. She twisted up her mouth in defiance.

Vivi stood speechless. Was that really how Honora thought of her? She stepped back. She wanted to lash out, defend herself, say something sharp and cunning to show her sister how strong she was. The last thing she had wanted was a knockdown-dragout fight with Honora, who was the most pigheaded witch she knew, but she couldn't let the jab go without one of her own. "This is exactly why I didn't come to you. Scarlet didn't tell me I was weak. She thinks I'm the one in the family with real power."

Vivi grabbed her bag and jacket and headed for the front door.

"Don't go." Clover chased after her. "Honora didn't mean it."

But Vivi was done listening. She pushed through the screen door and let it slam behind her.

"I'll come by the shop in a day or two to check on you," Clover called from the porch. "She didn't mean it."

But Vivi knew that Honora did mean it, and she also knew her sister had a point. Her magic *was* weak, but all that was about to change.

10

B Y THE TIME VIVI GOT home, she was livid. She was tired of being afraid of what was happening to her, about the things she saw and what they meant. She was tired of stuffing everything down deep inside. Ignorance was not bliss. She paced around her apartment, and before she realized it, she was digging through her closet, stripping out of her cute flimsy skirt and adorable flats that she had worn for a night of fun and tugging on a serious pair of jeans, a long-sleeved black T-shirt, and her butt-kicking boots. Twisting her hair up into a ponytail and winding it around into a topknot, Vivi grabbed her favorite cropped leather jacket and bounded down into her shop.

In the past, she would have stayed up half the night going on an emotional potion-brewing bender. She would have invented a magical concoction to make herself feel better and soothe her hurt feelings. And the worst part, or best part depending on how she looked at it, was that it worked. Her potions did make her feel better for a little while, but they wore off, and they distracted her from what she was really feeling.

Not this time.

Scarlet had been right. Mayhem witches were strong, but they were also proud. They were born kicking and screaming. Honora and Clover were powerful witches, masters of their crafts, but Vivi was not. She had been hiding behind the glittery potion bottles for too long. Her true magic had wilted from neglect.

Once in her shop, Vivi made a beeline to the shelves filled with magical wards, protection bubbles, and watch-your-back spells. She sold many potions to protect a witch from nasty gossip, backstabbing, and bullying, including more powerful potions to block attack spells. She also had shield wards to stop lesser wandwork, and a full-on protective bubble. Against typical-strength magic, they worked great, but the stronger the spell or the more powerful the witch, the less the potions held up. Her shop was not stocked for an all-out assault, but they would give her some protection.

Vivi moved quickly, transferring the

selected potions out of their pretty bottles into clear generic vials that slid nicely into the straps of leather on the bandolier. She kept moving; if she thought too much, she might change her mind. The time for sitting around meditating, talking, and thinking about what she should do was over.

She was going to use her *persuasion* to figure out what was really going on in the Dire Woods. Her sisters would be furious if they knew what she was planning. It was daring and maybe a little reckless, but she wasn't about to crawl into bed and go to sleep. She was heading out to the woods in the middle of the night to scout the area for clues.

Vivi was going hunting.

Before she locked up the shop, she grabbed a piece of parchment from under the counter and scribbled a note to Pepper, telling her where she was going just in case something happened and she didn't make it into work the next day. She was angry, but she wasn't stupid.

She navigated the dark streets, crossing over to Main Street and down a crooked alley. She saw the portal gate from a block away. It was a shellacked green door with a brass head of a boar on it. The door once belonged to a crotchety old wizard who adored his familiar so much that when the boar died unexpectedly, he'd had him bronzed and mounted on a plaque. After the wizard passed on, no one wanted his grubby little one-room hovel, so the place was turned into a portal. This gate would take her to the portal closest to the Dire Woods. Then she was on her own to find her way back to the crime scene.

Vivi pulled out her golden portal key and approached the door. She knocked on the wood surface and the boar snorted, his brassy eyes blinking to life.

"You're out late," he said. The wizard had also enchanted him with the power to speak. Seemed he had a sense of humor after all. "Got a hot date?"

"I need to go to Outpost 11," she said, matter-of-factly, which was difficult to do when conversing with a brass boar.

The boar snorted. "The Dire Woods. Tsk-tsk. I shouldn't be surprised, with you being a *Mayhem*. What happened, did all the trouble in town dry up, and now you need to go looking for it in the dark corners of the witching world?"

She hated it when the boar got chatty. "Yes, I'm hunting for trouble. Now, let me through or I'll yank you off your safe little plaque and take you with me."

With a snort, the boar announced, "Outpost 11." The boar's snout twitched. Snorting again, he advised, "Careful, girly."

Vivi slipped her key into the lock and

turned. The door opened with glowing magical warmth. She stepped off the sidewalk of the back alley in town and walked through a crumbling stone wall on the other side of Willow Realm that boarded the edge of the Dire Woods. She held onto the side of the archway for a second to get her bearings.

She was far from her destination and still had to traverse the forest. The last time she had been there, she'd had her arms wrapped around the strong chest of a handsome sheriff. This time she was on her own—no hover bike to take her.

A single brass lantern hung from the wall of the portal gate, the darkness encroaching on her tiny pool of light.

"Illuminus," Vivi whispered, and the stone in her ring glowed to life. She only had one idea on how she was going to get out to the Darklander territory.

Vivi pulled a potion from her belt, uncorked it, and swallowed before she lost her nerve and went home. It tasted like melted rubber and sour cherries. "Bleck," she said. She swallowed a few times to get the taste off her tongue. A strider potion was an acquired taste. The spell would last a few hours and made every stride triple the distance. If she picked up her pace, she could walk a fast mile in five or six minutes. Run, and she would be to the north quadrant of the Dire Woods in less than an hour. It wasn't as fast as flying—and it wasn't as graceful—but it was her way. And she was going to make it work.

Vivi breathed deeply and started to walk. She quickened her pace with each step, her eyes adapting to the darkness. Her body bounded through the crowded landscape of shadowy trees as if walking on air. The wind blew a cooling breeze across her face. Her lungs stung, but she pushed on. *I really need to exercise more,* she thought, trying to ease her anxiety. The sounds of night birds surrounded her. The woods were teeming with creatures that preferred the darkness, even if just to watch from a high perch. Claws, beaks, and talons were just a few of their weapons. The trees stood like ghostly sentries. Rumor had been out hunting, or she would have brought him for company and to warn her if she became the prey.

Vivi held her glowing ring up to chest height, careful where she stepped. She was in a jog, her breathing steady. Sweat beaded on her brow. She was getting closer. The dark magic of the scorched circle radiated toward her. It had left a signature of soot and charred blood salt, and when she let her senses drift outward, she could feel its sickening pull.

Within a few minutes she slowed to a cautious walk. Haunting red lights glowed ahead like the eyes of a dozen small creatures.

Alert, Vivi approached with delicate footfalls. The sheriff had marked off the area where they had found the old witch with a ring of glowing red illuma lights. The scene of the crime included the path the woman stumbled along and the charred circle where Vivi had found her. Technically, she was trespassing. Vivi gingerly walked around the lights, not wanting to disturb them and set off an alarm. Last thing she needed was the sheriff woken from his bed and hunting her down.

Her gaze drifted over the scene. Something wasn't right.

Then it hit her—the crime scene was unguarded. She let her senses open and drift around the immediate area. No wards, no boundaries, just a few glowing trip lights that, when she thought about it, were probably more for show than anything else. How hard was it to just walk around them? *Not very.* An emptiness washed over her when she realized the investigation at the scene was over. No one was there because the police were done collecting evidence. A witch had been tortured and left for dead, and now the site was abandoned.

A shiver went up her spine. *Stay alert.*

Vivi's attention was drawn deeper into the woods, to the sheer black obsidian rock of the Darklander's stone fortress, his mansion and home base. Surprisingly, it wasn't difficult to see in the dark forest since it was surrounded in glowing illuma lights hung in the trees like ghostly lanterns. Was it a coincidence Clarissa was found so close to the evil wizard's domain? Was that where the young witch was being held right now? It seemed foolish of him to be practicing dark magic so close to his own home.

Technically, the Dire Woods was part of Everland, and though the Darklander was on the fringe, he still lived within the rules of law of the council. It would be detrimental if he were implicated in black magic. He would be banished from Everland entirely.

The Darklander was anything but foolish. That wasn't to say he wasn't involved in suspect magical practices; most likely he was. He just didn't have a reputation for being stupid or for getting caught, and performing sorcery on a witch in your backyard was not only a heinous act, but really stupid.

Vivi wanted to widen her search. The police had done a thorough job clearing the crime scene of all magical evidence, and she expected no less of the sheriff. Her attention shifted to the mansion. Had Lance stayed away from it to appease the council? Taking a closer look might be her best bet of finding anything to help her cause. She inhaled the midnight air. No backing down now.

Vivi made her way closer and closer to the

mansion until suddenly a light flashed on, forcing her to advance in another direction, which set off another orb. For a second it reminded her of fireflies blinking on and off, but she realized the mansion was surrounded with motion sensors. She could only get so close before setting off an army of lights. Then who would be watching whom? The Darklander was certain to have an intense security field. In fact, when she opened up her senses to the surrounding magic, she could feel the pulse of wards. *Better not get too close unless I want to get zapped by his security wards.*

It was too dark to do a physical search, so Vivi found a large tree about fifty yards from the huge front door and sat in the perimeter of darkness. She rested her back against the bark, closed her eyes, and focused her attention. She quieted her mind and body, trying to become still and one with her surroundings. Vivi cast a net of intuition outward, sensing the velvety darkness. She was looking for magic, any pulse or residue. Minutes crept by. She pictured a grid of the area in her mind and searched each area section by section, beginning closest to where she sat and then moving outward. She had gotten about fifty feet before a flicker of magical energy caught her attention. Excitement filled her. It wasn't much, but it was enough to get her blood pumping.

Her eyes flashed open and she leapt to her feet. She moved cautiously in the direction of the magic, but it was waning, barely registering to her senses. Luckily, the magic was in the opposite direction to the mansion, and she avoided the security orbs. The area was more of the same—wooded, leafy, nothing special, only the fleeting pulse of energy to alert her. The ring on her finger glowed, and she projected the light in a search beam on the ground covered in leaf litter. She shifted the debris with her foot and was about to kneel and search the area by hand when she heard scratching, subtle at first and then furious like claws dragged across a tree trunk.

Vivi held up her ring against the darkness, fear pulsing through her.

A large creature flew in the shadows above the halo of light her ring cast into the darkness. Sharp wingtips dipped for a brief second into view and then retreated to the safety of the treetops. The beast rose, raking its body against the wiry tree limbs as it climbed higher. Vivi spun around, holding the creature with her gaze, trying to get a take on what the thing was. A hideous form swept through the trees, accustomed with its surroundings, turning her in circles.

Then the creature went still.

Her body tensed, her nerves on edge. She balled up her fist and moved the glow from her ring around the treetops like a spotlight. The creature clutched the tree bark about ten feet above her head. How long had it been resting there, watching her? She had never seen anything like the huge gray leathery beast that was double the size of an average vulture and had no feathers or fur. Its bony wing joints were folded as it sat perched in the tree with deadly sharp claws digging into the bark, leaving deep gouges in the tree's tender flesh.

The creature stared down at her with glowing red eyes. Its snout was flattened, similar to a bat's face, exposing a row of sharp, ragged teeth. Long strings of drool hung from its black rubbery lips. Worst of all was the way it studied her. This was no thoughtless animal. It appeared to be thinking, appraising her, recording her movements, waiting to see what she would do before striking.

Vivi crouched, giving it less of a target. She crawled slowly backward on her hands and butt, trying to put some distance between herself and the beast. She had heard stories of the Darklander's familiars being conjured from the bones of ancient creatures of myth and lore—dragons, reptiles, and bats—but she'd never believed they were real. Until now. Who would breed such a frightening thing? It shifted on its haunches. A musty stench filled the air. The creature began to growl.

"Good boy," Vivi said, her voice trembling. She backed up into a tree, pinned down like easy prey. Her heart pounded in her chest.

The creature made a terrible screeching sound and flew from its perch, making repeated swooping passes lower and lower, razor-sharp claws coming within inches of her head. Vivi's heart was in her throat as she dove out of the way. She tried to hold the creature in her sight. She had to get out of there. Ideas raced through her mind. Her only chance was to make a run for it. The portal gate was far, but with the strider potion still active, reaching it was her best option. The creature could easily swoop down, and by the way its eyes were studying her, it would be on her the second she ran, but it was a chance she was willing to take.

What she really needed was a diversion. Her best bet was to cast up a ward for protection and use the mansion's security system to her advantage, set off an alarm, cause a bit of chaos to distract the beast long enough to get a good head start, and then run like hell. Sounded like a plan.

The beast landed on a chunk of stone a few yards from her. It growled, watching her every movement. Trying to hide behind a bush, she sensed the flicker of magic again. In the commotion, she had almost forgotten about it. It was close, really close. She took a few steps toward the energy pulse and reached down until her hand brushed something cold in the ground cover. Waving the light across the area, she saw a thick silver band peeking out of the leaves. At first glance, it looked like a bracelet. Vivi inched her hand toward the piece of metal, her eyes locked on the creature's face. Its gaze shifted. It saw the bracelet, too, and then suddenly, in a flap of wings, dove toward the shiny object.

But Vivi was faster. She snatched up the bracelet and shoved it into her pocket. Backpedaling, she spun around, desperate for a hiding place, but there was nowhere to go. The creature lurched toward her, wobbling awkwardly on the ground, unable to walk well on its thick curved talons. Red eyes flared. A guttural growl came from its throat.

"Mine," she said in a show of defiance to the snarling creature.

It snorted and took flight, banking upward, avoiding a strike. Vivi felt a sigh of relief. Maybe it would let her go. Her fingers fumbled over the vials on her bandolier, grabbing a ward. Suddenly, the creature flashed into view in the spindly treetops, circling above her in a graceful arch. The potion was her best advantage over the beast. Huge wings swept toward her, sharp claws slashing the darkness. Vivi threw the vial to the ground and stomped on it with her boot. A spark ignited and an electric blue orb of light sprang to life, surrounding her in a protective bubble.

The thin transparent skin wavered, reverberating from the force of the magic, and Vivi hoped that it was strong enough to hold off the creature. It must have thought the same thing and took its chances, flying full force into the ward's surface, sending up a geyser of sparks. It reeled backward, stunned, tumbling in mid-air until it slammed backwards into a tree with a terrible high-pitched scream.

The spell held, for now.

The ward was the only thing separating Vivi from the clawed familiar, and she had made it angry. After recovering from the impact, the creature advanced with its talons raised. Claws scraped against the surface of the transparent bubble with a nauseating screech, and then it took flight to make pass after pass in a barrage of dive-bombing attacks, rattling Vivi to her core. The familiar banged against the magical ward over and over. As she stepped around, her movements caused the ward to weaken. Raking its claws across the thin surface, the beast sliced through the waning bubble, collapsing the barrier, and flinging Vivi to the ground in a sickening thud.

This time Vivi didn't have time to cast a new potion from her bandolier. There was no time to think as the familiar pounced and caught her within seconds. She tried to cover her head and curl up into a ball as the creature attacked. Claws tore through her jacket, slicing into her arm. Vivi screamed, rolled over onto her back, and kicked the creature in the belly with her boots, sending it flying backward in a dazed thump.

Vivi scrambled for cover under a grove of small trees. Her breath heaved in panicked gasps. She clutched her arm; warm blood seeped from between her fingers. The creature had recovered, and leathery wings filled the sky above her in a low circle. She grabbed a potion from her bandolier and broke it on the ground under her boot heel. A camouflage potion formed a haze, hiding her among the branches and underbrush. She was safe for the moment. The pain in her arm throbbed up to her shoulder, forcing her to bite back a cry.

A high-pitched whistle sounded. The creature pulled up and retreated. Huge wings whooshed through the air, pulling it toward the Darklander's house. She was only about fifty yards away and could see the outline of a wizard standing outside of the heavy wooden door, light flooding from the entryway. Vivi swallowed hard. She couldn't get a good look at him. He was a dark figure hidden by the light casting him in shadow, but she saw his arm raise, wand outstretched in his hand.

She stumbled to her feet and raced into

the woods before a barrage of sparks exploded against the trees around her. She pumped her arms and legs as fast as she could, but took a hit in the back from a stinger spell. A spasm of pain radiated through her muscles. She pitched forward, but righted herself on a tree and kept moving despite the pain until she reached the portal, lungs burning, covered in dirt and sweat.

Vivi had unofficially met the Darklander, ruler at the edge of Everland. He answered to no one and was feared by all. His sick creature had attacked her, almost fatally, but she had been out in the woods at night alone. Her judgment had been questionable. The Dire Woods was his domain. But even through her pain, it occurred to Vivi that if the Darklander wasn't responsible for the crimes against witches, then he probably knew who was.

At least she'd found a bracelet. Hopefully it would be something—another clue, a lead, a dangerous lure. At this point, she would take anything.

11

WHEN VIVI GOT HOME, SHE peeled herself out of her leather jacket and inspected the bloody gash inflicted by the freakish familiar. A huge claw mark had sliced across her upper arm, leaving a two-inch cut that was caked with congealed blood. She grabbed a vial from her belt and gulped down a pain potion. *It could have been a lot worse,* she told herself. She gritted her teeth and pressed a warm, wet washcloth to the ugly wound while resting on her bathroom floor, back slumped against the cool tile wall.

What had she been thinking? That she could take on whatever she found in the Dire Woods? She wasn't the type to go charging out into the night, scouting for danger like her little sister. She gave herself a half-hearted smile. It hadn't been all bad. At least she wasn't dead. Plus, she did hold off that drooling leathery beast for a while. She officially had her first fight under her belt, even though it was with a giant bat.

Vivi dug through her medicine cabinet and found a wound patch that she had picked up from a healer witch who frequented her shop. Bartering with other witches for goods and services was really paying off, and she couldn't be more relieved to find the healing pad to seal up the gash and keep it from scarring.

She peeled the wobbly brown gelatin substance off of the paper backing and stuck it to the washed cut. A cooling sensation enveloped her arm. The pain and swelling receded. She found some gauze bandage and wrapped it around her bicep. Vivi showered quickly, changed her clothes, and collapsed on the sofa for a few hours of sleep. She glanced at the clock before extinguishing the light and realized she'd be lucky to get three hours of sleep tops, as dawn was already creeping toward the horizon. *No rest for the wicked.*

Remembering that she had given Pepper the morning off, Vivi woke early, gulped a cup of strong black tea, and headed down to her shop, wanting to put her belt and potions away before she got ready for work. She was also curious to investigate the silver bracelet she'd found in the woods. Possibilities raced through her head. Had it been lost, dropped, or stolen? But most importantly, who owned it? Did it have anything to do with Clarissa? Vivi hoped the poor witch was recovering in the healing ward. She'd have to pay her another visit soon.

She dug through her potions and ran a few basic magical tests for about an hour, but nothing worked on the bracelet. What magic had been infused into the metal had all but drained away, leaving no clues as to what it had been used for and no residue to identify the owner, either. She got nothing. Rubbing the silver between her fingers, she admired the strange plain cuff. This little gem would need an expert opinion.

Vivi was just about to put on a pot of coffee when a knock sounded on the front door. She peered around the corner from the back room and her heart leapt. The handsome sheriff was peeking into the shop window. Lance cupped his hands against the glass and his gaze roved the room. What was he doing here so early in the morning? The knocking continued, only louder. Her escapades last night had left her bleary-eyed and frazzled. She cringed, feeling like death warmed over. She wanted to dive under the counter, but it was too late. He had spotted her. *No use hiding.* She padded over to the door, glad she had at least brushed her teeth.

He was slow to enter, eyes downcast. "Sorry to bother you. I tried your apartment, but you weren't there, so I figured..."

"No problem. What can I help you with, Lance? Do you need a potion?" She hoped he needed something quick, but by the look of him, this was serious.

"I was hoping you could come down to the station." He gazed at her sheepishly. Not his typical calm but firm demeanor.

"Am I in trouble?" Did he know about her little trip into the Dire Woods last night? No, that was impossible. "Has something happened?" Vivi stepped back, concern raising her hackles.

"You could say that."

"Do you want to come in the back and sit down? I'll make you a cup of coffee while I finish brewing up some stock for the store." She motioned over her shoulder and headed back, hoping to keep him at her shop, but he stopped in the doorway. The sheriff hadn't budged.

"I can't. I really need you to come with me to the station. This is serious." He crossed his arms over his broad chest.

"What happened?" she asked, her brow pinched with worry. Had he found the lost witch? Was she already dead?

"I should wait and tell you when we get

there." He moved to the threshold of her shop, imploring her with his eyes. The tiny string of bells on the door handle tinkled. His jaw was tense. "I can't tell you any more."

"What's this about, Lance?" They were in a standoff. Vivi drummed her fingers on the countertop.

He sighed and shook his head. "Stubborn Mayhem."

"Very."

He ran his hands through his hair. "Fine, I'll tell you. Hex Division has camped out in my station, and they want to question you about your *vision*."

"What? Why are *they* involved?"

She had never met a witch or wizard who worked for Hex, the special ops team the council assigned to the most serious and dangerous criminal magical cases. Her stomach lurched. She played the feeling off as lack of sleep and a decent breakfast, but she knew deep down that Hex Division was not an organization to take lightly. When they wanted an audience with a witch, she'd better well listen.

"Something bad has happened, and you aren't going to tell me what it is, are you?" she asked.

"I don't know. These Hexers are a tough group. They're keeping a tight lid on why they're here. I'll help you as much as I can, but that's all I've got right now."

A gust of cold air filtered in from the open door. No use holding out now. She rubbed at the bandage poking out from under her T-shirt, the wound beginning to itch.

"What happened there?" Lance nodded toward her arm.

"Just a stupid accident." Vivi grabbed a jacket and her purse and followed the sheriff. Her shop would have to stay closed. She crumbled up the note she wrote last night for Pepper and jotted down a new one. Her morning had taken a turn for the worse.

Vivi waited in an interrogation room at the back of the police station. The room was practically buzzing with protective wards. Her stomach growled, empty as a pit. She would kill for a cup of coffee, a donut, and a calming potion, in that order. She checked her watch. Only twenty minutes had passed, but it felt more like an hour.

A secretive group whose methods were shrouded in mystery, the Hex Division didn't show up unannounced unless the situation was serious. They had the full authority of the Witch Council and only investigated the most severe crimes. The witches and wizards of Hex were highly skilled with powerful *persuasions*, usually involving physical strength, intellectual cunning, stealth, and subterfuge—any magical skills that they could use to their advantage to capture witches who had gone dark.

Vivi's mind raced. This had to be connected to the Dire Woods and the circle of sooty black magic. Or maybe it was about that creep, the Darklander. He obviously wasn't above stinging a witch in the back, even if she was just out for an innocent midnight stroll in the woods, hunting for clues. Ha! The last thing this interview was going to be about was innocence. She pinched her shoulder blades back, trying to stretch out the muscle, the ache of the sting still fresh.

Finally, Lance escorted three Hex Division members into the room. Rumor had it that all Hexers traveled in threes. The first one was a young witch with white hair cropped on the sides, long on the top, and tied back at the nape of her neck. She had delicate features, a rosebud mouth, and a pale pink scar that slashed her cheek, wounding her baby face. The second Hexer was a huge muscle-bound wizard who looked like he could punch a hole right through a ward with his bare fist. Both wore stoic expressions and black leather jackets and pants, customary of the Hex Division.

"Meet Hannah and Adam," Lance said, introducing the Hexers. With a gruff demeanor, he glanced at Vivi briefly before nodding toward the final Hexer. "This is Division Commander Rye Finn. He has some questions for you today." Lance walked out of the room without another word. Obviously the sheriff wasn't happy the Hexers had infiltrated his station.

The other two Hexers had stood back when Rye Finn entered. He had a tall, muscular build. His features were angular, and his unshaven face and wavy black hair gave him a rugged appearance. He wore a metal wand carved with sharp swirls on his belt loop, but what was really fascinating about him was the collection of plain old rubber bands encircling his wrists.

"Are you an elemental?" Vivi asked, curiosity bubbling up in her. She had only met an elemental once. They were very rare, and the most powerful of witches. She didn't know much about how the magical science worked, but she had learned a little during her academy days. Elementals could control one or more of the elements—fire, water, earth, and air—and many used the weather as a power source. The rubber bands neutralized electricity.

"You're very perceptive, but no." His pale gray eyes more than looked at her; they studied her, peered into her soul in a way that made her shudder. "It's a pleasure to meet you, Ms. Mayhem. You can call me Finn." He set a glass of water in front of her.

"Why wear the rubber bands?" She gulped the drink, trying to steady her nerves.

"My mother was an elemental, but I'm not full strength. I'm training in conduction, pulling electricity, so I'm not official. Self-taught." His voice was deep and smooth, and he smiled with one side of his mouth. "My *persuasion* is a little subtler. I pride myself in being able to read a witch or wizard, detect deception. Understand their character."

"You're like a witch lie detector, is that it?" *One who pulled lightning down from the sky as a hobby. Wow. Talk about being a talented wizard.* Vivi swallowed. The room had gotten much warmer.

"Something like that." He sat across from her, and the other two Hexers flanked the doorway. "I just want to talk. The sheriff tells me you reported a crime you witnessed in a vision. Is that correct?" He leaned back in his chair. His stare grated on her nerves.

"Yes." *Keep it simple.*

"Curious. You aren't a registered seer, so your *persuasion* is a mystery to us. One you've been keeping a secret. Do you keep many secrets where magic is concerned?" His tone had shifted, forming an edge.

"I don't see why my magic would concern you. I'm sure as a Hexer you have more important duties." How did he find out about her vision? There's no way Lance reported her. Vivi glanced up, trying to see if the sheriff was in earshot. "What brings you way out here to Willow Realm? Are you assisting the sheriff with his investigation?"

Lance walked back in and dropped a pile of parchments onto the table. "I filed a report on the witch we found thanks to your vision." He rolled his eyes. "The Hex Division doesn't miss much."

Good, old, by-the-book Lance.

"That's why we like the sheriff. He's one of the most efficient lawmen I know. The report sent up a warning to us." Finn arched an eyebrow. "The case interests me." He nodded to the huge Hexer, who closed the door behind Lance as the sheriff left the room.

"Do you know who the young witch is? Is she okay?" Vivi asked. She tried not to fidget. It was the one question she wanted to ask, but wasn't sure if she was prepared for an answer.

"No, I'm afraid we don't. Another interesting twist to this case." Finn's stare practically bore holes into her.

"Interesting? How so?" Vivi asked.

"You went searching for one witch and you just happen to literally stumble onto a crime scene. I'm wondering if the witch even exists."

"The vision happened. I can only follow it." She swallowed hard, hearing Esmeralda's words echoed in her own.

Finn sifted through the parchments Lance had left on the table. There was also a pile of small clear evidence bags. Finding what he was looking for, he pushed a piece of parchment toward her. The image of the old witch appeared before her. Except in this photo Clarissa was bright-eyed and alert, smiling into the camera. Her complexion was creamy and bright, marked only with laugh lines and a burst of crow's feet caused by her wide smile. Stuffed into one of the plastic bags was the torn gown that she had been wearing, stained with blood.

Concern for the witch filled Vivi. "The healers are doing all they can for her."

Finn shifted a roll of parchment and something reflective caught the light. It was in a separate bag and was half hidden by the papers. Vivi picked up the photo and stared at it for a few seconds before retuning it to the table and using the edge to shove the pile aside, bringing the bag into view. Something metallic caught the light. She tried not to stare. Hexer Finn's watchful eye was tracking her every move. Buried under the piles of notes and papers was a silver bracelet in an evidence bag. Her heart leapt. It took all her strength to remain calm.

The bracelet looked identical to the one she found in the woods. Last night hadn't been in vain. She *had* found something.

"See anything familiar?" Finn asked.

"Of course, but you already know that. This is the woman we found in the Dire Woods." Vivi wasn't about to mention the bracelet until she understood what was going on, no matter how *persuasive* this Hexer was.

"Yes, but she wasn't the one you reported seeing in your vision. You claim to have seen a younger girl. Not the one currently in the healer ward. Correct?"

"Yes." Her voice came out sharp.

Finn opened a roll of parchment and stretched it out for Vivi to see. There was an image of a wizard with a shaved head, wearing an easy smile. His bright eyes squinted at the camera and flying goggles hung loosely around his neck. The name on the page was Maynard Luck. It sounded familiar, but Vivi couldn't place it. The photo showed him alive and well, but the one next to it was not so pleasant. His neck was raw, his eyes blank. But unlike the witch, Maynard was a corpse.

Vivi sucked in a sharp breath. Her hand flew to her mouth. She reached for the glass and gulped some water, averting her gaze from the dead man.

"What were you doing late last night, Ms. Mayhem?" Finn asked. All the charm had left his voice.

She closed her eyes for a second and considered her options. "I tested out a few new potions." Technically it was the truth. She had only used the strider potion once and had never used the protective wards against a lethal creature before last night.

"In the middle of the night?" His brow furrowed.

"Yes, I was in the Dire Woods. I wanted to get another look at the crime scene." Her shoulders relaxed. There was no use lying to him, especially if his *persuasion* detected it. "It wasn't the smartest thing to do. But I'm not sorry for it."

"I know where you were last night. You had a very close call with an unfriendly creature." He tapped his arm in the exact place where she was wounded. "Your conduct is suspicious at best, foolish, and potentially criminal."

Her body tensed. *Criminal?* She needed to be careful with him. "How did you know?" She was wearing a jacket, so he couldn't see the bandage. She thought she had been alone last night. Someone had been watching after all.

"Like I said, I can sense when a witch is being honest with me by sensing her state of mind and body. The fact that your body is injured was easy for me to detect. But what should really worry you is that you reek of dishonesty."

A shiver ran through her. She was speechless. She didn't like that he *knew* things about her, but he was right. She was hiding things from him. She had been less than forthright about her *persuasion,* but he was wrong about her intentions.

"I'm the one who reported the crime. I wanted to help." She had to make him understand.

"By traveling alone into the most dangerous woods in Everland? Who were you trying to help? Were you meeting someone?"

A hot rush of nerves washed over her face and neck. "I'm trying to save a witch. That's why I was in the woods. If you would do your job, I wouldn't have to." She struck back, not afraid to do a little antagonizing of her own.

"Your mysterious lost witch." An amused grin played across Finn's lips. "Who only you can see."

"I don't expect anyone to trust or believe in my visions. I realize I have no track record, so I went alone."

"You're right—I don't believe you. You hid your *persuasion* for years, and then suddenly you take the local police out to a crime scene, where you find a witch who had been tortured with black magic. Then you go right back to the scene of the crime in the middle of the night, claiming to be doing some concerned witchy detecting." He shook his head.

"Am I a suspect?" Vivi's throat was suddenly dry. That was why she was in this room, looking at crime-scene photos. This wasn't a friendly chat. He was interrogating her. She didn't know how to react to the angry turn the conversation had taken and was relieved when a scuffling sound came from the hallway. A loud commotion could be heard from outside the door. Lance was fighting with someone.

Finn jumped to his feet and pulled out his wand. The other two Hexers moved away from the door. The wood bulged inward. The ward was barely holding. Vivi pushed back her chair and moved out of the line of attack. Someone with more than a few magical tricks was ramming the door, trying to break through the magical barriers. How had the intruder gotten past Lance and his deputies?

Suddenly, the door exploded open. Sparks flew as one of the wards went down. The air crackled with magic.

The Hexers mumbled a spell, wands at the ready.

"Wait!" Vivi yelled, recognizing the witch who broke down the door.

Honora stood there, wand in hand, fierce determination in her eyes. "Out of my way!" Never one to take the subtle route, she had a way of making grand entrances. She was wearing her battered brown flying leathers and cap. Her goggles were still on, framing her large eyes.

"Damn you, Honora!" Lance hurried up behind her. "They're in the middle of an interview. Contrary to your belief, you don't own the place."

Her sister gave Vivi a nod. No wonder she got by Lance. No one had expected her to go charging into the room. "This little party is over." Honora practically snarled at Finn and the other two Hexers.

"I'm not done here." Finn glared at Honora but held up his hand to keep the other two Hexers from striking. "Your sister is being questioned on her whereabouts last night. We have reports of suspicious behavior in the Dire Woods, and she's hiding valuable information."

"You don't have any legal evidence to hold my sister on, so her presence here is voluntary. Am I right, Vivi?" Honora slipped her wand into her belt. She moved like a panther into the room. Vivi nodded. Her sister was in butt-kick mode. Something had really pissed her off, and Vivi had a feeling it had to do with the Hex Division's sudden involvement with the case.

"I see you're hungry for more action, Honora." Finn put his wand back into his belt but stayed in an aggressive stance. "Didn't get enough last night with my other team, so you decided to come up and visit me?"

"Your pathetic Hexers were following me all night while I was trying to run a case, and thanks to them I couldn't get any work done. Luckily for me, they weren't too hard to get rid of once I realized their agenda." She smirked. "You might want to get a smarter team."

"Next time a Hexer tells you to stand down, I suggest you do it."

Vivi's head spun. The Hexers had descended on Willow Realm, were following her sister, interrogating her, and yet were no closer to finding the witch from her vision. It was as if they didn't even care. The noise in the room was too much. She had to get out. "Enough. Please. It's been a long night, and I'm going home now."

The tension in the room wavered. Lance stepped aside to let Vivi pass, but before she could leave Finn grabbed her injured arm and squeezed, sending a jolt of pain to her fingertips. "I'm watching you." His voice was like sandpaper.

Vivi yanked free of his grasp and rushed out of the sheriff's station, not once glancing back. Honora hurried to keep up with her.

"What happened back there?" Vivi asked as they walked back to her shop. Her mind reeled over the encounter with the Hexer Finn. "Why are you being followed?"

"Remember that wizard I was looking for the other day when I was out here, Maynard Luck? The one I thought had nothing to do with the witch from your vision?"

"Yeah."

"Well, he turned up dead in the woods,

a couple of miles from the crime scene." Honora shook her head. "Somehow both cases are connected."

"He was killed." Vivi remembered the photo Rye Finn had shown her. That's why he seemed familiar.

"Hex Division thinks it's murder. It looks really bad with both of us digging around for witches who were juiced with black magic. Especially now that the Hexers are involved."

"I was a complete idiot last night. I was just so angry with you. I just plowed ahead," Vivi said.

"I have that effect on people. You know me. Brutal honesty has always been my downfall. I hurt people and I don't mean it." Honora gave her a sheepish look.

"Unfortunately for me, your honesty tends to be accurate. But it was my fault, too. I was overly sensitive. Sorry about Scarlet. I was wrong to go to her behind your back. I should have told you what was going on with me." Vivi linked her arm with Honora's. She was still a little angry about what her sister had said, but this was no time to hold a grudge. All sisters fought, and the Mayhem sisters had their share of family battles, but once they cooled down, they always made up.

"I was wrong. I shouldn't have said what I did about you and your *persuasion*. We're going to need it more than ever now."

"We're not going to worry about that now. We've got to find out who's harming witches before we get blamed for it." Vivi was relieved to have Honora by her side again.

From the looks of the pile of parchment Finn had on the table back at the station, this case was more complicated than Vivi had realized.

"What drives me crazy is we haven't done anything. If another witch was found in the woods, why was there no one out there last night?" Vivi asked. "There wasn't even one Hexer in sight, and yet somehow they knew I was there."

"My sources say Hex Division's under pressure to sew this case up fast."

Vivi and Honora walked around to the back of the shop. "Thanks for kicking the door in back at the station. I had just about enough of Hexer Finn." Vivi relaxed her shoulders. "Subtle, Honora. Real subtle."

Honora grinned. "The Mayhem sisters have found themselves in trouble once again."

12

ONCE THEY REACHED THE SHOP, the sisters said their goodbyes, and Vivi watched Honora lift off the ground and take to the sky. She was on her own now. As she made her way inside to get The Potion Garden opened for business, she noticed Rumor perched on the black mailbox stationed on the front stoop. He squawked and bobbed his head. Her heart fluttered and she raced over, flinging open the small metal door to find a rich parchment envelope that felt buttery smooth between her fingers. It had a thick gold wax seal imbedded with a cross insignia, which brought a smile to her face. Dax Cross had replied to her letter.

Vivi unlocked the front door and released the security ward. Once inside, she flipped the open sign and made her way behind the front counter, desperately wanting to rip open the letter and see what he had to say. Luckily, the place was quiet. It was still early, only a little after ten o'clock, so she wasn't too late getting the shop going this morning. She sliced through the envelope, her eyes impatiently scanning the letter inside.

Dax was gracious as always, inquiring about her business and her family, especially one family member in particular, his ex-love Honora. Finally, at the end of the letter he extended her an invitation to come and visit him anytime at Mender Corp, saying she could visit the facility during one of the many promotional tours they were currently running. Vivi grinned to herself and slipped the letter into her purse under the counter. The response was exactly what she'd hoped for, and she planned on taking Dax up on his offer, sooner than he realized.

After taking the morning off, Pepper strolled in at noon to relieve Vivi for her lunch break.

"Did you finish the novel last night?" Vivi asked.

"Nope. I was racing through it when I realized that once it was over, I would have to wait for the next novel, so I slowed down to savor the experience. I want to make the book last."

"Sounds like a good idea. Can you handle the shop for the rest of the day? I'm headed out on a little field trip."

Pepper raised her eyebrows. "Do tell," she said.

Vivi filled her in on the letter from Dax and her plan to get a behind-the-scenes view of the company. Afterwards, she ran upstairs to her apartment, changed her clothes into professional attire, and headed to the train station. Hopefully Dax meant what he wrote because she was on her way to Mender Corp, ready or not.

The magical Silver Train glided over the rails that crisscrossed the witching world like the spine of a great metal beast. Vivi rode in style, nestled into a first-class compartment, which she was bumped up into, since she was traveling alone. The plush seat melted around her body as she breathed deeply and relaxed. The train system had transformed Everland, bringing it into the modern age of witches, making traveling across the witching world quick and luxurious. A well-trained crew of elemental witches maintained the electrical power to run the high-speed rail system with the assistance of magical engineers to keep the trains moving effortlessly.

Vivi pulled out her journal and reviewed the notes she had taken on the case. Following the description of her vision were the details of the three witches—Clarissa Taylor, who they found in the woods; Maynard Luck, who was dead in the morgue; and the kidnapped witch, who only she had seen. Next to each, she wrote down their *persuasion*. Clarissa was an empath and Maynard was a flyer. Both were powerful witches who lived relatively solitary lives in isolated areas, making them easy targets.

She traced her finger over a crude sketch of the Mender Corp logo she had drawn in her notebook and reread the brief description she had written of the twins and the tragic accident that had left them orphans. Vivi had no idea what she was going to discover at Mender Corp, so her plan was simple—get a look around the lab, see the inner workings of the company, and learn as much as she could about the powerful healing *persuasion* that defined the mysterious twins, Mitchell and Miranda.

Outside the window, the landscape transformed from dense forests and farmland to villages and towns, finally giving way to crowded city blocks. Stargazer City never failed to take Vivi's breath away. The towering buildings shined like a jeweled metropolis born out of glass and metal. Additional train routes wove a labyrinth through the streets and gave the sense that a witch's feet never touched the ground.

Even though she wasn't a city girl, Vivi could easily see how her sister Honora fit right in with the glamor and shine. Exotic restaurants and cozy coffee shops dotted every street. The train zinged by dazzling shops filled with clothes and shoes—precious colorful knits, leather coats and boots, glittering sky-high heels. There were bookshops filled with rare grimoires that crowded the shelves with the latest popular novels. Magical artifacts filled the three-story glass windows of one shop. Magic had advanced into the modern commercial age.

At a routine stop, a potion shop caught Vivi's attention. Tables towered with identical gorgeous green potion bottles, and shelves were stacked with crystal vials of every imaginable cream and elixir. She would have been a little jealous except her shop had one thing the glamorous potion shop didn't: individuality. All the bottles here were mass-produced and exactly the same. The potions were also probably pretty generic. In her shop, all the bottles were hand-blown and no two were alike, and each potion was brewed in her big copper kettle.

The Silver Train dropped her off at a stop inside the enormous glass and chrome lobby of Mender Corp. This was no surprise since Dax was the genius businessman behind the train system and the newest investor in the healing company. She hoped to channel a calm and cool vibe as she made her way through the crush of witches and wizards hurrying to get to work. Pepper had twisted Vivi's hair into a loose chignon, and she'd opted for black pants, a pale gray sweater, and the blue leather jacket Honora had given her as a birthday present last year.

Vivi was in awe of the elaborate building and tried not to trip over her own feet while taking it all in. A huge Mender Corp sign and a painting of the famous healer twins—Mitchell and Miranda—hung on the far wall of the enormous glass atrium. Sheathed in black, both twins had lithe frames and looked like they could use a big bowl of stew and hunk of bread from Arnica's Nocturnes. Their black hair and pale skin gave them a striking appearance. Miranda stared down with huge doe eyes and wore a cropped black bob. Mitchell still wore the same mop of disheveled black hair and thick black-framed glasses he did in the photo from the paper when he and Miranda were first orphaned. They fit the eccentric genius look perfectly and reminded Vivi of the logo—two black birds haunting the vast empty sky.

The huge painting was creeping her out. Vivi averted her eyes and turned her attention to getting into the building. The reception desk looked more like a reception force from all the witches and wizards lined up to assist the throng of patrons entering the building.

"Can I help you?" a young wizard asked.

"I'm here to see Wizard Cross."

"Do you have an appointment?" His face was blank, completely void of emotion.

Vivi smiled. "No, but I have an open invitation." She pulled the letter from her purse and the wizard barely veiled his annoyance.

"You need an appointment to see him. No exceptions." He cleared his throat and glanced around her. "Next, please."

Dax probably had witches by the dozens trying to weasel their way in to see him. She just needed to explain her situation and he would understand. "Wait. I'm not finished. We're old family friends, and I'm not leaving until you send word to Wizard Cross that I'm here. I'm sure he'll understand." No way was she going to let this guy dismiss her like a common groupie.

He gave her a smug little smirk. "Wizard Cross is extremely busy, and I'm not going to bother him with a fan witch who wants to fawn all over him. Come back when you've made an appointment with his assistant."

Vivi twisted up her mouth. "This isn't what you think. If you'd just read my invitation, you'll see that." She passed the envelop across the desk to him, showing the cross seal, but the young wizard wasn't budging. Time to get convincing. She placed a hand on her cocked hip. "You should know that Dax, your boss, told me and my sisters a story once over dinner about an ambitious young wizard who refused to admit a business associate for an important meeting, angering Dax so much the poor wizard was demoted to working in *the pit*." She snorted. "And you know what they say—once you're in the pit, you never get out." Vivi wrinkled up her nose. "Who knows if it's a true story, though? You probably don't have to worry."

The young wizard's eyes widened.

The pit was Stargazer City's sanitation system and even all the scent spells in Everland couldn't make it smell like a rose.

"Oh," the wizard said after scanning the letter. He seemed relieved. "I'll call right away and let Wizard Cross's assistant know you're on your way up. You can go back. Top floor." He motioned to a nondescript corner across the atrium and handed her an old black key.

Vivi navigated through glass partitions to an elevator with huge brass doors off to the side that no one seemed to notice. She slipped the key into the lock and the doors dinged, swinging wide. Inside, elegant wood paneling surrounded her. She pushed the button for the top floor and was swooshed upward. The door to the elevators swung open, and she spilled out into a vestibule of dark wood.

The elegantly decorated office and sitting area was minimal, but the furnishings were plush and modern with clean lines and a cool color palate of dark blues, grays, and deep purples accented with glass and chrome. There was an invisible magical fountain off to one side that appeared to rain sheets of water from nowhere.

Vivi was drawn to the floor-to-ceiling glass windows. Staring out over the city, she figured she would need all the gold in Everland to buy a view from the top of this building. Stargazer City was laid out at her feet like a glittering jewel.

"Why am I not surprised to see you here?" A deep voice interrupted Vivi's moment of awe and she jerked around.

To say Dax Cross was handsome was an understatement. His impeccable black suit cut across his broad shoulders, giving him a commanding presence. He wore his brown hair combed back from his face. His skin was golden and his brown-eyed gaze piercing. He held a lacquered walking stick with a silver fox head carved into the handle. It was a good choice for a magical staff, and few wizards could have pulled it off without looking like they were trying too hard. Debonair suited Dax like a well-cut cloth, but most of all he exuded warmth, a rare quality among titans of industry. He was not a job-killing cutthroat. No wonder he was voted Stargazer City's most eligible bachelor three years in a row and

Honora and Scarlet had fought like wild cats over him.

Vivi had good memories of him and Honora dating through their days at Haven Academy. She remembered when he was young, hanging out in their kitchen, eating dinner as fast as their mother could make it. He was the smartest wizard in school and had the ambitions to match. His dreams were huge, and he was the kind of wizard who made them come true.

Vivi gave Dax a warm hug, and he motioned for her to sit on a sleek leather sofa. It was so soft Vivi thought she might sink all the way through to the floor.

"You don't waste any time, do you?" Dax asked.

"I hope you don't mind. I was excited to receive the invitation this morning." Vivi sat up. "I haven't been in the city for ages and wanted to get a look at your new company, now that you've invested with Mender Corp."

"Not at all, but I rarely get so lucky as to have a visit from one of the beautiful and entrepreneurial Mayhem witches." Handsome and charming, the wizard was good.

Dax gave her a sly grin. "You came down for an innocent little poke around, is that it?"

"Not exactly," Vivi said. "I was hoping to get a tour of the Mender Corp facility. For my potion making," she continued, coming up with a believable reason to get inside the lab. "I want to keep up with the new magic tech and production in case I decide to expand and open up additional shops. That's where you come in. I've read about your advancements in technology and wanted to check out a serious operation before expanding." Her explanation was a stretch, since she had no plans to grow her shop, but she didn't want to tip her hand by telling him about her investigation.

"Really?" Dax studied her. She hoped she wouldn't start to sweat under his charming gaze. "I never took you for mass-producing potions. Don't get me wrong. I think it's a great idea, but I always considered you an old-fashioned witch brewing up one potion at a time."

"A witch can change." Vivi was the definition of old-school potion making. She would rather eat a newt sandwich than create dozens of identical potions in the same little bottles, but she needed to see this company and satisfy her curiosity. "I'm coming into my own. Becoming a wise business witch. Mass production is the wave of the future." Vivi tried not to gag.

"Good for you." Dax stood. "Can I get you a drink?" He poured two drinks from a crystal decanter and handed her a glass.

Vivi gulped some of the warm amber liquid that oozed down her throat and through her body. "About that tour. I would be so grateful. I know how valuable your time is." She sipped the rest of her drink.

"I would love to accommodate you." He took a hard swallow. "But I'm afraid I'll be a terrible host. My schedule is tight." Dax leaned back. "It's a madhouse down in operations. We're working on an important production push of a transformative new magical device." His eyes gleamed.

"Sounds riveting. I always knew you would transform the witching world," Vivi said, and she wasn't just flattering him; she really believed it. "Just the thing I'm interested in learning about. For me to see how a groundbreaking operation works would be priceless. I'd really appreciate the favor."

"You're sweet." He paused and glanced over Vivi's shoulder. "Let me check with my assistant, see if I can't work something out. Callie, can you come here, please?"

A rail-thin, frantic-eyed witch wearing a storm-colored suit and huge glasses, carrying a roll of parchment tucked under her arm, hurried into the room. "Yes, sir."

"When's the next production tour on the schedule? I'd like to get Ms. Mayhem signed up."

She bobbled the parchment rolls and adjusted her glasses. "Right now, actually. Just started a few minutes ago. It's packed.

Not a spot left."

Dax glanced at her. "I'll take you down. I'm sure they won't mind one more witch. But I'll warn you, the Mender twins are on site, and they can get a little eccentric. They march to the beat of their own drums, if you know what I mean."

Vivi's curiosity was piqued. "Are the Mender twins in charge of all the healing magic or do you have a potions master?"

Dax ran his finger along the edge of the crystal glass. "The wizard in charge of operations is Dr. Fowler. He's a brilliant wizard, driven to exhaustion," Dax said. "We have inspections to get ready for. You know how strict the Healer Division of the council can be. They have such high standards for mass-produced potions. We even had to bring in extra staff to handle the workload."

Interesting, Vivi thought, setting her glass down.

Dax stood and whispered some instructions to his assistant. "I have an appointment in twenty minutes, so I'll walk you down, and we'll go from there."

"Perfect." Vivi smiled, trying to contain her excitement. It was everything she had hoped for. Like Esmeralda had told her—follow the vision wherever it leads, and currently her search continued for the two elusive black birds.

13

HOOKED TO HIS ARM, VIVI glided out of Dax's office. He guided her into the elevator, making her feel like a VIP witch as the assistant eyed her enviously. Within mere minutes the elevator whooshed them into the secret depths of Mender Corp. Vivi was practically giddy, for even though she wasn't entirely sure what she was looking for, she was getting a rare opportunity and gave herself a mental pat on the back. Spontaneous investigating just might work out for her.

A wash of cold crisp air enveloped her as she stepped out onto the sleek marble floor, sending a shiver through her. A long hall connected a hive of laboratories, humming with busy technicians who didn't seem to notice them as they entered the secretive domain of healing research. The company had a distinguished reputation for mass-producing many basic healing remedies, making them available to the public faster and easier. A witch didn't need to make appointments with healer witches and wizards when she could pick up a potion or capsule at the local apothecary to treat a headache or indigestion.

Suddenly, the hallway grew quiet when the technicians realized Wizard Cross was on the floor, but he didn't seem to notice the furtive glances and hushed whispers. Dax motioned for Vivi to go ahead, and she pulled her shoulders back, striding through the swinging doors at the end of the hallway. The sign on the door read: "Production," giving her a flutter of anticipation. Vivi's main goal was to follow the magic. Since the Mender twins' *persuasion* was healing, the ideal place to start her search was where the magic was literally put into practice—the lab.

Once through the doors, she was faced with glass-fronted laboratories lined up on both sides of the hallway. Inside the immaculate labs, witches and wizards, wearing head-to-toe white suits, hoods, goggles, and face masks, stirred giant bubbling vats of smoky potions with long wooden paddles. Brewing had never looked so efficient and sterile. Vivi cringed at the idea of wearing a hairnet and protective eyewear while she conjured up a batch of potions in the back of her shop.

Mender Corp was about logical scientific potion making. Here, the assembly line was king and made a lot more gold. This was the type of conjuring that would make the professors at Haven Academy proud, but Vivi was the kind of student who had blown up more than one kettle in her school days. She had always believed that potions, remedies, and healing came from the personal touch of a witch or wizard—the special creative juices a witch infused into the concoction. This magic might work well enough, but it had no soul. She shelved her opinion. She wasn't here to judge; she was here to observe and look for clues.

Witches and wizards hurried up and down the hall in a flurry of tense excitement. Dax wasn't kidding when he said the atmosphere in the lab was intense. He stopped a young witch who was scribbling data on a pad of parchment, completely absorbed in her duties.

"Excuse me, miss. Do you know where I can find Dr. Fowler?"

The busy witch's head jerked up, but she barely looked at them. "He's right behind me. But I'd steer clear. He's in a vile mood. Spitting nails."

"Is he on the rampage again? I'll be sure to watch myself. Don't want the good doctor angry with me." Dax smiled, and the witch almost dropped her notepad.

"So sorry, Wizard Cross. I didn't realize it was you." Panic filled her face as she quickly got her bearings, straightened her lab coat, and tried to cover for her previous comment. "The professor is hard at work. As I should be, too." The witch spun around, making a hasty retreat down the hall in the opposite direction.

"Are you sure this is no trouble?" Vivi asked.

"Not at all. It's like this all the time. They thrive under pressure." Dax stared at the frenzied activity with admiration.

The doors ahead of them swung wide and a white-haired wizard wearing a rumpled lab coat approached. Sensing someone's presence, he glanced up from his notes and gave them an exhausted sigh. He had bags under his bloodshot eyes and probably hadn't slept in days. "Good to see you again, sir. How can I assist you today?" The wizard gave Dax a cordial nod.

"We're trying to find the latest tour group, Dr. Fowler. Have they pushed through yet?"

"Yes. You missed them by about ten minutes." Dr. Fowler pulled his glasses off and pinched the bridge of his nose. "Can I assist you?"

"Dr. Fowler has important testing going on," Dax said to her and then addressed him. "I don't want to interrupt your progress. Perhaps one of your assistants could catch us up to speed, until we reach the group."

"Not at all. It would be my pleasure." He gave Vivi a half-hearted smile. She seriously doubted that. He looked like he wanted to get back to his work, but Dax was the boss, so he graciously complied. "I can walk you through the production stages and join up with the rest of the tour in a few minutes."

"Excellent. I knew we could count on you. You can start by explaining to Ms. Mayhem your role here at Mender." Dax gave the doctor a heavy pat on the back that almost knocked the poor man over.

"I'm the chief healer. I've been a healing wizard for over two and a half centuries," he said, beaming with pride. "Here at Mender Corp we are trying to do great things, pushing the boundaries of magical medicine, and meeting an ever-demanding clientele that expects the best. It's my job to see that it happens."

Vivi could tell Fowler was an experienced and powerful wizard, and working at the most advanced magical medical company in Everland probably meant he was a genius. "That's a lot of pressure."

"Nothing we can't handle." The doctor gave her a courteous nod, and they continued on through the facility, where he showed her the production process.

Vivi felt a twinge of sadness, seeing the sterile surroundings, conveyor belts, and rows of glass bottles ready to be filled with the next generic potion.

"Gone are the days of door-to-door healing, treating witches and wizards personally," Vivi said before she could stop herself. "Don't you miss it?"

"Miss the hands-on healing work I did as a young wizard?" He seemed to contemplate the idea. "Not in the slightest. I'm only one wizard and the population of Everland is constantly growing. We need assistance where we can get it."

"Tell me, what do you have going on here?" Vivi motioned to the gigantic contraption behind a wall of glass. Multiple levels of conveyer belts streamed by, carrying capsules in a tiny marching row.

"The herbal batches are transferred to this sterile area, where the potion vat is poured into a specialized machine and the healing tonic is either poured into a bottle or compressed into a lozenge."

The lab she had seen so far was crawling with magic techs, engineers, and healing wizards and witches hard at work. The operation was impressive, but Vivi wondered what it had to do with her vision. She wasn't seeing anything that might connect Mender Corp to anything evil or illegal, just the opposite, and she was getting a bad feeling this whole endeavor was for nothing.

Dax's stressed assistant had slinked up

behind them and had managed to pull him away with a stack of parchments for him to sign. He hung back as the witch talked incessantly and shoved a plumed pen in his hand. "Keep going. I'll be right behind you," he said and waved them onward.

"He's very busy," Vivi said.

"Aren't we all?" The doctor turned to continue the tour and his wand slid out from under his arm and fell to the floor, skidding down the hallway. Vivi leapt to grab it before someone stepped on it and handed it back to the doctor.

"Thank you. I forgot I was carrying it." He slipped the wand inside of his coat and that was when Vivi noticed the doctor's hands for the first time. The pads of his fingertips and nails were a sooty gray color as if they had been washed repeatedly, and the doctor had been unable to remove the stain.

He noticed her staring. "Oh, this." He inspected his fingernails. "I was installing a new charcoal filtration device in the lab and the spell backfired, covering me in black gunk. I can't seem to get it off my hands no matter how hard I scrub. I blame the spell combination."

"Try washing with vinegar," Vivi said. The dark wizard in her vision had fingers that were stained worse than that, but still, the sight made her suspicious. Maybe he was telling the truth and couldn't bother with the stain, but it was still suspicious. She would definitely keep an eye on him. "Are you working on something new? A new magical device?" she asked, already knowing the answer, but seeing if he would tell her something about the company's newest breakthrough. "I enjoy experimenting with potions, so I find this all very fascinating."

"I'm not at liberty to discuss developmental magic. The Mender twins are the real visionaries behind the company. They've dedicated their lives to the healer's craft. Advancement is important to them at any cost."

At any cost—what a strange thing to say, Vivi thought. "Ambition has taken them far," she said.

Vivi and the doctor filed out of the production area and entered a packing facility where a group of young wizards was loading up crates for delivery. Glass jars filled with lozenges and liquid potions were lined up and being stocked for shipping all over Everland. A side door was open, and a hover delivery vehicle was ready for pick up.

A young wizard wearing a hoodie and a jean jacket ducked in through the opening. He rushed up to Dr. Fowler and handed him a roll of parchment. Bouncing on the balls of his feet, he stared eagerly at the doctor, who with an annoyed glance tucked the papers under his arm. Dr. Fowler barely suppressed his disapproval of the guy's presence. "Not now, Paul. Come back later."

"You're going to want to see my new results." Paul's hands shook as he grabbed the parchment from under Dr. Fowler's arm and unrolled it for the doctor to read. He poked nervously at something on the page with his gloved finger. "I've done it. You have to check out these findings. This changes everything." His eyes were wild with excitement.

"I'll look at the tests and get back to you as soon as time permits." The doctor rolled up the parchment and squeezed Paul's arm. "Can't you see I'm busy here?" He motioned toward Vivi, trying and failing to subtly communicate with him.

"The tests were ordered by Miranda. She'll want to see them, if *you* don't." His gaze turned downcast like a wounded puppy's. *Talk about immature,* Vivi thought.

"I'll make sure she sees them. Now, please excuse us." Dr. Fowler turned his back on the young wizard.

Vivi made eye contact with the pushy wizard, but he averted his gaze and darted out of the room as quickly as he had come. She had only gotten a brief glance at his face, but was certain she had seen him someplace before, but she just couldn't remember where.

"He seemed excited," Vivi said, trying to be

kind. "I'm sure you have many witches and wizards vying for your attention."

"Unfortunately, yes. It causes a stir."

Vivi could tell he was being modest. Working with Fowler was a career maker.

"Though a little unpredictable, Paul is one of my smartest apprentices. He's very ambitious. He'll do anything to succeed, even interrupt me no matter what I'm doing."

"Where does the company go from here?" Vivi asked, sincerely curious. "You've revolutionized healing. What's next?" Vivi had a feeling there was more to Mender Corp, much more that the doctor wasn't telling her.

"Right this way. I'll let the visionaries show you for themselves." The doctor motioned to two huge silver doors elaborately carved with the official healer's seal. As Vivi approached, the doors parted and he ushered her into a hushed theater space where a small group of witches and wizards sat in rows of chairs, facing a lectern on a small stage. Vivi spun in a circle. "I should wait for Wizard Cross," she whispered, not wanting to disturb the presentation going on. She glanced around, but Dax was nowhere to be seen.

Dr. Fowler gave her a small bow. "I'm afraid I must be going. Do enjoy the rest of the tour." He was done with his polite hosting duties.

She had no choice and quickly found a seat in the back row of the darkened room as the other attendees began to stir, crane their necks, and shoot her annoyed glares and a few shushing sounds. From the expensive clothes and well-coiffed appearances, Vivi realized she was in the company of a wealthy group. She also noticed a few scholar robes from the advanced magical academy and figured the tour must have been tailored for investors and academics. *This must be a very private tour,* Vivi thought. She settled down in her seat and tried to blend. Flanked by two uniformed security wizards, the large doors swung shut. *Guess I'm on my own.*

Mitchell Mender stood in a circle of light at the front of the room, addressing the group. Her stomach plummeted. Tall and thin as a needle, he went silent, and his gaze pinned her to her seat like an arrow. She swallowed and tried to sink down in her chair.

"Welcome. Why don't you join me up front? I was just about to ask for a volunteer," he said. Vivi suddenly realized he was talking to her.

The Mender twins were an imposing duo. Off to his left, Miranda sat perched on a stool, gazing at her like a curious bird. She looked resplendent in a fitted skirt and loose silk blouse. Mitchell wore a black sweater and black jeans. Coolness oozed off them. His gaze shifted quickly over Vivi as he extended his hand to her. She felt briefly suspended in time, remembering the photo she had seen in the old newspaper of the two wide-eyed, black-haired twins holding hands after the terrible demise of their parents, and now here they were all grown up and still together. A mix of awe and sympathy for the orphaned geniuses filled her.

Vivi cleared her throat. "Thank you, but no. I'll sit and watch."

"You want to be a good sport, don't you? Join me. I might surprise you," Mitchell said with a mischievous grin. He directed her to the chair positioned at center stage. "Please take a seat."

Reluctantly, but seeing no way out, Vivi walked to the front of the group to the sound of light applause. An ominous table covered in spellcasting supplies was positioned to the right of her. *What kind of demonstration was this?*

"Tell us, what brings you here today?" Mitchell was in performance mode.

Vivi smiled and played along. Might as well make the best of it. "I'm a potion maker and I was curious about your operation."

"Trying to steal our secrets?" Miranda asked as the crowd chuckled. "Be careful. You know what they say about cats and curiosity."

As if on cue, a side door slid open, and a sleek black panther strode across the stage and stood next to Mitchell. The animal's long tail twitched back and forth. Its coat shined a beautiful glossy black under the spotlight, and its eyes were the color of sulfur.

"Xavier is our familiar. He's a little protective," Miranda said.

The twins *shared* a familiar. Who had a bloodthirsty carnivorous panther as a familiar? The Mender twins did—that's who. It was over the top, but if you were two of the most famous witches in Everland with superior healing *persuasions* at your fingertips, what are a few animal scratches?

"I'm not here to steal anything." Vivi blushed under the attention. "I'm an admirer and wanted to witness the production process firsthand. It really is legendary." Perhaps a little flattery would ease the tension.

"Now, this lovely witch has wandered into our tour, and by doing so agreed to be the guinea pig for our latest experiment." Mitchell's brow raised and the crowd laughed again. "It's so hard to find willing *volunteers* these days."

Dax had been right when he said the twins were eccentric.

"What kind of experiment?" Vivi's gaze drifted over the tools. She noticed a scalpel with a razor-sharp blade as well as additional nefarious laboratory instruments. Mitchell and Miranda both smiled at the same time in a creepy twin way.

"It's just a little test," Mitchell said. He shifted in front of the metal table, inspecting beakers filled with salt, ground powders, and liquid essences.

"A test for what?"

"For *persuasions*," Miranda said, sauntering across the room. "They are the most powerful magic in the witching world." She held her head high elongating her neck as gracefully as a swan. "They are the defining magic of our age."

"I doubt my magic is up to your high standards," Vivi said with a hard swallow. The last thing she wanted was her *persuasion* tested.

"Don't be embarrassed, dear." Miranda glided over and placed a firm hand on Vivi's shoulder. "It'll just take a second." These two were really starting to creep her out.

Miranda and her brother moved in concert, pouring liquid and powders into a copper bowl and heating the concoction over a tiny flame ignited from a shiny black rock. They were so in tune with one another it was almost like watching a single person. For a moment, Vivi could have sworn she smelled lavender.

"At Mender Corp our mission is the greater good of witch and wizardkind." Mitchell stared down his thin nose at her. "It's obvious to me now that you are the kind of witch we want to help."

"What kind of witch am I?" Vivi asked, trying to keep her voice steady.

"A hardworking witch with minor power. You probably dabble in potions, but you are eager to get ahead. Visiting our facility today shows us just how ambitious you are, but you need help." Condescension oozed off him. He pitied her. "Perhaps you were even hoping to one day apply for a job here."

Hardly, Vivi thought.

What the twins lacked in warmth, they made up for with snobbery and arrogance. Vivi just needed to keep her cool, hope the experiment wouldn't be too humiliating, and get out. She could play along if she had to. "Not every witch can be as powerful as the two of you. That's how the witching world stays in balance," Vivi said.

"This is going to hurt a bit," Mitchell said, loud enough for everyone to hear. "Though not as much as a panther bite." Sliding up next to her, he picked an instrument from the table, and quick as a snake, pricked Vivi's finger.

"Ouch!" she yelped and took a sharp breath, but it was too late. The wizard had drawn blood, and before she could pull her hand away, he grabbed her wrist hard and squeezed a few drops of her blood into a porcelain bowl. "Hold still," he hissed in her ear.

The blood droplets were bright as a cherry

against the snowy white bowl and reminded her of a fairy tale from her childhood, prompting a question. "Did you do experiments together like this when you were growing up?" Vivi asked, playing to the audience. She rubbed the tip of her wounded finger.

"After our parents' tragic death, magic was all we had, all we could count on." Miranda shot her a warning glare. "Alone in a crumbling orphanage, wearing tattered clothes and eating scraps not fit for dogs, surrounded by *strangers*." She emphasized the word as if it left a bad taste in her mouth. "We realized power was essential for survival."

Magic made them feel in control.

The room had grown uncomfortably warm. Vivi's head ached.

Miranda continued, "Once a *persuasion* is isolated, we can assess the magical properties, study them, and eventually harness them." She raised her arms in triumph and the crowd applauded. That was when Vivi noticed a thick silver bracelet on Miranda's skinny wrist. It looked exactly like the one she had found in the woods. Her heart raced. Finally, she had found a connection between them and the case.

Miranda positioned herself between Vivi and her brother so she could watch him work, but Vivi couldn't take her eyes off the bracelet. It was so close she could touch it, and she inched her hand closer until the soft side of her hand grazed the piece of jewelry and sent a sharp current of magic through her fingers. "Ouch!" Vivi yanked her hand back as if stung by a wasp.

Ignoring her, Miranda turned to the crowd, cool and calm as ice. "We think our new science will become very popular in the near future."

Vivi rubbed her stung fingertips on her pant leg. Sweat beaded on her brow. The bracelet was obviously more than it appeared. The one she found in the woods had no magical properties to it that she could tell, but Miranda's was so loaded with magic that it caused a spark.

Sweat beaded on Vivi's brow. Something was wrong. Was that lavender she smelled? Suddenly, Vivi wasn't in the auditorium, but in a dank, dark basement, and at her feet on the cold earthen floor was a trail of cherry-red blood drops. Curiously, she followed them, drop by drop, up a flight of wooden stairs as if picking up a trail of breadcrumbs.

Once at the top, she stood inside a cottage with a sitting room and clean, quaint kitchen. A fired popped and crackled. A kettle hissed on the stove. It would have made a charming setting if it weren't for the dark smoke that seeped under the front door, pooling, and then morphing into the shape of a wizard who sat with a hunched back over a workbench, concocting a spell. A scraping sound filled her ears. She winced.

What was he brewing up? Vivi moved closer and closer to him. Sensing someone was in the room with him, he jerked up, turned around, and right as she was about to peer into the black hood and finally glimpse his face and learn his true identity, he blew a gust of black ash and red salt right in her face. She screamed.

Vivi woke covered in sweat and jerked up in her seat.

"Hurry, Mitchell. Lift her head." Miranda's cold fingers patted Vivi's cheeks, trying to rouse her. "She's awake. Just a little stage fright. Afraid of seeing her own blood. Give her a round of applause for participating." Miranda clapped her hands limply. The audience buzzed with chatter.

Vivi blinked rapidly and stared around the room full of strangers. She straightened in her chair as Mitchell dabbed at her forehead with a damp cloth that smelled medicinal. "You fainted," he said loudly as if she had gone deaf. "Drink this. It will make you feel better." He poured a potion down her throat before she could protest, and she swallowed with a cough.

"Fainted?" It all flooded back. *The vision.* "Get your hands off me." Vivi stood up with a mixture of shock and embarrassment. "I'm done with your experiment." Whatever sympathy she had felt for the two orphans had quickly dissolved.

A burst of sparks exploded from the back of the auditorium and the double doors swung open. The panther leapt to its paws and bounded down the aisle. Dax entered the room with an angry glare, immediately firing off a spell from the head of his cane to stun the charging cat.

Gasps filled the audience. They were certainly getting a show.

"Seems the door was locked from the inside." Dax gritted his teeth and ran his hand through his hair, trying to compose himself in front of the distinguished tour group. His eyes widened when he saw Vivi and the makeshift experiment. "It's time for our guest to be leaving." But Vivi was already heading out the door.

"I wasn't done with my test," Mitchell whined. "We were in the middle of a demonstration. It's not my fault she freaked."

"Sorry to disturb the show, but we're wrapping up for today." Dax pointed his cane at Mitchell in a dare.

"By all means. Thank you all for joining us," Miranda addressed the crowd.

Dax whispered a spell and the big cat stirred, rose to its giant paws, and glided back to its masters' sides. The armed guards walked behind Vivi and Dax down the hall and to another elevator. "I'm sorry about that. I didn't realize how long I was taking. I got caught up in business," Dax said. His shoulder sagged. "I hope I didn't ruin your day."

"No, not at all," she said. "The twins are *fascinating*. A little eccentric, too, like you mentioned. And a bit creepy."

He sighed. "They went too far. I had no idea they were doing experiments on the tour or I would have never let you go. Did they hurt you?" Real concern filled his eyes.

"No, just a little prick. Don't worry." The potion Mitchell had given her wiped out her headache, and she felt surprisingly well. Vivi was very glad to be out of that room. "I fainted, that's all. I ruined their experiment." She had no idea what the vision she'd just experienced meant, only that she was getting closer and closer to an unpredictable darkness.

"Let me make it up to you, please. We're holding a lavish party in a few days. No experiments, just champagne and music. I promise. We're launching the new product, and you can see firsthand what all the excitement has been about. You should come. I'll send an invitation. Bring your sisters. It'll be fun, like old times." He gave her shoulder a good-natured squeeze.

"That's nice. I'll think about it. Thanks

for everything."

The train ride home was a little more crowded. Vivi shared an open car with a group of young witch commuters and mentally reviewed her day. It had been a surreal experience at Mender Corp, but it wasn't entirely fruitless. The vision of the cottage was an interesting development, but she had no point of reference for it. She recorded the vision in her notebook and decided her first stop when she got back to Willow Realm was The Charmery to do a little research on the other big development of the day. She had a lot of questions about bracelets.

14

I T WAS DINNERTIME WHEN VIVI got back to Willow
Realm, but she was too excited about the
bracelet to stop and eat, so instead she
grabbed a couple of overstuffed sandwiches
and side salads from Nocturnes and headed
down the street to The Charmery. The sound
of tinkling chimes filled the air as she pushed
open the door with her hip, her arms filled
with the food bag and her oversized purse.

Every inch of The Charmery was bursting
with metal objects used as vessels for magic.
Charms were spells that needed a conduit
to hold the magic. The magic was infused
into an object that was then carried by the
person wanting to benefit from the spell. The
most popular charms were small and worn
on bracelets, necklaces, rings, and anklets.
A charm could be infused in any metal, but

silver and gold held the spell the best, since they were soft metals and were easy to melt down into jewelry, making the perfect wearable magic spell. The silver and moonstone ring that Vivi wore was infused with a charm that created illuma light.

Charms of all shapes and sizes filled the glass cases. One case contained a menagerie of silver animals, another held golden flowers and leaves, whereas a third case displayed metal beads, headbands, and bangles. Vivi placed the food bag on the counter near the back of the shop and drifted around, finally having time to browse the beautiful merchandise her friend and fellow shop owner, Lavender, displayed.

"What's that delicious smell?" Lavender poked her head out from the back. "Hey, Vivi. Haven't seen you since the gala. How's business?"

"Can't complain."

Petite and curvy, Lavender wore colorful knit sweaters that could be seen from the end of the block, sensible shoes made of natural materials, and patchwork jeans. She had been making jewelry and working with metal since she was a young witch at Haven Academy and now was the most coveted metal artist in Willow Realm. She pulled off her leather work gloves, revealing short fingers and neatly trimmed nails, and dug into the food bag with hungry urgency.

"I hope you brought some of this food for me because, as you can see, I'm helping myself." Lavender held a paper-wrapped sandwich up to her nose and smelled. "Roasted veggie on focaccia, melted mozzarella, and balsamic dressing. Be still my heart." Her eyes closed in a moment of silence for the delectable treat.

"The roast beef and cheddar is for me. I'm feeling very carnivorous tonight," Vivi said, giving Lavender a wink. The shop owner was a vegetarian with a sense of humor.

"To what do I owe the pleasure?" the petite witch asked after they had eaten about half of their sandwiches.

"I was hoping you could take a look at a bracelet for me. I think it might have held magic at one time." Vivi took a bite of pasta salad, flavored with sun-dried tomatoes and artichokes.

"Right up my alley."

After they had eaten, Vivi and Lavender examined the bracelet. The charm expert carried it over to her station and pulled a magnifying mirror attached to an adjustable arm over the piece of jewelry. If anyone could decipher its magical purpose, Lavender could. Her brown hair was a halo of curls hovering over the lighted glass as she squinted and rotated the bracelet, examining every crack and crevice as if it were a puzzle to solve.

"Interesting," she said, extinguishing the illuma light. "Well, first off, there's no magic in it currently, but you probably knew that. Secondly, I've never seen anything like it." She waved Vivi closer. "This little gem was made for a distinct purpose. And I seriously doubt that purpose was vanity. This isn't an ordinary charm vessel."

"Tell me more. I barely touched the one Miranda was wearing and I got zapped."

"Take a look at this." Lavender flipped the cuff over and pointed out the interior rim. The underside of the metal was carved with thin bands that wove around the circumference, looping back and forth.

Vivi had noticed the grooves, but thought they were part of the construction.

"I'm guessing those aren't for show."

"The grooves are the conduit for the charm. This little guy was designed to hold a lot of magic, more than just a simple spell or ward."

Pretty and powerful, Vivi thought, squinting at the design.

Lavender moved the magnifying glass over, so she could see the details. "The grooves form bands that hold the spell. Simply put, the more bands, the more magic," Lavender said.

"How powerful are we talking?"

"Very. I'll have to examine at it closer, maybe even take it apart if I can. I also have a few spells to penetrate the metal. I might be able to give you a better idea after I've taken a good look inside. Maybe even get a trace of the charm it once held."

"Could it be a defensive spell? Or maybe a restraining spell?" Vivi asked. The memory of the witch's bound wrists was still fresh in her mind.

"Do you think this bracelet was used to handcuff someone?" Lavender wrinkled up her pert nose at the piece of metal. Restraining spells were restricted to law enforcement unless a permit by the council was granted. "Bracelets would be a logical choice."

"I'm not sure." Vivi twisted a strand of her long hair around her finger, contemplating the use of the bracelet. "I guess I'll wait and see what you can find out about the thing before I pass judgment on it." But Vivi already knew the bracelet had been found near one victim. She was lucky to have found the one she did, and since Miranda had been wearing one, too, there were probably more of them. An idea crossed her mind. She hated to ask, but what choice did she have? "Lavender, you don't happen to know any witches or wizards who make this sort of piece, do you?"

"Do I know a witch who makes charms for illegal binding spells? What exactly are you asking me?" Her brow creased, her expression stern. "What kind of witch do you think I am?"

Vivi stepped back. "Sorry to offend you. I

don't mean to get personal, but I really need to know."

She cracked a smile. "Don't worry, I'm just messing with you. I don't know anyone off the top of my head. Let me check around with other charmers and see if I can dig up some dirt."

"Excellent. I knew I could count on you." Relieved she had Lavender's help, Vivi leaned against the case and noticed the news parchment, *Witch World Daily,* unfurled on the counter. The paper was filled with the most current news, gossip, and happenings of Everland and was delivered by scroll twice a day. A familiar image of Willow Realm peeked up from the front page. It was an image of her shop! Her heart fluttered. She had always dreamed of getting a feature article in the paper to expose her shop and reach more customers, but she had a bad feeling this wasn't the kind of advertising she had been hoping for.

"What's this?" Vivi picked up the parchment, scanning the headline.

"It's nothing. Oh, don't worry about that," Lavender tried to snatch the parchment out of her hand.

The front-page article was a scathing exposé, which in loose terms detailed the entire ordeal from poor old Clarissa found tortured and near death in the Dire Woods to Maynard Luck's tragic murder. Worst of all, though, it implicated the Mayhem sisters, implying they were linked to the tragic events that befell both witches. Vivi and Honora were also mentioned as *involved* in the investigation, and not in a good way—in a 'mayhem-causing' kind of way. There was even a quote from Hexer Finn saying he was *watching* the investigation and monitoring *certain* witches closely. *Swine,* she thought, but her stomach clenched. *Stupid article.*

"How could they print this? We haven't done anything wrong."

"It's just gossip, a sensational story. You know that. They always embellish the truth to sell more papers." Lavender scanned the counter, snatched up the bracelet, and held it up like it was the answer to Vivi's problems. "This little beauty has a story to tell, and we're going to find out what it is. Mark my word. Let them print that in the paper."

Vivi gave her a thankful smile. "You're right. This isn't over." She sighed. "Let's keep the bracelet just between us, okay? The less attention, the better."

"I'm here to help."

She dropped the parchment back on the counter. Her head ached, but her resolve was unshaken. "Just be careful. Trying to help was what got me in this mess in the first place."

After saying her goodbyes, Vivi headed home for a good night's sleep. She changed out of her clothes and sipped a cup of warm milk with a touch of cinnamon, reflecting on another day as an amateur sleuth. She couldn't get a read on Fowler. He was obviously under a lot of pressure at Mender Corp with the new product launch. Sure, he was a little overconfident and had strong opinions, but with his experience, who wouldn't? He had earned his station in life, but still, his stained fingertips made him worth keeping an eye on.

Then there were the creepy Mender twins and their mounting ambition and magical tests. Images of the bracelet, the Dire Woods, and the victims shifted across Vivi's mind's eye. When she closed her eyes to meditate, it felt as if she were lost in a thick fog. She couldn't see the missing witch anymore, but only heard a faint voice, saying the same thing over and over—*help me*.

The dark wizard was growing more powerful, while the witch was sliding away. Vivi's dreams were dark and empty. Nothing came to her in the night, not even the cottage. And that scared her more than any nightmare. At least in a nightmare, she had something to fight against, but this new darkness was hollow, and she feared that emptiness most of all.

She practically sleepwalked through work the next day, and after closing up the shop, Vivi sent Rumor with a message to both Clover and Honora. It was time to dig into the family's magical treasure trove. Time to do a little spy crafting the old-fashioned way.

15

THE SISTERS NEVER KNEW THEIR father. All they had was a grainy photo of a dashing young wizard, his thick dark hair windblown, his eyes sparkling with mischief. Their mother went glassy-eyed and daydreamy when she talked about him, but was light on personal details and heavy on stories of exotic trips they took together. They'd had a whirlwind romance that led the young couple all over Everland, before Elspeth returned to their grandmother's house with a baby due and a boyfriend who would disappear five years later.

Elspeth kept nothing of his. Not a scrap of clothing nor a snip of hair. Not one memento of their time together existed, except for three young daughters. They were too young when he left to remember much about him. It was like being fathered by a ghost.

Elspeth was a restless witch. She had a wandering soul that pulled her all over Everland, traveling and mapping every inch of the witching world, often leaving her daughters with their grandmother for weeks at a time while she ventured out, wrapped in her felt green traveling cloak and carrying a tall carved wooden staff. Not one inch of Everland remained uninspected by her. But the witching world became a cage, and when her daughters were grown and out of school, Elspeth packed up her bags and left to explore the world beyond.

She had been gone for a decade. Occasionally, messages scribbled on parchment would arrive, sometimes accompanied by mysterious twine-wrapped packages containing wondrous gifts: a giant yellow-stained tooth, an old whiskey bottle filled with fairy dust, a necklace made of foreign coins. She once sent them a journal filled with drawings and notes from her travels as a testament to her life on the road, and the sisters treasured it.

They accepted their mother as much as they could—gypsy scholar that she was—and loved her. Vivi was proud of her mother's spirit and her life of adventure. Clover lived vicariously through the journal and the promise of a storybook world. Honora had the hardest time since she was the youngest when their mother left; she felt she missed out on time with her and harbored resentment toward her for leaving them, but at least they always had each other.

Since Clover had the most storage space in her house, she became the keeper of the family heirlooms and treasures. Currently, the three sisters were gathered in her musty attic. Clover kneeled on a threadbare carpet that lay across the cluttered wooden floor. The necklace that hung around her neck cast a faint illuma light as she dug inside of a giant old steamer trunk. Her sweater quickly collected smears of gray dust on the sleeves. "I know it's in here somewhere," she said with a sneeze.

"This is a terrible idea. Tell me why we're doing it again?" Honora asked, sitting in an antique chair with her leg thrown over one of the carved wooden arms. She looked like a bored noble woman, if royalty wore tight black jeans and an irritated stare.

"Because I need to get another look around the woods where I found my best clue." Vivi heaved boxes out of the way and positioned a worn velvet ottoman in the center of the rug.

"The bracelet. I get it, but you could ask Lance to take you back during the day. Kill two birds with one stone." Honora propped her feet up on the ottoman and flashed her a sly grin.

"He's cute and single." There was a smudge on Clover's nose.

"I know, but I don't have time for handsome sheriffs right now. I'm more curious about the Darklander, as bad as that sounds. Something's going on out there and I need to figure out what. Like you said, it's probably nothing, but I want to know for sure."

"If this keeps you from going to the Dire Woods alone, then I'll do it. Don't you ever do that again," Honora said. "You could have been seriously hurt."

Clover gave Honora a warning nudge with her bare foot. "We're here to be supportive, not to lecture."

"I'm sorry. I don't mean to be so harsh. I get upset because I love you. You're the middle sister, the sweet creamy filling in the Mayhem sister cookie sandwich. We need you. You're our center," Honora said.

Vivi smiled. "You're right, going out in the middle of the night in the Dire Woods was kind of stupid, but I took a risk and found my clue. Now I've got to keep pushing."

"I don't want to mess with a sinister wizard like the Darklander. There's nothing he wouldn't do to protect his world," Clover said.

"He knows something. I can feel it." Not wanting to worry her sisters, Vivi kept the painful stinger spell from the Darklander a secret. She knew firsthand what he was capable of.

"Here we go." Clover pulled an antique mirror out of the depths of the trunk. She blew dust off the surface and sneezed again. Many families passed down heirlooms like jewelry, clocks, or a set of china from generation to generation, but leave it to the Mayhem family to pass down a dangerous magical artifact with a dubious past.

Clover beamed. "I knew this bad boy was in here somewhere."

A nosy aunt who loved to keep an eye on her neighbors had created the scrying mirror, which was a powerful magical tool used to see what was going on in another location. It was a little bit like spying. Or a lot like spying, depending on the witch's intent. Vivi liked to think of using the mirror as magical snooping.

Honora wrinkled her nose. "I hate that thing."

"I would think as a private investigator you would love using scrying mirrors," Vivi said. She positioned the mirror on the ottoman.

"No way. I do surveillance the old-fashioned way, out in the open. Plus, I don't like to get caught. That thing is going to cause a disturbance. We're so getting busted." Honora shook her head. "Scrying is easy. Doing it anonymously is the hard part."

That was the downside of the scrying

mirror—it exuded a magical signature, a pulse that could be detected. There was also the problem that scrying was technically illegal, since the Magical Privacy Act was issued about two decades earlier. The only reason they were allowed to keep the mirror was because it was created prior to the law and was a family heirloom, sort of a magical grandmother clause. Still, using the mirror was dangerous. That was why the thing was buried in Clover's attic.

"We'll be quick. Plus, it's the woods. It's not like we're peeking in any windows or bedrooms. No one will see us." Vivi wiped the dust from the surface of the milky glass. "It's worth the risk."

For the mirror to work it needed a reference—something taken from the place or person to be seen. The mirror homed in on the place and reflected the scene back. Their aunt might have been nosy, but she was also a smart spellcrafter.

Vivi opened a paper bag containing the reference material she'd brought with her from the woods. She hoped she'd been able to pick enough leaves and debris from her jacket and hair after sitting on the ground and fighting off the familiar the other night to activate the spell.

The three sisters sat cross-legged in a circle around the ottoman. Globes of illuma light cast eerie shadows across the rough-beamed ceiling. Clover gave Vivi an encouraging nod.

"Let's do this," Honora said.

Vivi scattered the leaves around the rim of the mirror's surface. The sisters placed their fingers on the gilded edge and focused their attention. Vivi whispered the activation spell their grandmother had taught them as little girls. It was an old-fashioned witch's rhyme.

Glass of light. Mirror of the night.
Show me what I wish to see,
The place these leaves used to be.

The mirror hummed to life, warming under their fingertips. It was like peering down into a frost-coated pond. Something moved under the crackling surface. Black clouds billowed across the glass. The smell of damp earth, leaf rot, and decay filled the attic. Vivi wrinkled her nose. Clouds parted and a scene appeared. Slender trees stood sentry in the Dire Woods. The night was quiet. The moon's pale light filtered through the blackness.

They stared for minutes, saying nothing, watching. There was nothing to see—no movement, no one at all. Vivi focused, tried to see something, strained to sense the missing witch, but the woods were empty. She bit her bottom lip to fight the frustration, her own sense of failure.

What else could she do to make tonight a success?

What she really wanted was to see the Darklander and ask him a few probing questions about what was going on right outside his mansion, but he wasn't wandering the woods or standing on his doorstep. He was probably locked up tight behind his heavy wooden door, the thick stone walls protecting him. She imagined the hideous creature he kept as a familiar perched on the back of his chair. It probably still had her blood under its claws.

Vivi had nothing of the Darklander's to use as a reference to him. *Except...*

She fingered the cut on her arm, wrapped under gauze. Her glance shifted between her two sisters.

Clover raised her brow. "What are you thinking?"

"Yeah, I don't like that look," Honora said.

"Could we use my blood?" Vivi asked, a spark of excitement flaring inside her. Maybe tonight wouldn't be a total loss after all.

"What do you mean, your blood?" Clover drummed her fingers on her knee. She was wearing her favorite patchwork jeans and loose sweater. "We aren't using blood." Her lips pinched into a knot on her pretty face.

Vivi reached out and touched her sister's hand. "There's nothing in the woods. We need to see inside the Darklander's mansion, and I don't have anything of his, but his familiar slashed me with its claw. I'm sure it took some of my blood with it." She rolled up the short sleeve of her T-shirt and examined the bandage.

"Blood magic? This is getting a little too dark for my taste." Clover crossed her arms over her chest.

"It's not dark magic. My blood just happens to be a reference point," Vivi justified. "It's not the same and you both know it."

"Okay, it's not black magic, but it's still insane," Honora said, blowing her bangs out of her eyes. "You don't go peering into the Darklander's mansion like a witchy Peeping Tom. Do you have any idea what he would do if he caught us?"

"Why do you have to be so negative? Give it a chance. I'm running out of options."

"Vivi, Honora has a point. He would take it as a sign of aggression." Clover shifted her weight and wrapped her arms around her knees. "Dark wizards live for retaliation."

"He already saw me in the woods. He knows I was there," Vivi said, frustration building in her. "I've hit a wall, and he could know something." She stood and spun in a small circle. "I have to help this girl before she ends up dead like Maynard. Don't you both see that? I was the one who saw what happens to her. You're both right, and under normal circumstances, I'd listen, but I'm getting desperate. I need you guys."

Honora sighed. "Or you'll do it on your own."

Clover wiped the mirror clear of leaf debris with the edge of her already dusty sweater sleeve. "We can try. I don't know if it will even work. Right now all we're getting this mirror to show us are trees and more trees."

"What did we expect? I told you this was a bad idea. That mirror is trouble," Honora said.

"Zip it," Vivi said. "I want to try."

Honora was not going to scare her out of this. Vivi pulled her bandage back. The wound was healing nicely. All that was left of the cut was a thin red line, and now she would have to open it up again.

Clover handed her an antique letter opener and shrugged. "It's all I have up here and I don't want to haul my butt down and up those stairs again."

Vivi took the knife and rested the dull edge against the wound.

"Oh, please." Honora pulled a long thin blade out of her boot and handed it to her. "Here try this. That antique letter opener is so dull it wouldn't open a *letter*."

Vivi slid the blade into the wound with a wince. Blood blossomed against her pale skin. A thin red trail dripped down her arm and pooled onto the mirror's surface. After she stanched the blood and readjusted the bandage, the three sisters placed their hands on the mirror and repeated the spell.

The glass trembled and shuddered. Then nothing.

"It's searching for your blood out in the world," Clover said in a loud stage whisper.

"I hope you haven't used any blood in your potions." Honora smiled. "That would be awkward if we ended up in a customer's bathroom or bedroom."

Her sister's levity was comforting. "I don't use blood," Vivi said. "Until this second."

A screeching sound filled the attic. Barnaby, Honora's owl familiar, and Rumor were perched in the rafters and something had set them both off. Vivi jerked as the mirror shook beneath her fingers, and she had to clutch the edge to hold on. The glass surface bubbled with gray smoke and the smell of soot and ash filled the room.

The spell had worked.

It was like peering over the hunched shoulder of a gargoyle, staring down over its domain. They had found the beast. Vivi had been right. The familiar still carried her blood embedded under its claws, and from the view of the roofline they were seeing through the mirror, the creature was currently perched on the edge of the mansion's gutter like a lookout, waiting and watching.

"What is that thing?" Clover asked. Her face scrunched in disgust. "Where did the Darklander find such a weird and creepy familiar?"

"I don't think he found it. I think he bred it," Vivi said with a cringe.

"Shh." Honora pointed at the scene in the mirror. "Look, someone's coming."

A hover bike appeared out of the misty woods and pulled up to the mansion's front door. The familiar was perched at an odd angle, so it was difficult for them to get a clear view of the rider. A wizard dressed in black dismounted the bike and pulled his helmet off, revealing shaggy dark hair and a strong stubbly jaw.

"Who is it?" Honora asked. Her silky dark hair fell like a tent over her head and shoulders, obscuring Vivi's view of the mirror. "I can't see his face."

"Neither can we with your hair in the way," Vivi said, sweeping Honora's mane of hair off the glass. "His face is in the shadows."

Suddenly, the view in the mirror shifted when the bat creature took flight on its leathery wings. It rose up into the night sky, expertly skirting tree limbs and circling the mansion once, twice, giving them a view of the gigantic house and grounds. There was an enclosed courtyard lit with torches and a twisted maze garden with a strange iron fountain in the center. There were also numerous adjoining buildings making up the compound—not to mention about a half-dozen black-hooded security wizards walking the grounds.

"Awesome." Honora's gaze was trained on the mirror. "Did you see the way it glided through the air? Talk about aerodynamic."

Clover pointed, her attention captivated. "It's flying toward the mansion. We're going inside."

Goosebumps cascaded over Vivi's arms. She didn't know anyone who had ever seen inside the dark wizard's mansion; there were no rumors, not even whispers, of what existed behind the stone walls. And she was getting pulled inside, getting a bat's eye view. The familiar flew into a tall vestibule lined with windows and down an expansive hall. Wrought-iron chandeliers hung on thick chains from the ceiling. Illuma lights glowed from the tips of tall waxy tapers though not a drip of wax fell on the dark wood floors. The walls were lined with tapestries woven with historic scenes of witches being tortured, burned, and hung.

Vivi shuddered. What kind of wizard hung such disturbing images on his walls? At the end of the hallway, the familiar entered a sitting room adorned with plush red velvet sofas, brocade-covered chairs, and wooden tables. A fire crackled in a huge stone hearth large enough to roast a pig. The three sisters were given a perfect view of the room when the familiar perched on one of the wood beam rafters. The sound of a door opening and closing down the hall filtered into the room, followed by approaching footsteps.

An imposing wizard stood in the threshold. Clover gasped. Her hand went to her mouth. The wizard was impeccably dressed. One side of his face was handsome with a strong jaw, but the other side was covered in scars that ran from his collar to his hairline. Viciously creased and puckered, his face was painful to look at and appeared to have been burned. His black hair was cut short, exposing ears that came to points, the way a fairy's or elf's would, but which seemed unnatural on him.

For a second, Vivi wondered if the wizard might be part goblin. What kind of magic had he been using on himself to create those ears? *A glamor?* she wondered.

The wizard's gaze drifted skyward, locating his familiar, staring right at them.

"Do you think he senses we're here?" Clover whispered.

"Hopefully not. But we don't have much time." Vivi couldn't stop staring, mesmerized by the wizard. "We get as much information as we can before he senses us, and then we break the spell. I want to see the wizard who just arrived. There's something about him that has my hackles raised." Vivi rubbed the back of her neck.

"We make it quick, see who the wizard on the bike is, and cut the connection," Honora pushed defiantly. "One look."

Her sister was right, of course. But it was hard to resist a tempting opportunity to see inside the forbidden lair. Vivi felt so close to an important piece of information. Additional footsteps came from the hall and the door swung open.

The man from the bike drifted into the room. He slipped off his jacket and dropped it onto a chair. A black T-shirt clung to his well-developed torso and biceps. Black jeans and heavy boots completed his outfit. He helped himself to a drink and swirled the amber liquid around inside a crystal glass. Sinking down onto the sofa, he propped his boots up on the coffee table with his back to them. Vivi's gaze drifted to his belt holding a metal wand that she recognized. Then she saw the rubber bands around his wrist and put it together.

Her mouth suddenly went dry. She knew him. "It's Rye Finn!"

"Who?" Clover asked.

"He works for Hex Division. He questioned me about my vision at the police station. I can't believe it. He practically accused me of being a suspect and now he's sitting in the

Darklander's house sipping expensive booze."
She fumed, both shocked and confused.

"What a pompous jerk," Honora said. "This
is unbelievable." She shook her head.

The Hexer glanced over his shoulder and
she got a good view of his angular face and
sharp nose. She had no doubt. The Darklander
poured himself a snifter of amber liquor and
joined Finn.

"What does this mean?" Clover asked.
"Why would a Hexer be meeting with
the Darklander?"

"He looks a little too comfortable to be on
official business," Vivi said, realizing that the
Hexer was alone, without his two associates.
She bit her lip. "I knew there was something
up with him. He was more curious in what I
knew about the case than wanting to find the
missing witch."

"Let's give the guy the benefit of the doubt
before rushing to judge. Hexers have to do a lot
of things against the Witch's Code. He could
be undercover." Being a private investigator
gave Honora a sympathetic perspective.

Vivi wasn't buying it. She didn't trust
Hexer Finn one bit. She focused on the scene
and realized they had started talking. "Shh, I
want to hear this."

The three sisters leaned in to listen.

"This is unacceptable. I'm not bargaining."
Finn gulped his drink and sat the glass down

with a loud clank.

"You don't have a choice." The Darklander's voice was smooth and deep. "You do what I say."

"Ha! Hardly."

"For now we keep to the terms of the original agreement."

"Sounds like they've done business before," Vivi whispered. Her hands were slick with sweat against the mirror's frame.

"Fine." Finn sighed. "What about the other matter? Any word?"

"The magic is varied, inexperienced and advanced at the same time, but the wizard wasn't stupid enough to leave anything useful behind. I am afraid, for now, I have nothing to offer you on that front."

"There has to be a good reason the Darklander's keeping quiet. He knew I was in the woods. Why doesn't he tell Finn?" Vivi swallowed, her nerves on edge.

The familiar's head jerked up as the door opened and a group of black-clad minions entered the room. A wizard with twisted horns and a curly goatee led the way. One had a tattoo covering the side of his neck and half his face in the markings of a Druid. Another had bleached white hair and the pointed ears of an elf. It was rumored that the Darklander and his followers were against the separation of species and wanted the borders of Everland opened up to the Otherworld, welcoming fairies, elves, wolves, and all the creatures of the Otherworld, including humans, into Everland. Many of his supporters used magic spells to mimic the features of other species like the elf ears, goat horns, and tattoos as a sign of solidarity.

They lugged a long rectangular wooden box into the room and heaved it onto the table in front of Finn and the Darklander as if it weighted a ton. The side panels were carved with ancient woodwork and intricate markings Vivi had never seen before. The Darklander wiped the surface with a damp cloth that came away covered in dirt and cobwebs. The box had been hidden away for a long time.

The followers jostled for position around their master, curiously peering over each other's shoulders to glimpse what they had unearthed. An elaborate lock with two interlocking metal serpents graced the lid. The Darklander waved his wand over the twisted metal snakes and the lock slowly uncoiled.

A hushed silence filled the room.

The lid lifted. The hinges creaked. Nestled inside the box on a bed of crushed blue velvet was a row of colorful glass spheres. Each small globe was about the size of an egg, with a transparent surface revealing a swirling cosmos of light and color leaping to life inside of the balls.

"Wow." Vivi gaped.

"What are those?" Clover asked.

"They're impossibly rare. I've only seen them in diagrams at the Academy archives." Vivi was riveted. "Amazing."

"Elaborate, please," Clover said. "Besides being spectacular, you still haven't told us what they are."

"Spectacularly dangerous. If I'm right, those little babies are elemental spheres. The balls are used to control elemental forces as well as the weather. The red ones are sky fire. The blue ones channel water. Gold controls the earth; white the air. I think the silver one must harness electricity." Elemental magic had always fascinated Vivi. This had to be about Rye Finn and his desire to know more about the volatile magic.

"Where did they get them?" Clover asked. "But more importantly, what are they planning on doing with them?"

"Probably the black market," Honora said. "You don't want to know the kind of stuff traded in Stargazer's seedier sections of town."

"That's heavy-duty magic, and it isn't good. The Witch Council outlawed the spheres a century ago. They could screw up our whole world. Can you imagine someone controlling the elements?" Vivi said.

"The Darklander would control the entire witching world," Honora said. "He must have stolen them. Or traded them for something equally terrible."

Clover narrowed her eyes. "I understand why the Darklander would be involved. Selling illegal magical devices for profit seems right up his alley. But what's the Hexer doing here?"

Vivi stared at the rubber bands he wore on his wrist. "He's not an elemental, but his mother's one. He has some power," Vivi said. "But I'm guessing he wants more."

"Now he has a whole lot." Honora snorted. "Never trust the Hex Division. They're always out for themselves. Who knows what plans they have for the spheres?"

"Could the council be after them? Maybe he's working for them." Clover shrugged, always the pragmatic one, giving everyone the benefit of the doubt. "We should wait until we know more before we condemn him."

"Maybe, but you never had the pleasure of meeting him. The spheres need to be destroyed or at least locked away by the council. No matter who has them," Vivi said. She was really starting to dislike this guy.

Finn picked up one of the balls from its velvet bed and held it up to the light. The ball swirled with energy. After inspecting the magical fireball, he reached into his jacket and pulled out a pouch and dropped it on the table—gold. Vivi's stomach clenched. He was here to make a deal with the Darklander.

"Does this mean that the Darklander isn't involved in the witch attacks?" Clover asked.

"I don't know." Frustration washed over Vivi in a wave of heat. Every time she got a little bit closer, she took a step backwards. She didn't know what this meant, except that it complicated things. "I don't think the missing witch is in the Darklander's mansion. I can't feel her at all."

There was a buzzing sound in the room.

"What's that?" Honora asked.

"The mirror's vibrating." Vivi grabbed the edge.

"Magical power surge," Clover said. "This old thing is unpredictable."

The minion with the elf ears looked up suddenly and pointed to the rafters where the Darklander's familiar perched.

"They're onto us," Honora said. "I told you two this mirror was trouble."

They had been so distracted by the elemental spheres they had forgotten that the mirror caused a disturbance in the scene it was viewing. After a short amount of time, the magical energy would be felt and even seen, the mirror becoming a window, enabling the wizards in the room to peer right through. The veil separating them thinned, turning transparent.

"One more second." Vivi needed more information.

Finn slammed the case shut and the Darklander stepped in front of the table. The minions snapped to attention and went into a surround formation to protect their leader. Suddenly, the sisters were staring down at a small gang of wizards with their wands raised, ready to strike. The Darklander pulled a long thin wand that looked like a crooked finger bone from the interior pocket of his jacket. A dark phrase poured from his lips. It wasn't a curse, but it was a strong spell that leapt in a spark of sharp energy from the tip of his wand upward into the rafters. The familiar screamed as the spell exploded inches from its head.

"Shut it down." Honora lunged for the mirror, but she was too late, for Clover had spoken the counter spell, and with a spark, the mirror went black.

"That was close." Honora brushed the hair out of her face.

"Too close," Clover said.

"I just wanted answers. The Darklander has to know something about the witch attacks." Vivi held her head in her hands. "Nothing happens near his house without him knowing. His familiar flies through the trees at all hours. He knows, and he's not telling anyone. He trades in stolen goods, and I bet he trades in information, too."

"What about Hexer Finn?" Honora asked.

"If he's an elemental or wants to be a stronger one, we're in trouble. Plus, he knows we saw him committing a crime. He's not going to be too happy about that."

"A Hexer might have gone rogue. That's all you need." Clover picked up the mirror and placed it back in the old trunk where she had found it. "I hope this wasn't a bad idea."

"At least we know more than we knew before. It just wasn't what we were hoping for," Vivi said.

16

THE FOLLOWING MORNING THINGS WERE slow at the shop. Pepper was holding a potion-conjuring workshop with a few friends from Haven Academy, and Vivi didn't want to get in the way of eight overly excited young witches brewing up love potions, so she headed over to Nocturnes, craving a cup of tea and a warm cherry almond scone. After her peek through the scrying mirror last night, when she spied on and got caught by one of the most powerful and deviant wizards in Everland, she needed time to clear her head and figure out her next move.

Lavender waved madly from the front window of The Charmery, tapping on the glass to get Vivi's attention as she walked down Main Street. She had planned on stopping by later that day, but from Lavender's reaction,

Vivi figured she must have exciting news about the bracelet, so she picked up her pace and headed over. Once she was inside the shop, the excited charmer latched onto her arm and pulled her into the back, telling her assistant to watch the store.

"I'm guessing you have news," Vivi said, pushing past a drape and into the workroom.

"You bet I do." Lavender peeled back a piece of black velvet, revealing the ominous silver bracelet.

"It's still in one piece." Vivi eyed the jewelry, wishing it had been carved up, so she could peek at its metal guts.

"I didn't cut it up or melt it down. I used a view casting spell to see inside like a magical x-ray." Lavender wiggled her eyebrows, practically giddy with excitement. "Want to know what I found?"

"Of course." Vivi felt as if she would jump out of her skin. The charm witch's enthusiasm was infectious. "Tell me."

"Well, you were right about it containing a binding spell. But that isn't the interesting part. Let me explain. The purpose of a charm infused into jewelry is to gradually transfer the magical spell onto whoever is wearing it. For example, a binding spell controls or binds the witch wearing it."

"Right," Vivi answered. "So Miranda, the witch I saw wearing a similar bracelet, was using it to give herself more magic. It was a charm, but this one is binding." That didn't surprise Vivi. She held up the bracelet, turning it in her hand.

"Not exactly. That's what's so exciting. This charm bracelet isn't just a vessel to hold magic or bind someone. It's a siphon." Lavender's face lit up.

"Wait, you mean it was made to draw magic out of a witch?" Vivi dropped the bracelet back onto the cloth and gave it a suspicious glare. "Is that even possible?"

"I know witches who have tried. I've heard of experiments to help witches with too much power." Lavender sat next to Vivi. "If a witch's *persuasion* is too strong, it can cause problems. Some elementals have to siphon off magic prior to working with fire or air. The elements are stronger than witches, so to handle the magic, they siphon some of it off to keep from hurting themselves."

"That's interesting. This bracelet could be used to pull magic from a witch in a good way. Hexer Finn is trying to learn elemental magic. Could something like this help him?"

"Not necessarily. He would need magic if he's going to control it, and if he isn't a natural elemental, I don't see how this would help him. As for the bracelet doing good, it depends on the intent; it could be used for good or bad. I haven't been able to get any signature of what kind of magic the charm held, except for the remnants of the binding spell, like I said."

Vivi picked up the bracelet. It looked harmless, but looks could be deceiving. The bracelet was a device that yielded to the magic and the witch wielding it—good or bad.

"Thanks, you've been a big help."

Lavender wrapped up the bracelet and handed it back to her. "I hope you know what you're doing."

"Me, too. I just can't stop thinking this thing is a key to what's been happening."

"Always trust your instincts."

A surge of excitement filled Vivi as she left The Charmery. Finally, she had another piece of the puzzle. It made sense and explained why Clarissa Taylor was empty of magic when they found her in the woods. The dark wizard siphoned it off and left her for dead. A pulse of anger hit her when she thought of the poor witch lying in the healer ward. At least now she knew how it was being done. Finding out who was behind it was another story.

Her list of suspects was short.

The twins had to be involved. There no way Miranda's bracelet was a siphon. She was too hungry for power and control. But why would they steal magic? They were already powerful and wealthy. It didn't make sense. Could they be using it for a new healing remedy? The lab was buzzing with some grand new product. But what motivated them? That was the question.

Vivi rubbed the tip of her finger with her thumb, recalling the drops of her blood Mitchell had taken for his test. She knew from her own potion-making experience the Menders would naturally have to test all products before selling them to the public. Testing was the norm. But how far would they go? The twins' involvement didn't explain the black magic found in the Dire Woods. She couldn't picture Mitchell and Miranda traipsing around the forest, using blood salt, *unless* the experiments and tests weren't working, and they became desperate. But she had no proof against Miranda. A bracelet wasn't enough.

The vision she had at the lab only confused her more—a lovely cottage in the woods, but inside the idyllic home, the blackest magic was being performed. Where was it? Vivi remembered the tapestries hanging in the Darklander's home. Terrible things had been done to witches in the past, but that was by humans. Vivi knew better than to think that witches and wizards were that different. They had many traits in common and the desire for wealth and power was just one of them. The Darklander was the type who had no problem with using black magic. She was left with still more questions.

She crossed the street and headed into Nocturnes. The lunch crowd hadn't descended yet, so she had her pick of tables and chose a prime window seat location that stared out over Main Street and ordered a hot mocha tonic. Her hunger was gone. She couldn't eat, but the drink was rich and soothing, warming her whole body from the inside out. Wanting to confide in him, Vivi contemplated heading over to the sheriff's office to see what Lance thought about her recent discoveries, but if she told him about the bracelet, she would also have to tell him where she found it, and that would lead to the Darklander and the scrying mirror. She wasn't ready to turn in Hexer Finn without knowing more about his dealings with the Darklander and the elemental spheres. Maybe Clover was right and Rye Finn was working for the Hex Division on a secret mission.

The shops on Main Street were all coming alive for another day, opening their doors to the oncoming shoppers. Nocturnes was great for witch watching. Vivi eyed witches and wizards walk by on their way here and there. That was when she noticed a familiar face—a wizard wearing a jean jacket with the black hood of his sweatshirt blown back from his head. He had a stubbly jaw, lightly scared from acne. His eyes darted up and down the street as he crossed, making his way to Nocturnes and passing the window without a glance. She knew she had seen him before. Butterflies erupted in her stomach when she remembered him.

It was Paul, the young wizard she'd seen at Mender Corp, lurking around the lab, talking to Dr. Fowler. Then it clicked. She'd also seen him at the Cassandra Reason book signing. He was the nervous fan who dropped his books. Seeing him at the company, she'd assumed he lived in the city, but she realized he must live out here. It made more sense. Maybe he would give her the inside scoop on his bosses, she mused, prompting her to pay her check and dart after him before he could get away.

She spotted him immediately and hurried to keep up, but hung back, watching. There was something about him that interested her, and she had a feeling he might be of help to her. He didn't go into any shops, but took a right turn down the crooked alley. He was headed for the portal, so she quickened her pace. Casually following someone down the street was one thing, but following the wizard through a portal was verging on stalking. This was her only chance to ask him a few questions.

"Excuse me," Vivi said, reaching his side. "Hello. I hate to interrupt you, but I was hoping to talk to you for a second."

Paul stopped abruptly and gave her a suspicious glance. "What about?" His hair was shaggy and hung across his forehead into his eyes. Clad in worn jeans, he drove his hands into his pockets and scanned the street.

"I saw you at Mender Corp the other day. I was on a tour. You work with Dr. Fowler, right?" She smiled, hoping to put him at ease.

"Oh, is that all?" He shrugged, looking relieved. "Technically, I don't work with him. I do freelance research for the lab. Pick up jobs on the side. Sometimes I feel like I do all the work for them, and they take all the credit." His voice was laced with sarcasm.

"It must be exciting, a great opportunity? I'm a potion maker. Nothing major like the work they do there, just small stuff, but I'm a big fan of the Mender twins. Do you ever get to work with them? You know, see behind the scenes?" She was betting on her fan-witch routine to get some dirt on the healers and their operation.

"Sure, sometimes. Mostly Miranda, when I can reach her. She's very selective of who she works with." His gaze was calculating. "If you're looking for a job, I can't help you. Sorry."

"I wouldn't dream of asking."

"Do you have any idea how hard it was for me to get a meeting with Fowler? It took years, and I still have to come in the back door." He shrugged.

"Good to know. Tell me, what's he really like to work with?"

"Guy's real hard-nosed. Cocky, too."

"Why? He didn't seem all that bad to me. Kind of gruff, but he's the head healer so I imagine he's under a lot of pressure."

"Pressure." Paul shook his head. "He's the problem. Always pushing for results and never satisfied. I'd stay away from him if I were you."

"Really?" But, if Vivi recalled, it was Paul who was pushing the doctor to read his paper. "I hear he's working on some breakthrough magic. That he's a genius."

"Like I said, stay away from him. You haven't seen what he's really like. He's got this back room to his laboratory that no one knows about, but I saw it one time when he didn't realize I was there. It's like a *dungeon* where he takes *volunteers*." His expression turned serious. "I've heard things, terrible cries. Strange things go on down there." He glanced around, making sure they were alone. "I even saw some jars filled with black ash once."

Vivi couldn't believe what she was hearing, so she challenged him. "Now you're just trying to scare me." She narrowed her eyes, remembering Dr. Fowler's black fingertips. Could the *volunteers* be the witches? "Have you told anyone?"

"Why would I do that? I'd lose my job. I don't care what that crazy wizard does in his spare time as long as I still get to work and get paid."

Obviously, Paul cared more about his career than about the ethical standards at Mender Corp. It seemed impossible to know for sure, and accusing the doctor or the Mender twins of a serious crime was going to be difficult enough. She tried to imagine the doctor as the wizard from her vision. He definitely had the experience. And who knew what motivated him? But she pressed on. "The twins are healers. It's hard to believe they'd let anything bad go on in their lab," Vivi said.

"Who knows? They're all about sacrifice and the greater good, hard work, and the grind. They've got an orphan complex. They see the sacrifice as necessary."

"Miranda seemed like a control freak if ever I saw one," Vivi said before she could stop herself.

A smile spread across the young wizard's face. "I'll give you a piece of advice for getting a job with the company, no charge. The Menders like strong witches. Power attracts them. Real power."

"What do you mean?"

Paul tilted his head to the side and contemplated her question before answering.

"Let's just say I have a sense about people. I

know their true nature. Take you, for example. I know you pretend to be a potions master. Don't get me wrong. You seem smart, but you hide what you really are. You've been doing it for years. But you can't hide it from me." A strange little smile twisted up his mouth. "They would like you. The real you."

"What are you talking about?" Vivi was shocked. Who did he think he was, taking one look at her and summing her up? He didn't know her at all, and yet he knew there was more to her than potions. "Are you an intuitive? What's your *persuasion*?" Vivi asked.

"Don't get mad. It was a guess." He gave her a devious grin. "Nice talking to you." He turned his back and headed over to the green door with the boar's head portal.

Vivi wasn't sure if she could trust anything he had told her. Something was off, but she couldn't decide if he was telling the truth or was just a cocky wizard talking trash. She turned to leave, but lingered, waiting to see where he went. Paul walked over to the boar's head portal. "Fox's Rock," he said and disappeared into the swirling energy.

Fox's Rock was an old haunt. It was nestled on the outskirts of Willow Realm, between the village and the Meadowlands. Witches gathered at the outcropping of rocks for festivals, harvest moons, and solstices. Huge boulders jutted up out of the clearing, creating stony ridges and plateaus, making perfect places to sit and have a picnic or get away from the world, relax and kick back. It was a nice quiet place to live.

Turning back, Vivi hurried to her shop to get ready for tonight.

17

HONORA DUG THROUGH VIVI'S CLOSET with a look of mortification at her meager offerings of evening attire. Earlier in the day, another buttery cream envelope had arrived with Dax's telltale cross wax seal. True to his word, he invited Vivi and her sisters to the exclusive Mender Corp launch party. The minute she got the invite, Vivi sent Rumor with a note for her sisters to see what they thought, and if they would be interested in going. Clover was her go-to witch for emotional support, and she knew if there was anyone who would give her sound investigating advice, it was the great and *persuasive* Honora.

"Paul sounds weird," Honora said.

Rumor cawed from his perch, clearly in agreement.

"I think he just tries too hard. He desperately wants an opportunity to work with Mender Corp, and who wouldn't? It's a career maker," Vivi said, recalling her impromptu conversation with the young wizard. "Granted, he's eager to get ahead, but he knows more about the company than we do."

"I get that, but he implicated Dr. Fowler, who he supposedly admires and is his boss," Honora said, fruitlessly sliding hanger after hanger across the practically barren wooden rack.

"True. But, remember, Dr. Fowler's fingertips were stained black, just like the wizard in my vision."

"Hope the building schematics I brought help." Honora nodded to a roll of parchment on Vivi's nightstand. "I had a copy made from the public records before leaving the city."

Vivi unrolled the map. It was just what she was hoping for—a detailed diagram of the inner workings of Mender Corp. After a few minutes reviewing the plans, Vivi knew the quickest route to Dr. Fowler's personal workspace.

"The only way to know for sure is to check out what's in the lab. Paul said suspicious things were going on down in Fowler's *dungeon*. That's why I need to get a peek in his back room." She traced her finger along the route to the lab, committing it to memory.

"I must admit a party is a good distraction."

Honora smiled, a fresh glow on her face. "Plus, let's face it, I wouldn't mind seeing Dax again. It's been a while.

"He's as hot as ever, and I know one of the reasons he gave us this invite was to see you." Vivi was both happy and a little jealous of her sister. The kind of passion that Honora and Dax experienced had eluded her so far in her life.

"I can believe that," Clover said, muscling her way into the bedroom. Her arms were loaded down with a large garment bag and a couple of shoeboxes. "Dax's been mad about our little sex kitten sister his whole life." She smirked and tossed the boxes on the bed.

"I'm not looking forward to seeing Miranda and Mitchell." Vivi's brow wrinkled. Another encounter with the creepy twins was not going to be fun. "My plan is to steer clear of them and maintain a low profile."

"Don't worry. We'll be with Dax. Plus, I won't let them lay a finger on you. They probably won't even notice us with the big announcement planned," Honora said.

"You're probably right. Tonight it's Fowler I'm interested in, anyway."

Honora pounced on the garment bag. "Thank the natural world. You brought clothes. Vivi's got nothing in this wasteland of a closet that's remotely wearable for the party tonight."

"Hey, I've got a black wrap dress in there somewhere. It's cute." Vivi sat on her bed, knowing full well there were slim pickings in her closet.

"Yeah, and it was really nice the first hundred times you wore it. Now it's faded, and there's a hole in the elbow." Honora let out a good-natured cackle. "Sister, I need to take you shopping, and soon."

"Fine, after this case is over, I promise to come to Stargazer City and hit some stores with you. Happy?"

"Wait till you see what I brought," Clover said and unzipped the bag.

Vivi gasped as a flowing gas-blue gown with a crystal-beaded bodice spilled out to the floor. "It's the most beautiful thing I've ever seen."

"I know," Clover gushed. "I saw it about a month ago when I was at the seamstress getting some pants hemmed, and I had to buy it. I figured I'd wear it when I'm Cassandra Reason to some big industry event, but when I got your note about the fancy cocktail party, I knew you had to wear it."

"Are you sure you don't want to come with us?"

"No, thanks. I'm all partied out with the book launch. You two will have your hands full without me."

Vivi jumped off the bed and fingered the

silken fabric. "You should keep the dress for yourself."

"Don't worry. I'm going to wear this baby, but there's no reason you can't take it for a test drive." Clover pulled the dress out and held it up to Vivi so they could admire it in the mirror.

"Gorgeous. You might even look better than me," Honora said with a wink. Her younger sister had a healthy appreciation for her own charms. She opened the shoebox and pulled out a pair of to-die-for strappy silver heels. "Clover, you've outdone yourself. I was getting worried after a few minutes in Vivi's closet, where dust bunnies go to multiply, I wouldn't find anything for her to wear." She smirked.

"Hey, it's not that bad." Vivi laughed and then cringed. "Okay, it's pretty dusty in there, but it's not like tonight is a total social outing. We got lucky Mender Corp's doing a private launch. Once inside, it's up to us to figure out how to get into Fowler's lab." She rolled up the parchment map. "Knowing where it's located is the first step. Getting past security is the next one."

"Are you sure you don't want to take Lance as your date?" Honora asked. "He could use his badge to strong-arm his way into the lab."

"No, I don't want to get him involved yet. I'm going on a tip from a freelance employee. It could be nothing. He would never trust me again if I gave him wrong information." Vivi paused. "I've been thinking, and I want to become a registered seer one day, so I need to be sure about my sources before involving the police. I don't want to be the witch who cried wolf. Gaining Lance's trust is important to me."

"True. Plus, you do have little old me to watch your back." Honora bowed dramatically. Clover nudged Honora aside.

"Vivi, that's great. I'm glad you're taking your *persuasion* to the next level. And don't worry. The sheriff will come around. Now sit down and let's do a little magic with that hair of yours."

Vivi plopped down in front of her dressing table and watched as Clover pulled out her wand and wove it through her long brown tresses. Out of all the sisters, Clover performed hairstyling spells the best. She had about a dozen committed to memory, and within minutes created a masterpiece of hair art—curled, pinned, and twisted on top of Vivi's head, exposing her neck. Tiny tendrils of chestnut curls framed her face.

"Gorgeous," Honora said, coming out of the bathroom wearing a shimmering gold cocktail dress that showed off about a mile of toned tanned legs. Her hair was stick straight and glossy as a black lake.

"Wow. Dax is going to drool all over you,"

Vivi said.

"I aim to please." Honora inspected her killer figure in the mirror. "Plus, I hope to drop off a few business cards while mingling with the elite. Only Stargazer City's finest are invited, and I bet more than a few of them could use an investigator."

"You never miss an opportunity. What's the occasion of this swank party?" Clover asked, holding up a pair of dangling aquamarine teardrop earrings to Vivi's lobes.

"A product launch. Mender Corp is introducing a new magical device to stockholders and members of the Healers' Council. Then they'll eat, drink, and dance till late into the night. It's perfect. I'll get a chance to peek inside Fowler's lab while the announcement is going on," Vivi said. "I don't know if I'll find anything, but at least I'll have tried."

"I hope you're right and the missing witch is there. The police need to catch whoever is behind this, so all of this can be over. Witches are afraid. There's talk," Clover said.

"I read the *article* in *Witch World Daily*. Trust me, I want this over with, too, for her sake as well as ours." Vivi stared at her reflection in the mirror, hoping she could pull this off. It was going to take more than a pretty dress to infiltrate the laboratory of the most powerful healers in Stargazer City. "We'll find her, if not tonight, then soon. We're Mayhem sisters. What could possibly go wrong?"

All three sisters let out a cackle.

Before leaving for the party, Vivi grabbed one of the tiny wishful-thinking potion vials she had made the day before, slid it onto a simple silver chain, and draped it around her neck. It was a beautiful swirling glass orb and was a simple and yet perfect addition to the elegant dress.

"Stunning," Dax said. His eyes roved over Honora's entire body when he arrived to escort the sisters to the party. "You look lovely, also, Vivi." He smiled, but offered Honora his arm as they got into the luxury vehicle. Nestled in Dax's personal hovercraft, they glided through the velvety night air between the towering skyscrapers of Stargazer City. Talk about a witch's feet never touching the ground. They arrived at the party in style. Never in her life had Vivi attended a swank gathering like this one, and she took in the scene with awe. Tiny twinkling illuma lights filled the atrium of Mender Corp like dozens of fireflies dancing across the dark sky. Music floated on the air. Once packed with busy commuters and employees, the room was filled with elegantly dressed witches and wizards sipping flutes of chilled champagne and nibbling canapés topped with fresh crab, lobster, and smoked salmon.

After escorting the sisters inside, Dax excused himself to do his obligatory mingling with the shareholders. Vivi's plan was simple—make a few rounds of the party, watch and observe, then at an opportune moment, slip down into Fowler's personal lair to see if there was anything to Paul's story. No way was she going to implicate him if the *dungeon* was all in his imagination.

She and Honora blended into the crowd, casually listening to conversations to pick up any information on the mysterious device and sampling the delicious buffet. Just because Vivi was on a serious mission didn't mean she was immune to the night's festivities. Her mouth watered at the delectable sights and smells, so she snatched a canapé off a passing silver tray and stuffed it into her mouth. The last thing she needed while poking around Fowler's lab was a rumbling stomach.

The twins were stunning, sheathed in their trademark black. Mitchell wore an expensive suit and tie, and his hair had the casual disheveled look. Miranda donned a curve-hugging dress with a plunging neckline. A handsome young blonde wizard clung to her side like a piece of butterscotch arm candy. Vivi breathed a sigh of relief that the two were on the other side of the room, well out of arm's length. She stayed as far away from them as possible and made another pass of the room, searching for the entry down to the lab.

Vivi almost choked on a salmon puff when she saw the dubious figure of Rye Finn standing guard at the only stairwell down to the lab. Her gut tightened. He looked annoyingly dashing in a crisp white shirt topped off with a long leather duster. His dark hair was slicked back and showed off a widow's peak, which accentuated his strong brow. His gaze was brooding, and his eagle-eyed glare suspiciously scanned the crowd. Luckily he hadn't seen her, and she darted behind a column like a guilty school witch cutting class, pulling Honora with her.

"When did Hex Division start doing private security?" she asked with a squeak, her plan suddenly made more complicated by the wizard's presence.

Honora's smooth brow wrinkled in concern. "Sorry, Sis. If you're going to get to the lab, you'll need to get by Hexer Finn."

"Any ideas of how I'm supposed to do that?"

"Well, if it were me, I'd try to seduce him, lure him into a dark corner, and plant a long lingering kiss on him. Make him think of me instead of his job. But that's not really your style."

Vivi gulped down the rest of her drink. She glanced at Finn's full lips and imagined their taut softness against her own. *Not going to happen.* She shook off the idea. Strategic seduction was not her forte. Plus, he would see right through her, since they could barely stand each other.

"I think I'll try the direct approach." Now, that was an interesting prospect. There was no way she could avoid him, so perhaps she could convince him she wasn't a threat, at least not that evening, and see if he would let her slide, especially since she knew about his dealings with the Darklander. "I've got to try, but if it doesn't work be prepared for plan B."

"What's plan B?" Honora asked.

"That's where you cause some kind of colossal distraction." Vivi raised her eyebrows slyly at her sister. "I did bring you for a reason."

"I can do a distraction just as long as I don't ruin the presentation. I promised Dax I had turned over a new leaf and was trying to stay out of trouble."

"And he believed you?" Vivi gave Honora a playful smirk and a little finger wave as she headed over to the staircase and Rye Finn.

Two burly security wizards flanked the Hexer. He spotted her before she even made it halfway across the room, his dark gaze clinging to her every move. Vivi would have been flattered at how he stared her up and down, but she knew he was probably trying to sum her magical prowess, assessing if she was armed and dangerous, which he knew by now she wasn't. Pity that such a handsome wizard with a prestigious job and killer shoulders could be so untrustworthy.

Vivi snatched a glass of champagne off a passing tray and continued on her trajectory to the stairwell, slinking up to Finn. Bubbles tickled her nose. She gulped the last swallow of her drink and handed the empty glass to one of the other guards, going for confident and nonchalant. The drink made her feel warm and fuzzy, and she suppressed a hiccup.

"I didn't expect to see you here tonight, but then again I wouldn't expect to see you in a lot of places. You sure do travel in interesting circles." Vivi held her chin high while opening up her clutch and pulling out a small envelope.

"I'm not going to take the bait." Finn shifted his weight, squared his shoulders. "Tonight's an important job, so as for you and your sisters' little game of spying the other night, don't think it went unnoticed, but I've got more important work to do. I suggest you stay out of events that don't concern you." He averted his gaze and scanned the room.

"You're right. I should leave illegal activities and cover-ups to the professionals." *Meow*, she thought.

"Meddling doesn't become you. And tonight you look very becoming."

Vivi ignored the compliment, not taking his bait either. "I didn't come over to chat with you. I need to drop a note off to Dr. Fowler. He was kind enough to give me a tour the last time I was here. So, if you don't mind, I'll leave it in his lab." She held up the envelope. The thank-you note was her best idea to get past security. She turned sideways and tried to squeeze between the Hexer and the doorframe.

"The lower levels are off-limits." Finn crossed his arms over his chest and spread his stance, trying to block her descent.

"I'm sure you can make an exception," she said, scrambling to come up with a more convincing reason to get downstairs.

"Sorry, no exceptions, not even for you. I'm sure you'll see the good doctor tonight." Finn motioned to the crowd. "He's here somewhere."

Time to think fast. Vivi opened her purse, only this time she pulled out a tiny vial and showed it to Finn. "I have a potion to drop off for business purposes. I'm trying to get his opinion on a new formula I'm working on. It would be inappropriate for me to ask at the party. It'll take me two seconds to run down and leave it. I'll be right back." It was a long shot, since she wasn't his favorite witch in the world.

"Aren't you ambitious? But I can't let anyone down there." One of his eyebrows arched seductively, and she got the feeling he was flirting with her. "A Mayhem sister on the loose is the last thing I need tonight," he added under his breath.

Vivi was forced to retreat. There was no easy way she was getting down those stairs. Plan B, it was. She slipped away from the Hexer and tried to locate her sister in the crowd. "I wish he hadn't said that," Vivi mumbled to herself. "Because *mayhem* is exactly what he's going to get."

Luckily, Honora's glittery gold cocktail dress was easily spotted through the crowd and Vivi rendezvoused with her at an area beside the stage.

"Dax is going to give a presentation. He said we should be near the front and it'll be unforgettable." Honora beamed.

"Sounds intriguing," Vivi said. "We still need a way to get past the Hexer squad over there." For now, she turned her attention to the stage.

Dax tapped on the microphone and a hush fell over the crowd. The bewitching Mender twins were positioned to his far left at a place of honor, conspicuous as ever, seated with Dr. Fowler, who looked more bored than excited. A twitchy, wide-eyed wizard with a pale complexion and a line of sweat trailing down his neck into his collar stood by Dax's side. He gave the nervous wizard a reassuring pat on the back and began his speech.

"We are gathered here tonight to celebrate the latest magical wonder brought to the witching community by our esteemed visionary leaders, the Menders." Applause and cheers filled the room. "It's thanks to their genius and sacrifice that we are here today, and once again I'm proud to showcase yet another breakthrough in magical technology."

Dax pulled a small wooden box from his jacket pocket and cracked it open, revealing a piece of shiny metal on a velvet bed. He pulled the jewelry out and held a silver cuff high into the air.

Vivi gasped. "What's he doing with *that*?" She grabbed her sister's arm.

Honora's eyes went wide, but she hedged. "Wait and see what happens."

The charismatic wizard smiled. "I'm more of a watch man myself." Everyone chuckled at the joke. "But my brave friend here has offered to demonstrate exactly what this little gem can do for him and for witches and wizards across Everland."

The nervous wizard stepped forward and stuck his arm out in a stiff gesture. Dax took his wrist and attached the silver band.

"This can't be good," Vivi said, giving her sister an anxious stare.

The man's body suddenly jerked, but Dax continued his speech. "We call this new invention the 'gift of *persuasion.*' It will be the company's greatest accomplishment."

Honora's body tensed. "I don't like the sound of this."

"I told you," Vivi said. "Gift of *persuasion*? More like the theft of *persuasion.*"

"Now all of us will have the opportunity to sample other *persuasions* that we were not given at birth. This first band is in the testing phase and is currently called five-minute flight."

Honora's face went pale. It was a look of fear in her eyes Vivi had rarely seen on her. "He's kidding, right?" she asked, grabbing Vivi's arms. "This isn't possible. That bracelet can't make someone fly, can it?" She sucked in a sharp breath.

The wizard hopped tentatively, drawing laughs from the crowd. His face went red and Dax gave him a nod of encouragement. The nervous wizard drew a deep breath and made a few bounding steps until he reached the end of the stage and leapt into the air. The crowd gasped.

The wizard was airborne.

His mouth hung wide open as a cascade of emotions from disbelief to wonder crossed his face. His arms flailed, his feet kicked wildly like he was drowning in midair, but after an excruciating few seconds, he gained his bearings and took flight, soaring skyward above the heads of the gathered dignitaries.

"Holy Hazel," Honora said. "This can't be happening. This isn't right."

"They've done it," Vivi said. "The twins have created magical *persuasions*. I didn't think it was even possible." A rush of panic filled her as she watched the wizard awkwardly circling the room.

"He's going to hurt himself. Vivi, it took me years to learn how to control my *persuasion*. Flying isn't a game you just pick up. It's dangerous. If everyone suddenly started flying like it's some party trick, there would be some serious accidents." Honora never took her eyes off the wizard.

"I agree, but how do we stop the most powerful witches in Everland? When news of this gets out to the general public, the Menders will be unstoppable. Everyone will want to try this new invention."

"I'm going to talk to Dax. He's got to know this is going too far."

Vivi followed as Honora made her way up onto the stage. Never afraid of speaking her mind, Honora grabbed Dax's arm. "You have to stop that guy. Get him to come down now," she implored.

The wizard had gotten the hang of flying and was making wild loops around the room, diving and banking left and right, soaring higher and higher across the open air of the glass-enclosed atrium.

"He's loving it. Everyone's loving it." There was a joyous gleam in Dax's eyes. "I never dreamed this was possible. And now look."

"It's dangerous," Vivi said, backing up her sister. "He's going to get hurt."

"This isn't right, Dax." Honora's voice rose.

"What do you mean?" His expression changed, and he grabbed Honora's arm. "I pushed this through for *us*. Now we both can fly together. Think of everything we can explore. It'll be brilliant." His eyes gleamed. Vivi had never seen Dax this excited before.

Honora pulled away from him. "It isn't right. *Persuasions* are individual. You shouldn't mass-produce them like shoes. It will cause an imbalance in the magical order."

"Why not? Why should only some witches be able to fly? Why not all of us?" Dax didn't wait for a response, but turned his back on them and continued to watch the show.

"That didn't go well," Vivi said. Dax was totally on board with selling *persuasions*. Was he right? Were they overreacting?

Murmuring among the crowd grew frantic. A gasp suddenly filled the room.

The flying wizard banged against a glass window, sending a shudder through the crowd. He waved, acknowledging that he was all right, but he clutched at his arm. Unsteadily, he made another pass over the crowd, lower this time, brushing against a huge flower arrangement and sending roses tumbling to the floor in a shatter of glass when the vase crashed. He wobbled in the air as he struggled to gain control of his flight.

"He needs to come down." Honora tracked the wizard with her eyes. "He can't control his directional navigation. He's going to crash." Her voice was firm.

Dax grabbed her arm. "Leave him be. Let him have his fun. It's only for a few minutes. Or is that it? You don't want to share your power with anyone else because then it won't be special. It won't make you better than others."

"That's rich, coming from one of the most intellectually gifted wizards in the world. What happens when all of us can have instant magical knowledge of everything?" She put her hand on her hip.

"That won't happen. This device is for popular magic," Dax countered.

"Is it? Or do you mean profitable magic? *Persuasions* you can sell."

"Enough, you two." Vivi interrupted their quickly escalating argument. It was all becoming clear to her. "What about the cost to witches' lives? That *persuasion* was ripped out of a wizard," Vivi said, thinking of the flyer, Maynard Luck, who was dead thanks to that device. "It's unethical, not to mention deadly to the wizard being sucked dry of his magic."

But Dax and Honora had stopped listening. They were watching the flying wizard. Currently, he was tangled in an enchanted web of illuma lights that had been draped over the entrance to the room. "He needs help," Vivi said.

Honora rose off her feet and flew up to untangle the poor wizard. A wave of relief washed over his face when she reached him, and from what Vivi could tell from the ground, her presence was having a calming effect on him. Her sister was talking nonstop to the wizard, trying to offer advice, pointing to the ground. Once free from the illuma webbing, the wizard took off, seemingly over his little accident, totally ignoring any words of caution that Honora may have given him.

The guy is nuts, Vivi thought. Or he was just too excited with his new *persuasion* to heed the warning.

Dax returned to center stage and spoke. "Within a very short time, we at Mender Corp hope to offer an array of different temporary *persuasions* to our customers." Applause filled the room. "That ends our display portion of the evening. Please enjoy the festivities and have a wonderful night."

The lights in the hall flickered, signaling a cue, but the young wizard kept up his flight. Honora watched him from a perch on one of the crossbeams. The man was halfway across the room on a routine pass when he dropped a few feet before regaining his elevation. He needed to land; even Vivi could see the magic was wearing off. He shook his wrist, but his body jerked as he tried to fly higher, intoxicated with his new abilities.

He wasn't going to make it. Attempting to reach the safety of a beam, he suddenly plummeted, falling right toward the crowd. Screams erupted. Dozens of guests scrambled to get out of the way of the flailing wizard. In a stunning move, Honora swooped down and snatched the man up in her arms right before he crashed into a group of partygoers. Gasps and relieved cries filled the air at the daring rescue. Honora hauled the man's body up and hung him from the edge of a huge statue, where he dangled like a bug about six feet from the ground, the metal statue impaling the man's expensive jacket. It appeared to Vivi that Honora wanted to teach him a lesson in the dangers of flying.

"Stop this!" Mitchell yelled. "Help him down! Now!"

The Hexer security staff went into action, racing forward. Finn was on the move, his wand raised, ready to strike. The wizard was safe thanks to her sister, so Vivi grabbed the opportunity to sneak by them. There was only one guard left blocking her way down to Dr.

Fowler's lab. Commotion continued when the wizard struggled to free himself from the statue. Finn motioned for the rest of the guards to approach, and the one blocking the stairs abandoned his post.

Right as Vivi was about to descend the stairs, she glanced over her shoulder and saw her sister trying to pry the *persuasion* bracelet off of the wizard's wrist. Dax was not going to be happy.

18

CHILLS RACED UP VIVI'S SPINE as she hurried down the stairs and through the darkened labs. Pale blue illuma lights glowed through the empty hallways echoing with clinical silence. She crept along, senses alert. Her pulse quickened. She still had her doubts whether the doctor was involved in hurting witches, but she had to go where the clues led her, and right then, they led deep into the labyrinth of Mender Corp. Luckily, she had memorized the route from the building schematics, or she would have never found his workspace.

The plain wooden door was out of character in the gleaming modern laboratory. He grabbed the handle, but the door was locked with a black wrought-iron bolt. She fished through her purse and pulled out the potion she'd flashed to Hexer Finn. The little bottle actually contained a lock-releasing concoction, which she had brought just in case, and was glad she had.

She popped the cork and attached an atomizer she borrowed from an old perfume bottle. Holding the nose of the bottle up to the lock, Vivi gave it a quick spray, releasing the potion into the metal keyhole. She pulled her wand from her purse and tapped it against the lock, whispering the spell. To her relief, the latch clicked, and the old bolt shifted.

"That was easy." She stepped tentatively inside the room. "Hopefully not *too* easy."

Vivi thought Paul was being melodramatic when he called Dr. Fowler's lab his dungeon, and she couldn't have been more right. The room was neat as a pin. The metal tables where spotless, the shelves were orderly arranged, glass beakers all lined up in gleaming rows. A tall metal chair was positioned like a throne at the end of a row of tables. Vivi could see nothing weird or unusual. No sounds, no torture chamber, or bound witches. Her source was looking less reliable by the second.

She heard the soft padding of paws across the polished marble floor. The hairs on the back of her neck rose. She jerked around. The swish of a black tail caught her attention. Her stomach lurched. How had *the familiar* gotten down here? The panther swayed lazily down the aisle between a long row of metal tables. Vivi froze. Running would only set the creature off. The carnivorous cat leapt up onto a table in one fluid movement, watching her the entire time with eyes the color of sulfur. A diamond-studded collar reflected the low light. Even the panther got dressed up for the party. It would have been cute, if not for the fact it could eat her like an appetizer.

The big cat growled, its mouth filled with sharp fangs. Vivi stumbled backwards, her heart racing. It jumped to the floor, herding her, and she had no choice but to back into the throne-like chair stationed at the back of the lab. "Nice kitty," she said, her entire body trembling. If curiosity killed the cat, then what did the cat do to a curious witch? Rip it to shreds with its razor-sharp claws. *Get it together.* She swallowed hard and slid back into the seat as the panther held her pinned down.

The sound of high heels clicking across the marble floor drifted toward her.

"So nice of you to join us this evening." Miranda glided over to them and stroked the silken back of her deadly familiar.

"Nice to be invited," Vivi said, trying to remain calm.

The twin was not whom she'd expected to encounter. Tension rose between them as Miranda made a slow appraisal of Vivi, as if eyeing up her prey. She had foolishly lost track of Miranda during the evening, thinking she would be preoccupied entertaining her guests. "Your familiar has caught me snooping." Vivi smiled politely, disguising her nerves.

"Of course you were. Just as I had hoped." Miranda pulled out her wand and gave it a violent flick. The door to the room slammed shut and locked.

"Me? How did you know I would be here?" Vivi asked, but she had a sinking feeling she'd been set up, and the fact that her question was answered with peals of laughter from Miranda only confirmed her suspicion.

Once she regained her composure, Miranda patted the metal lab table, and the giant cat leapt up, sitting near its master in an attentive posture. "I knew you would be here because I know everything that goes on with my company. Especially when someone is meddling, my darling little witch."

Vivi had walked right into a trap. That pipsqueak wizard Paul was working for Miranda. She never should have trusted him. It had all been a little *too* convenient. The information Paul provided was exactly what she'd wanted to hear. Vivi had desperately wanted to believe him, needed to do whatever it took to find the witch, and he knew it. There was no dungeon laboratory or terrible cries or black ash.

Now Vivi was alone with an insanely ambitious witch and her deadly familiar, and no one but her sister knew where she was. After the commotion she'd witnessed upstairs, Honora and the Hexers had their hands full. Vivi doubted anyone would come looking for her anytime soon. "What do you want with me? I can't hurt you or your company. I'm nothing to you." Vivi tried to hold her ground, but the devious witch had other plans.

"You underestimate yourself. You're a powerful witch with a very covetous *persuasion*." She slapped her wand in her palm over and over. Her gaze narrowed, as if contemplating what to do with her new toy. At least Vivi knew what this was all about—her *persuasion* and the *test*. Mitchell had taken her blood, tested it, and now the twins knew about her *real* magical abilities. If anything, her *persuasion* had been nothing but a curse. Miranda could have it. See how she liked being dragged into nightmares she couldn't stop.

"You have no idea what you're talking about," Vivi said. "Some magic only looks good from the outside."

Miranda gave her a sympathetic turn of her head as if Vivi were the simplest witch alive, and she pitied her. "At the hands of an experienced witch, magic can perform miracles." Her voice was as slippery as oiled glass.

Vivi rolled her eyes at the witch's arrogance, but her gaze followed Miranda curiously as she reached over and adjusted the cat's collar and something shiny attached to it caught the light. The sudden realization of what the witch possessed was a jab to Vivi's heart.

"You've got to be kidding me!" Panic flooded through her veins. She jerked around on impulse, immediately seeking a way out, but she was pinned to the chair, cornered with no means of escape.

Coy as a snake, Miranda held up a silver bracelet. "I have a present for you. It's like mine, except this bracelet will take some of that precious magic of yours and give it to me."

"You're insane," Vivi blurted. Time for some brutal honesty. "You can't just go around hurting witches, robbing them of their powers, and leaving them near death or dead." *Or could she?*

"So dramatic. You don't know what you're talking about. Everyone should have whatever *persuasion* they want. Magic should be for all of us." Her temper rose, her voice turning rough. Miranda wasn't listening to her.

Vivi had to make her understand. "Life is about more than power. Please, you've been mislead about the bracelet. It's a siphon. It's dangerous."

Miranda's brow creased, but she continued

on the same path. "This miraculous device will take a sampling of your *persuasion,* and by the end of the evening, it will be mine. Your sleeping body will be found. Too much champagne will be blamed. It's a party. These things happen. You'll be embarrassed, but no one will think anything of it." She had this all planned.

"That *thing* is too strong." Words flooded out of Vivi. Her muscles tensed and sweat streamed down her back. Miranda had no idea the device was killing witches. But how could she not know? Vivi didn't have time to figure it out now; she had to convince her. "The bracelet is volatile. The magic isn't safe."

Miranda turned on her with a vicious glare. "Stop it! Shut up!"

With sheer muscular power, the great cat pounced at Vivi's feet and held its heavy front paws on either side of her lap. Its muzzle was so close to her face she could feel its hot breath on her check. Vivi froze. Miranda waved her wand and uttered a spell, causing thick bars to jut out of the chair and wrap around her chest, strapping her down.

"Foolishness. Lies. I won't hear it." In one swift motion, Miranda snapped the bracelet around Vivi's wrist, and a jolt of pain flowed up her arm like a river of fire.

Vivi screamed as the icy silver enveloped her wrist with a searing pain. The magic pierced her skin like a needle pulling thread, pulling her essence from her. Her body jerked. She struggled against the bonds, but the metal band only tightened around her chest, causing her breathing to spasm in deep gasps. "No! Don't do it! You're better than this. You're a healer." Vivi's eyes welled with hot tears that slid down her cheeks.

"It only hurts for a few minutes. Then all the pain will drift away." Miranda stroked her hair in an odd show of affection.

"Is my life worth it?" Vivi pleaded, her back pressed hard against the chair. Sweat beaded on her brow as the bracelet slowly drained her energy. Her mind reeled as the image of Clarissa, lying in the healer ward empty of magic, of her essence, of her very soul, filled her mind. Vivi had to think of a way out. She couldn't die like this.

Miranda bent down to Vivi's level, her eyes wide. She clasped Vivi's face in her cold hands. "I want the power to see the future. All my life I've helped other people to feel better, healing them. But I want more out of life. I'm tired of serving others. I want a *persuasion* that serves me. Nothing is more powerful than the *persuasion* of prophecy."

"Is this what you did to the others? Lured them here with promises? Just tell me one thing. Where's the other witch? What have you done to her?" Vivi asked. She had to know what had happened to the young strawberry-blonde witch from her vision. She hadn't sensed her when she entered the lab, and now she realized, she might never find her. "Please tell me what you've done to her?"

A flicker of confusion crossed Miranda's beautifully evil face. "I don't know what you're mumbling about. There's no one here but us. No one to stop me." She lifted her arms and turned around in a dramatic gesture.

"What about the other witches, the ones who suffered to give you the *persuasions* you think you deserve?"

Miranda's expression twisted in a moment of confusion, but she brushed it aside. "You've had too much champagne. No one is going to get hurt. It's a very simple procedure. Witches will be lining up to offer their *persuasions*." Miranda gave her a self-satisfied smirk and turned her attention to the panther. The giant black cat had leapt back up on the table, and Miranda showered the animal with affection.

If Miranda didn't know about the other witches, then who did? Was someone else at Mender Corp behind the siphon's power? Was it *really* Dr. Fowler, after all? Had he hidden his nefarious testing from the Menders? The pain in her wrist surged. Vivi's head was killing her, but she had to focus her attention. Her eyelids felt heavy as lead. There had to be a way out. She couldn't let Miranda steal her magic and her life.

Then Vivi remembered the tiny vial she wore around her neck—the wish.

It was a long shot. The potion was not a strong punch of magic. The wish wasn't a weapon or a ward. It was just a simple wish. Her eyes fluttered. Her chest and upper arms were pressed tightly against the chair, but her forearms were free. If she could bend her head down, she might be able to reach the dangling charm. She took a deep breath and feigned a coughing attack. Reaching up to cover her mouth, she lowered her head and the necklace dangled within reach. In a swift motion, Vivi broke the chain and held the tiny potion bottle in her closed fist. So far so good.

Loud noise from the party upstairs distracted Miranda. Vivi formed the wish in her head. She only had one shot, so she'd better make it a good one. She decided on a big loud, party-ruining disruption.

"I wish the fire alarm would go off and not stop. Right now," she mumbled under her breath while pulling the stopper out of the bottle. From between her fingers, the potion activated and a pale purple cloud drifted out of the vial and caused a swirl of color and sparks. A second passed and then another, but the silence was shattered when a blaring alarm and glowing red illuma lights lit up the room. Vivi figured a colossal disturbance was her best chance to get Miranda out of the lab and to alert her sister she was in trouble.

"What's happening?" A look of panic washed over Miranda's face. The panther jumped off the table and stayed close to her side.

"How should I know? It's your alarm."

Shouting and movement stirred above them. Miranda waved her wand and the door flew open. She muttered a litany of spells, but the blaring alarm continued, causing her to curse under her breath. The giant cat paced across the room, tail twitching, head lowered. Miranda stormed over to the door and peered up the stairwell. Within a few seconds, a wash of sounds poured into the room—loud voices, heavy footsteps, clanking of doors. With an agitated glare, the witch spun around and hurried back to Vivi.

"Problem?" Vivi asked, satisfaction welling inside her. She could barely hold her head up and her eyelids were thin slits, but she had beaten the witch, and it felt good, even through the pain.

Miranda made a few angry swipes with her wand, muttered a spell, and the restraints on the chair released. Next, she quickly yanked the bracelet off of Vivi's wrist and slipped it back onto the panther's collar. From her purse, she pulled a small metal flask and poured the contents into Vivi's mouth and down the front of her dress. Vivi coughed violently when the strong liquor went down her throat, but she was too weak to fight Miranda off. She grabbed Vivi by the back of her hair and yanked her head up. "I don't know what's going on, but we aren't done here," she hissed in her ear and hurried out of the lab, followed by her familiar, who wasn't so ferocious with an alarm scaring it. Vivi closed her eyes, dazed and weak as time slipped by.

About twenty minutes later, Honora raced down the stairs and rushed to her side. Vivi tried to stand, but was hit with a wave of nausea, so she decided sitting was best.

"What happened? I'm sorry it took me so long. I got hung up with the Hexers blocking the stairwell. Finn finally let me through when I told him you were down here. He was talking to the Menders last time I saw him." Honora brushed a strand of hair from Vivi's face. "Who did this to you?"

The bracelet had been so draining that Vivi just listened to her sister and nodded. Her reactions and thoughts were slowed. "It was Miranda." Her tongue felt thick in her mouth.

"Miranda! Are you kidding?" Honora asked, fury filled her face, but she breathed slowly. "What about the missing witch?"

"She isn't here. Miranda tried to use the bracelet to steal my *persuasion*. I don't think she knows about the tests. She thinks the stupid bracelet is harmless."

"Can you stand? I'll try and get you out of here," Honora said. Vivi was beginning to feel a little better with every passing minute the bracelet was off, but she imagined that wearing the thing for an extended amount of time would be a nightmare. Her fear of finding the witch alive intensified.

Hexer Finn and the security team stormed the lab. A swarm of witches and wizards surrounded her, some wearing lab uniforms, some wearing the Hex Division black. A healer witch went to work on Vivi, checking her pulse and eyes, giving her a soothing potion and a restorative tonic. While the investigation proceeded around her, Vivi's mind started to clear and her thoughts sharpened. Her wrist was sore, but there was only a small red mark as any evidence the bracelet ever existed. "Miranda took the siphon with her. The bracelet's gone." Her shoulders slumped.

"I need to get you home," Honora said, her brow creased. Vivi could sense she wasn't telling her something, so she nudged her sister.

"Spill it. I'm feeling much better. I'll be fine."

"Dax is furious with me." She shrugged, but Vivi could tell her sister was disappointed. "We just can't connect. But he's always a gentleman and lent us his car and driver to get you back to Willow Realm. I made arrangements with him while you were being treated by the healer."

"Tonight was a mess," Vivi said. "I need to think this through. Something isn't right." Pain shot through her temples. "Ouch." She pressed on the sides of her head with her fingertips.

"Don't worry. We'll figure it out," Honora said. "I'll go make sure the car is ready, and we can get out of here. Will you be okay until I get back?"

Vivi nodded and her sister headed off. She peered through her half-opened eyes as Finn walked her way. The illuma lights were bright little daggers. "What'll happen to Miranda?"

"Nothing's going to happen to her," Hexer Finn said, striding over to her. "Are you feeling up to talking? I've got some questions that need answering."

"What?" *Impossible.* Her head spun at the thought of the witch walking free. "Miranda tried to steal my magic. She used that thing, that torture device on me, and you're not going to arrest her?" A pulse of anger flared deep inside her. "Finn, she's involved. I'm a witness and can prove it. You have to do something."

"We're proceeding with caution. The investigation will continue, and if we have enough evidence, then actions will be taken." Hexer Finn's gaze swept over the lab. "The Menders suspect there was a break-in."

"Are you saying that my word isn't enough against hers?" Vivi asked. She couldn't believe what was happening. She gritted her teeth to keep from screaming at him.

"Miranda claims she was never in the lab this evening, and she has a room full of guests who swear she was with them all night. No one saw her leave. She thinks you may have been drinking too much." Finn cleared his throat. "I saw you down two drinks, and by the smell of you, I have to agree with Miranda."

"It was Miranda who did this to me. She poured liquor out of a flask down my throat and dress." Vivi slowly stood and stared right into Finn's face. "You don't believe me? There are security spells all over this place. They'll show our magical signatures. They'll prove I'm telling the truth."

His expression was stoic, unbending. "We've already checked. There were no signs of Miranda on any of the security wards. They only show you. But that we already knew."

"Unbelievable! She was here!" Vivi yelled. "You know I'm not lying."

"Collect your things. You're coming with me. The healer witch cleared you for travel." The Hexer took Vivi by the arm. Two more officers closed in as backup. "I'm taking you in for questioning, and your *sister* isn't invited."

Vivi felt her legs buckle, but she held her ground. Her night was far from over.

19

VIVI HALF EXPECTED FINN TO blindfold and drag her off to some secret Hexer interrogation cell and was a little shocked when they arrived at the Willow Realm Police Station, which was the last place she thought he'd take her. Once inside the building, Vivi immediately noticed a change—the energy in the room was electric as chatter rose and fell. The usually sedentary receptionist, Honey, hurried around distributing flyers from a stack of parchments clutched to her chest. A group of enthusiastic witches and wizards huddled in a tight circle, listening attentively to the sheriff's directions. Lance's uniform was wrinkled, his sleeves rolled at the elbow. A coffee stain marred his usual pristine white shirt. It looked like it had been a long night for everyone.

Juniper stood in front of a large map of the town, dividing up sections and piercing the surface with pushpins. Wiping her sweaty bangs with the back of her hand, she turned and made eye contact. Her face was drawn and tired, but brightened when she saw Vivi. She mouthed the words, "You were right."

What? Vivi's stomach lurched. She grabbed Finn's arm as he led her down a hall. "What's going on?" Her voiced filled with urgency.

"One step at a time. This way." He opened a door and motioned her inside.

Vivi had no idea how he could be so calm, especially with something big obviously going on. *He must be part cold-blooded reptile,* she thought. She slapped her purse on the table and spun to face off with the Hexer. "Start talking, Finn. Something's happened. Tell me."

Hexer Finn pulled out a chair and slowly sat. He set a packet of parchment on the table's smooth surface and flipped it open. She wanted to strangle him. He was going to take his sweet time. "Is this about tonight at the party? You already made it clear you weren't charging Miranda. Not enough evidence. Did the twins put you up to this? Do they say 'jump' and everyone flies into action?" Vivi collapsed down into a chair. Her upper arms and chest ached from the restraints worn earlier that night. Her head spun. That bracelet had really done a number on her.

"Are you done?"

"No." Vivi had to speak her mind. She recalled what she and her sisters had seen the other night through the scrying mirror when Hexer Finn was meeting with the Darklander and wondered if she had gotten a little *too* involved in his business. "Are you angry at me because of what I saw through the mirror?" Vivi asked. "Let's stop pretending. I saw you with the Darklander, and when the spell collapsed, you saw me and my sisters."

He shook his head. "The scrying mirror you and your sisters were using has been banned. Using it will get you into trouble." He narrowed his gaze, but he didn't seem angry.

"The mirror's a family heirloom, and it's registered, so technically it isn't illegal," she countered. "That doesn't explain what I saw."

The Hexer was a hard wizard to read. His gaze was intense. "You have no idea what you saw the other night." His jaw clenched. "You could have ruined my investigation with your meddling. You and your sisters should change your names from Mayhem to the Meddling Sisters."

Vivi gave a small bark of laughter before she realized he wasn't joking and that he *was* working on a serious case. Clover had been right. Hex was investigating the dark wizard, and they'd almost screwed it up. "I wasn't going to say anything about what I saw between you and the Darklander." Truly, she wasn't entirely sure what was going on with him and the Darklander, besides the exchange of elemental spheres.

"This isn't a game. Lives are at stake, and this isn't my *only* case." He stopped and stared at her, pinning her to the wall with his eyes. "Do you want to know why you're here or not?"

Vivi nodded.

Finn flipped through his papers and pushed a photograph across the table. It was a young witch with a dimpled smile and long strawberry-blonde hair. Vivi grabbed the photo with a surge of energy. "It's her! It's the witch from my vision!" Her heart was racing. She had been right. About...*her vision?*

"She was reported missing earlier today by her parents." Finn's expression remained neutral.

Finally, Hex Division acknowledged the witch. Her vision wasn't a fluke. Everything made sense—the frantic activity in the police station was a search for the kidnapped witch. They were looking for her. But a feeling of relief mixed with fear and panic flooded through her when she realized the ramifications. "How long has she been missing?" Vivi asked, focusing her thoughts.

"We don't have an exact timeline, but we've

narrowed the window to about five days ago." He drummed his fingers on the table.

"That's only a few days before I had my vision." Her timing had been close.

"Looks like it."

Part of Vivi wanted to jump up on the table and scream *"I told you so"* at the top of her lungs, but it was hard to gloat when she was right about the terrible fate of another witch. After getting the bracelet slapped on her for a few minutes, she knew exactly what the witch was going through. Finding her was more crucial than ever.

"Who is she? Do you have a name?"

"It's Sabine Monroe. Early twenties. She works as a teller at Golden Bears Bank. Lives in Willow Realm," he read down his list of notes.

Vivi's heart ached. *Sabine,* she thought. Finally, the witch had a name, but she was so much younger than Clarissa and Maynard. Someone would have missed her. "Why wasn't she reported missing sooner?"

"Her parents were away on vacation. It took them a few days after they returned to realize something was wrong when they couldn't get hold of her. Plus, they live on the other side of Everland. That's why it wasn't reported until now."

"Have you been to her house? I should go and see where she lives. I might be able to get a read on her."

Finn swept up the pages with an air of finality. "I'm not giving you the address. We have a team there now. The whole station is searching for her. You've done enough."

Vivi ignored his stern expression and continued with her thought, "You said she works at a bank?" Something wasn't sitting right.

"Yep."

"That doesn't make sense. The other witches were taken because of their powerful *persuasions*, so what exactly does she do at the bank?"

"She's a teller. Mostly does customer service."

"But I doubt that's why she was kidnapped. What's her *persuasion*?" Vivi asked.

"It took a while for her parents to finally tell us. She was keeping her magic a secret to everyone but her family and closest friends." He paused.

"Well? Are you going to tell me or not?" Vivi asked.

He glanced up from his papers. "Levitation." The word brought an appreciative smile to his face.

"No way! That's a great *persuasion*. I'm assuming she can do it totally wand-free." Admiration for the witch bloomed inside her. Levitation was not only rare, but it was seriously cool. Most witches learned a couple of basic levitation spells at the academy, but it wasn't as easy as it looked and almost always required both a wand and spell. Unfortunately, the allure of her *persuasion* was what had gotten her kidnapped.

"From what her parents say, she doesn't need a wand or spellwork. She does it on will alone. It's her gift."

"Power. That's the one thing they all have in common—power and proximity. What else do you have linking the cases to give us more information?"

"You mean besides you? You're the only other link I have."

"Me? Come on, I can't still be a suspect." She rolled her eyes. He had to be kidding.

"You are until you're not, and right now you're still a witch of interest." He was serious. What was it going to take to convince him she was on his side?

Vivi leaned back and closed her eyes. "You can't be serious. That bracelet, which everyone at the party saw, is the latest Mender invention. Question them. They have the most to gain by stealing *persuasions*."

"We did, and Miranda says she knows nothing of anyone being hurt by her device. In fact, she seems to think that you are trying to implicate her in the crimes."

"And you believe that?"

"We're searching the lab. Miranda gave us

full access." He shrugged.

"Sounds like the Menders have you jumping through hoops."

"You think you have Hex Division all figured out." He snorted.

"I think Hex Division won't risk upsetting one of the most powerful business owners and investors in the world and that's dangerous."

"Did you ever consider the ramifications of your actions if you're wrong? The damage a false accusation would cause? The Menders, who up to this day have lived exemplary lives, have dedicated themselves to healing witches and wizards—you want to storm their labs and find evidence lying around so you can point your finger, save the witch, and be a hero." The speech had been a good one. He was right. She hadn't considered the fallout from her actions because she had been so sure of herself and focused on finding the witch at whatever cost.

"You have a point." Vivi bit back her emotions. "But I'm the one who got burned tonight." She held up her wrist.

"I'll check into that personally. After all that's happened I don't think you're directly involved in the case." His shoulders relaxed. "But I have to be sure."

Vivi had an idea. If she couldn't beat him then she would propose a working relationship. "As much as you hate to admit it, you need me. So, as I see it, we can either work against each other, or we can help each other and work together. We want the same thing—to find the witch."

Finn glanced at her for a few seconds, as if trying to make up his mind about her, before finally giving in. "Tell me everything you know about her and the visions you've had."

Vivi told Finn everything about her visions and her notes on the Mender twins, Dr. Fowler, Dax, Miranda, and the bracelet. As the words poured out of her, it felt like a huge weight was lifted off her shoulders, but he seemed less impressed.

"Why were you snooping around the lab tonight?" he asked, not reacting to anything she'd just told him. "I was right there. You could have told me the truth."

"Ha! Hardly. You never would have believed me. You needed hard proof, like the parents of the missing witch coming forward, in order to trust me."

He leaned back in his chair. "That's fair, I guess, but it doesn't answer my question as to why you were there."

"I was following a tip I got from an employee of Mender Corp, and I wasn't sure it was valid."

"A tip?" His brow rose. He tapped his pen on a page of notes. "Tell me about this employee."

"A young wizard who does freelance for the lab suspected Dr. Fowler of being involved."

"We have a team at the lab now. We're checking the whole facility, and I can send a team to check out Fowler's residence to see if your tip pans out."

"We have to hurry. She doesn't have much time." Vivi swallowed.

"You have to trust us. We've done this before. It's our job. The sheriff and his staff have been searching and will continue to do so until we find her. This isn't over."

Vivi was overwhelmed. She choked up and took a deep breath. Hot tears streamed down her face—finally, they believed her. She had been waiting to hear those words, to get this kind of action. "All I wanted was your help."

"I know. You were right—there, I said it." He gave her a smile. "Now, you need to go home and get some rest. You've had a rough night. Plus, you're a little overdressed." He eyed her up and down. "Go on."

Vivi was still wearing her sister Clover's beautiful dress, which looked a lot less glamorous in the police station, and was now stained with expensive booze. Hopefully, she knew some cleaning spells. But no matter what condition her clothes were in there was no way she was going home now that they finally believed her. "I'm staying."

"Not happening. Leave this to the professionals."

"But I can help. I know this case better

than anyone. Let me at least try."

"No, you're too close. Plus, you need some sleep. Come back tomorrow and check with the sheriff. I'm sure he'll have some volunteer opportunities for additional searches." He pushed back his chair and stood.

Vivi was too exhausted to go another round with him. She needed to get some sleep and a change of clothes.

He turned away from her and rapped his knuckles against the door, which swung open. "Hannah will show you out. Go home. Get some sleep. Are we clear?"

"I get it." Vivi fished her shoes out from under the bench and rammed her feet inside. The strappy heels had lost their sparkly charm. Finn disappeared down the hall, and one of his Hexer sidekicks ducked her head in the door. It was the pretty girl with the cropped blonde hair and terrible scar that ran down the side of her face.

"Are you ready?" Hannah asked, and even gave her a small smile.

"To get out of here? No, but I have no choice," Vivi said. She'd seen her with Finn on that first day they met in the Willow Realm Sheriff's Department, except today she wasn't wearing a long coat. Her arms were bare, exposing a crisscross of healed pink scars that covered her pale skin.

Following the Hexer out, Vivi wondered what had happened to her. Had she been wounded in some terrible accident or magical battle? The Hexer wasn't trying to hide her wounds, and Vivi admired her for it. She could have used a spell, potion, or charm to try and disguise the ugly jagged scars, but she didn't.

"He's not so bad," Hannah said.

"Finn?" Vivi snorted. "He's starting to grow on me, though I still think he's a little stubborn."

Hannah's smile widened. "I guess you're right. He's opinionated, and he always thinks he's right. But he's a good guy. It might surprise you to know he's a great Hexer. One of the best."

"Now *that* doesn't surprise me. He seems the type to do anything for his job." Vivi sighed. "I don't know if I fully trust him. And I can't figure him out."

"Hex Division's a tight group. We have our orders. It can be hard to understand unless you can see the whole picture." They had reached the front door. "Goodbye. And be careful out there. Whoever took the witch is still on the loose."

"Finn's lucky to have such a loyal partner."

"He's been there for me my whole life. But I guess that's what brothers are for."

Brother. Now *that* was interesting. Vivi repressed an urge to ask Hannah a million questions about Finn, but it wasn't the time or place. The young Hexer waved to Vivi as she exited the station.

20

RAINED, VIVI DRAGGED HERSELF UPSTAIRS to her apartment, slipped out of Clover's dress, and collapsed onto her bed. She had hoped to go over her notes and piece together the events of the evening, but she hadn't realized the toll the bracelet had taken on her until she woke up the next morning with glaring sunlight pouring through the curtain onto her face. A familiar beak tapped on the window, reminding her it was time to get out of bed. She jerked up, still groggy, her mouth dry and cottony.

"Rumor," she croaked and stumbled over to the window to let him in. "I learned a couple new lessons yesterday. One—never wear jewelry from a weird genius. Two—snooping has its price."

He flew to his perch, nodded his head and

gave her a good morning squawk, which she took for him saying, "You're a lucky witch. Now get going."

Vivi showered, dressed, and headed over to Nocturnes. Just as she expected, the café was buzzing with activity. News traveled fast, and talk of the missing witch was on everyone's lips. After grabbing a cup of coffee, she snagged a seat at the counter and sifted through the morning's edition of *Witch World Daily*. A photo of Sabine Monroe stared up at her from the front page with the headline: *Missing witch identified, the search continues.* She scanned the article, but most of the contents she already knew. The police were asking for volunteers to search and distribute flyers. The search was a good start, but as she sipped her coffee, she couldn't help but want to do more. Frustrated, Vivi knew that with her powerful *persuasion* she had to deliver results. *But how?*

Arnica was stuffing a wicker basket with food—waxed paper-wrapped sandwiches, slices of cherry almond quick bread, and apples. She caught Vivi's attention and said, "It's for the volunteers. I want to do my part to help out."

"I know the feeling. Hey, do you know when the teams head out and where they plan to search?" Vivi asked.

"Not exactly. I've overheard too many

conversations today to give you an accurate location, but you could just ask the sheriff. He's found a nook in the back. Been up all night and needed a little breakfast to get him going this morning."

Vivi picked up her coffee and headed toward the rear corner of the room, curious to see how the investigation was going. Looking rumpled, Lance leaned his head against the side of a high-backed chair, eyes closed, hands folded over his stomach. The plate in front of him had been practically licked clean. She hated to disturb his sleep, but pulled up the chair next to him and sat down.

"Morning, Sheriff," she said.

"Yep." His eyes sprang open and he glanced at her without lifting his head. "Oh, it's you. Hey." He smiled. His uniform appeared clean enough, but from the state of his bloodshot eyes and general weariness, she doubted he'd slept much.

"I hear you had a long night."

"And it just keeps going." He stifled a yawn with an apologetic look as he begrudgingly sat up. "I suppose you've heard the news."

"I'm here to help. I want to see this through." Vivi sat on the edge of her chair.

"Volunteers are always welcomed."

"The search is great. You'll get dozens of volunteers. What else can I do? Have you questioned the Menders and Dr. Fowler? They must know something."

"Even if I wanted to, I can't share information on an active case with you. I'm sorry. However, I can tell you the Mender twins and Dr. Fowler have been more than cooperative." He hunched over, elbows on knees with his head in his hands. "Just between you and me, besides the bracelet, I haven't been able to link them with any of the victims. But the Hexers are in full swing. They're practically running the show."

"What about the tip? Has it helped find anything in the lab?" Vivi thought about the mysterious young wizard Paul.

"Nope. Tell me, what else do you know about that guy?"

"He's hard to figure out—ambitious, awkward, and according to Dr. Fowler, he's brilliant. He does freelance research and brings his results to Mender Corp, but he doesn't work in-house, from what I know. I saw him give a paper to the doctor the other day. I think it was data on some tests he's doing, but I'm not sure. He's a fan of *The Spellbinder Series*." Vivi smirked. "I saw him at a Cassandra Reason signing."

"Likes romance novels and working by himself. I don't know how much of a help that is, but it's good to know. Thanks, I'll check him out."

"I know I'm not a registered seer, yet, but

I'd like to come to the station and dig deeper into the case. I could try and sense the witch, especially if you have something personal of hers from her parents I could use as a reference. I know I can see more."

"I think it's best if you stick to physical searches for now. Hexer Finn is pretty tense already. We're under a lot of pressure right now."

"You two are so stubborn. Neither one of you will let me in on this case." Vivi tensed as frustration surged through her. "I get it. I'm not registered. But I'm the one who saw her. Come on," she pleaded.

"Maybe it's for your own good." Lance put his hands on her arm and a cooling sensation filled her body. It felt as if his touch was extinguishing a smoldering fire inside of her. Her anger lessened.

"What was that?" she asked, sensing he was using some kind of spell on her.

"What?" He played dumb, badly.

"What you just did to me. It was magic, wasn't it?" Vivi had the sneaking feeling there was more to Lance's *persuasion* than he was letting on.

"Not much, just a little trick I know to create calm in people." He shrugged.

"Nope." Vivi shook her head. She wasn't about to let him off the hook. "It was more. Stronger. Like a *persuasion*. What are you hiding?" She put her hand on his arm and squeezed.

"Nothing. You know I'm the sheriff. My *persuasion* is keeping people safe, investigating crime, bringing the guilty to justice."

"You're more than that." Her eyes widened. "You're a *peacemaker*. That's it. Why didn't you tell anyone?" She felt a pang of guilt for confronting him, but also genuine awe at the powerful *persuasion* he was hiding.

Lance pulled his arm free. The chatter in the room seemed a million miles away. A small fire crackled in the hearth. "I can't hide anything from you." He smiled.

Peacemaking was a genuine *persuasion* of great significance and one of the most valiant and important ones. Peacemakers were revered and honored. If it were not for some of the early peacemaking witches and wizards, Vivi didn't know how Everland would have managed to transition from the human world to a world of its own. Witches and wizards are very opinionated. In the early days of forming the Witch Council and creating the doctrine that would rule their world, the peacemakers were vital in establishing trust and stability. Everland wouldn't exist without them.

"Why are you still here in Willow Realm? You could move to the capital. You'd be amazing. A truly great leader." He was an even better wizard than she realized.

"Well, for one, I happen to like it right here in Willow Realm. I'm a small-town kind of guy. I guess you could say I never wanted the attention that went with my *persuasion*."

Vivi bubbled with warm laughter. "Now *that* I can totally relate to." She smiled. Perhaps they had more in common than she knew.

"It's simple. I want to help my village and the witches and wizards who live here, and I don't want the glassy-eyed, adoring stares given to the others like me. I was born with my *persuasion* like you were born with yours. I didn't earn it. I'm not better than anyone else."

"Not everyone feels that way." She raised her brow.

"That's part of the problem we're having right now—witches and wizards who aren't happy with the power they were born with. They want powerful and exciting *persuasions,* no matter the cost. I'm here to tell you the grass isn't always greener."

"I guess we all have our secrets when it comes to magic." Vivi felt like she was so close to figuring something out, but she couldn't put her finger on it.

"Will I see you later at the volunteer rally?" Lance asked, standing to leave.

"Yes, I'm headed over to open my shop to get things squared away with Pepper, and then I'll meet you there," she said.

Vivi and Lance parted ways as they headed

out of Nocturnes. Once at her shop, she entered through the back door and immediately noticed the security ward had been deactivated, so she assumed Pepper had already arrived. She walked into the back room and something crunched under her feet—bits of buttered toast and broken pottery—a ceramic mug had shattered. It looked like someone's breakfast had fallen on the floor.

"Pepper!" she called out. "Are you here?" Her throat went dry. "Pepper!" she yelled again, worry building. The shop was eerily silent. Her senses prickled. "Pepper! Answer me!"

Her assistant was never late to work, and at a quarter to ten would have already arrived. She should be there by now, humming a tune, being her usual cheerful self in the morning. Within seconds, Vivi raced to the front of the shop. Dozens of potion bottles were upended and scattered on the counter.

Pepper was on the floor, unconscious. Vivi knelt down at her assistant's side. She was sprawled on her back with her head facing the ceiling. Her eyes were closed, but she was breathing. Vivi gently patted her cheek. "Pepper, can you hear me?"

Vivi heard heavy footsteps across the wood floor. Her head jerked up as she realized she wasn't alone, and she cautiously peered over the counter. A wizard wandered the front of the store, but all she could see was the back of a hooded sweatshirt he wore under a jean jacket. The hair on the back of her neck rose, and she fought the urge to run and get help from Lance. She was torn, fighting her fear, but there was no way she was leaving Pepper hurt and alone on the floor.

The intruder must have sensed her presence and thrown a spell because suddenly the shelf behind her exploded, causing shattered supplies to rain down all around her. Vivi dove to cover Pepper.

"That was a warning shot. Make any sudden moves and the next one is a direct hit," he said. "Now get up off the floor and put your hands on the counter where I can see them."

Vivi slowly got to her feet. He turned a corner and walked down the aisle as if he were a customer, casually browsing the merchandise and taking his pick of potions. His hand knocked over a row of potions sending them scattering like gems. His fingertips were blackened, the nails split and ragged. Their eyes locked. Vivi's heart raced. He had always seemed so harmless. Paul masked his intentions well behind his youth and ambition, but now a slow, burning anger flashed in his eyes, and her impression of him shifted in an instant.

Vivi had not been born a master potion maker, but she had built her shop with hard work, studying late into the night, cooped up in her tiny Haven Academy room. She had given up parties and vacations with her sisters and friends to save every gold coin to make her dreams come true, and this little swine was traipsing across all she built like it was nothing. But when he had hurt Pepper, he'd crossed a line.

Vivi fingers curled into tight fists. She had had just about enough of this arrogant, self-important wizard.

"She'll be fine in a few hours."

Anger pricked at the back of her neck. "What did you do to her?"

He sauntered forward. A pretentious little grin played across his lips. "It was priceless. I used your own potions." He motioned to the array of bottles scattered on the work surface. Vivi grabbed a few of the empty bottles to see what he had forced on her—a deep-sleep potion and an anxiety-soothing potion. Relief washed over her. Pepper would be okay in a few hours. She would have a killer headache, but she would survive. What a cowardly weasel. She fought the urge to rip the wizard's head off with her bare hands.

"What do you want?"

His face was pasty and flushed. Sweat ringed his hairline. His hands trembled. Vivi noticed a silver band around Paul's wrist. Not good. All she needed was a power- hungry wizard pumping dangerous magic through his veins, making him more unstable than he already was. She had no idea what kind of magic he was drawing from the bracelet, but if she had to guess, it was the strongest possible.

"I have a proposition for you. Think of it as a business deal." He drummed his fingers nervously on the counter.

"I'm listening," Vivi said, calming her voice. She instinctively knew to get him out of the shop and into the open before he did any more damage.

"You'll come with me, and I won't hurt your assistant or your sisters." He tapped the silver cuff on his wrist. "I've recently acquired some dangerous magic, so for their sake I suggest you do what I say."

"Let's talk this through," Vivi said. This was going to be difficult. She would do whatever he said if it saved her sisters and Pepper, and he knew it. Talk about having no leverage.

"Shut up! You'll do exactly as I say or you'll regret it." His scowl hardened.

"I'm not going with you," she said, but her voice trembled, giving her away.

"Potions make terrible weapons. You've got nothing here that can hurt me." His voice was flat, void of emotion.

"Potions aren't meant to hurt people."

"No, but this is." He held out his hand to her. Resting in his palm was a clump of brown hair. A sadistic smile crossed his face. "I made it especially for you."

"A witch's snare," Vivi blurted. Once she saw the tangled knot, she knew she didn't have a chance. Knot magic was old school, an ancient art of weaving spells with thread, yarn, or in this case, hair and fibers. Like most magic, not all knot magic was bad, but once cast, a witch's snare was almost impossible to escape. An enchanted blade was the only thing strong enough to cut through the fiber, and they were hard to come by. If she didn't think of something fast, she was going down.

She panicked. Her heart pounded in her chest. Paul was right. There was no potion in the shop to hurt him, but what he didn't know was that Vivi had grown up in a house with three other women and only one bathroom. In the Mayhem household, sisterly hand-to-hand combat had been the norm when wrestling for a hot shower or a moment of privacy. It had often gotten ugly and very physical. She readied her stance.

Paul lifted his wand, but in close quarters, Vivi had the advantage when it came to a sudden attack, and without hesitation she lunged, hitting him square in the stomach with her shoulder. They both went flying to the floor with a hard thud. She scrambled, pinning him down with her knees and sat on his chest. Honora had used this tactic on her more than once growing up, and finally Vivi was putting the experience to good use.

Paul gasped for breath and bucked like a wild horse, but Vivi grabbed his throat and pushed on his windpipe. It took all her strength to hold him down. Her muscles trembled, and she didn't know how long she could control him. "Stop!" she screamed.

He went still. His eyes bulged. His skin was slippery with sweat under her hands.

Esmeralda had been right all along. The seer had warned her about the witch's snare, and here it was—the future catching up to her in real time. But where the trap had gone in the struggle, Vivi had no idea.

"He is stronger than anyone realizes." The words echoed in her memory.

"Don't do this, Paul. You don't have anything to prove to Dr. Fowler or the Menders," Vivi said, trying to quiet him.

He choked back a gurgle and she loosened her grip on his throat. "That's where you're wrong. Don't you get it? This is my invention."

"Your invention kills. You aren't a killer." Reason was all she had left to bargain with. "There's still a way out. Let me help you stop this."

He went quiet and still as a stone. Something in his eyes changed. They stared at each other for a few achingly long seconds, until he nodded. "Will you talk to the sheriff?"

"Yes."

"You're lying."

"No, I promise to speak with him. We'll help you end this."

"Okay, but on one condition." His voice was low and hoarse.

Vivi leaned closer. "What?"

"I want your magic first," he whispered, his hot breath against her ear. Suddenly, he screamed the activation spell, calling the knot toward her. The fibers sprang off the floor, alive with magic. Vivi tried to jerk away, but the trap sprung instantly. Coarse hair shot out of the tiny knot and spun around her, sealing her in a cocoon of hair, thread, and fiber. Paul rolled out from under her, shoving her as far away as possible.

The snare was rough against her skin and smelled like a wet sheep. She dropped to her knees and then keeled over. Her limbs were pressed tightly together as the fibers twisted, rendering her completely immobile and at his mercy. This was what flies must feel like when they got caught in a spider's web, spun up until they're served for dinner.

"Where are you taking me?" she asked.

"Someplace where no one will find you." Paul pulled a black hood out of his pocket and covered Vivi's head.

The world went dark.

Paul mumbled a phrase of spells and Vivi

was lifted off the ground. Her body floated and she struggled, but it was no use. He was moving her. She felt a hard thud against her hip as she was dropped onto a flat surface. Then a whooshing sound from the magical thrust of a hovercraft filled the darkness, but where he was taking her, she had only one guess—Fox's Rock.

She had underestimated him. It was all so clear now. He lived in the area, just like all three of the victims. He had access to both Dr. Fowler and Miranda. He could easily be providing them with the magical formulas for the device, and they would never be the wiser to how he was obtaining the data.

Vivi's mind raced. Pepper was out cold and Honora was in Stargazer City. With the search in full swing, everyone would be busy and would probably assume she was out looking for Sabine. She had to accept that no one was coming to help.

They didn't travel far. He moved her again, lifting her like a doll and leaving her in a cold place with loose earth beneath her.

"Paul! Paul!" Vivi yelled. The hood was claustrophobic, causing her to panic. Sweat poured down her face. The snare tightened with every twist and turn.

"What?" he asked. The sound of his voice was close.

"I can't breathe," she gasped. The fibers

were strangling her, cutting into her skin. "Too tight. I'm being squeezed to death."

He yanked the hood off and gazed down at her. "Damn, your face is turning blue." He let out a sigh. "I guess I could cut you loose. Don't want you to die yet." He snorted. Something brushed her side and Vivi jerked. "It's just me. You're so jumpy," he said. "You're just lucky I have the knife on me. These snares are impossible to escape." He tugged at the rough hair. She heard scraping and cutting sounds, and the knot loosened.

Vivi kicked free and untangled herself from the snare. Relieved, she collapsed onto the ground and rubbed the circulation back into her legs. She rested her head on an earthen wall and looked around. Paul's face was shadowy and hollow. The tip of his wand glowed in the darkness of a tight underground tunnel. "There's no way out of here, so don't even try to run." His breath was hot on her face as he leaned in close.

"Is she here?" Vivi asked. "The other witch. Her name's Sabine, in case you were wondering."

"Shut up about her," he snapped. "Can't you stop?"

"No, I can't. I can't stop seeing what you did to her. That's what having my *persuasion* does to me." Vivi had to keep him talking while she figured a way out.

"There's plenty of pain to go around. Pain made me stronger. Gave me purpose." In the low light of the tunnel, he looked like an animal.

"You steal *persuasions*. You kidnap, torture, and kill. That's not power."

"That was an accident. I didn't mean to kill the flyer." Paul turned away from her, unable to face what he had done. "Sacrifices have to be made for the sake of magical science." The line was an excuse to ease his guilty conscience.

"What will you do with my *persuasion*? You can't just peer into the future."

"I don't want it for myself. It's a gift for Miranda. I told you, she loves power. Soon she'll need me. I just have to prove to her how much. I knew the minute I met you in the alley. You were the one." He smiled.

"Empathy. You were using Clarissa's magic." She had walked right into his plan.

Vivi reached out her hands, feeling the hard-packed ground beneath her fingers. The walls were made of rough earth. There was no door, no window, no discernible way in or out of the small space. He tapped the low earthen ceiling with his wand and whispered a spell under his breath. The ground parted, and a row of earthen steps appeared. Sabine hadn't been buried alive; she had been kept in the ground, stored like a nut for winter.

"We're inside a rabbit hole," Vivi said. "Is that where you're keeping her?"

"Does it look like it?" Paul held out his hands. "Just sit there and be quiet. I have something special in store for you," he said cryptically and hurried up the steps, leaving her underground.

A rabbit hole was old-world magic. It was an escape spell used in the days when witches were hunted in the human world. The spell created a burrow in the earth with no way in and no way out. The witches used them to hide from hunters and would stay hidden for hours or days until the hunter left. It was kind of ingenious. Only the witch, or wizard, in this case, who cast the spell, could open the burrow. What Paul lacked in natural magical talent, he more than made up for in intelligence and creativity. Too bad he was such a psychopath. His talents were going to waste.

Vivi closed her eyes and reached for an image of Sabine with her mind. All she wanted was a sign that the witch was still alive and close by. But it was an image of the basement she'd seen in her vision at Mender Corp that flashed into her head. Vivi felt Sabine's presence almost immediately, but Sabine wasn't in the ground like she was; the young witch was being held in the basement. Then, Vivi gagged as her own throat tightened. She reached her senses further out to the young witch. This time Vivi felt Sabine cough and grab at her neck. Paul was hurting her, draining her, but not with the bracelet, with something else, more powerful.

Something heavy and tight hung around the young witch's neck—a collar.

The purpose of the collar made sense to Vivi when she thought about it. Paul had taken his magic to the next level. By creating the collar, he had created a powerful siphon to obtain higher amounts of magic to store. That was why he was still holding Sabine, pulling more power from her. The metal bracelet wasn't enough. He needed a stronger device. With a cuff, the magic only lasted for a short amount of time, as demonstrated by the flyer at the Mender Corp party. By design, the collar pulled more magic from the witches, but it also left them as a shell or dead. The thought sickened her.

He was going to drain Sabine dry, killing her in the process, and then he was going to collar Vivi. Panic sharpened her focus. The good news was Sabine was still alive. Now all Vivi had to do was figure out a way to trick Paul into letting her out of the rabbit hole. That's what made them perfect hiding places. The only way out was when Paul opened up the hole to enter.

Vivi ran through a list of spells she had

learned from her days at Haven Academy. When she first learned basic magic spells with her sisters and classmates, they all wanted to have spells at the tips of their wands. Then they realized how hard it was to memorize and retain the spells, and the list dwindled. It wasn't like she had an encyclopedia of spells in her head, and she knew of no spells strong enough to break out of a rabbit hole.

Basic spells for lifting heavy objects, opening and closing doors, and turning on an illuma light just weren't going to help her. Neither would movement spells like propulsion or shifting. Being underground didn't help. She didn't want to shift or move the ground. The last thing she needed was a collapsed burrow, raining earth down on her, burying her alive. The only thing she could think of was to make it so miserable out there for Paul that he would have to open the rabbit hole. All she needed was for him to open the burrow for a few seconds. The fire alarm had worked well at Mender Corp, but she was in the woods and needed more than an alarm. Perhaps what she needed was a natural noisemaker with claws, one that was feathered and not so friendly like a flock of angry squawking birds.

Vivi had never excelled in music, so there was no way she could send out anything elegant or enchanting, but she could call out for help. Having a bird for a familiar had its advantages. She knew a lot of birdcalls, and they could be really compelling and annoying, especially when amplified with a magic spell, and so she pressed her lips together and blew. Then she coughed. It had been a while. She licked her lips and tried again. She whispered the spell to amplify the sound and then blew. This time a lovely tune filled the burrow. She repeated the tune over and over until her throat was hoarse.

Black birds, lots of black birds, she thought. If the spell and song worked properly she was conjuring up a swarm of angry black birds, pulled out of their own habitat and into the woods, surrounding Paul. Within minutes, caws filled the air above her. The spell was working. Vivi intensified the spell, agitating the flock. She was hoping Paul would be overconfident enough to open the burrow.

Suddenly, the ground shuddered and the earthen steps appeared, but he didn't descend. "What do you think you're doing down there?" Paul's voice was exasperated. The burrow immediately filled with the screaming of birds and sound of ruffling wings. "Call off those stupid birds."

Vivi was ready and, in a split second, yelled a tumbling spell that knocked Paul off his feet, followed by a pulling spell that yanked him violently forward. He tumbled down the stairs, and she leapt around his body, raced up the earthen steps, and exited the rabbit hole. She squinted at the bright light. She was in a wooded clearing with a small, thatched roof cottage that appeared to be near Fox's Rock. Her suspicions were right. Paul had been here all the time, hiding right in Willow Realm. She ran in the opposite direction of the cottage, but was suddenly and violently thrown to the ground. Her body was dragged across the rough surface, and she grabbed wildly at the underbrush, but it did no good. Paul had chased her down and was pulling her back. Her escape attempt had been futile. Once returned to the clearing, Vivi rolled over and sat up.

"I can move anything. *Anything*. Even you." Wearing a crazed expression, Paul held out his hand, and Vivi's entire body levitated off the ground. She hovered two feet off the ground. She gasped and flung her arms out for balance, but she didn't need it, for he held her perfectly still, pinning her arms down to her side. Paul had obtained one of the strongest *persuasion* in Everland. "It's brilliant and it's mine. Oh, I'll make some cuffs for minor *persuasions* to keep Mender Corp happy, but the really valuable magic will be mine alone."

"You can't do this. Look at yourself and what it's doing to you. All that magic isn't safe. It takes years to master a *persuasion*.

They're meant to be a part of us, to grow and develop with us, so that we know how to use the magic." Vivi tried to reason with him, but he released her body with a wave of his hand, and she plummeted to the ground with a hard crash.

"Says a witch with power."

Vivi crawled to her feet. "I would gladly let you take every drop of my power, but I can't. I have it for a reason, and I have to learn to use it, to keep it. We have to be the witches we were born to be with whatever magic we were given. It's how the witching world works. I'm sorry if it's not fair."

"I wasn't born with a strong *persuasion*. I've had to learn everything. What am I supposed to do while the rest of you have all the advantages?" He held up his wrist. "This is what I did. I made this happen when Fowler couldn't." His eyes gleamed with pride.

"Sounds like you're doing pretty fine without magic. You've made tremendous advancements in the lab with little or no help. You just have to keep doing that in a positive way. You were succeeding. You just can't do it like this."

"That's a nice speech. But I don't care anymore. About you or anyone else." His face had gone blank. He held up a collar.

Vivi stumbled backwards. Paul was done talking. "Sorry, this is gonna hurt."

Before he could reach her, black clouds filled the sky. The wind picked up. The birds erupted from the trees and flew away in a burst of wings. A storm was coming, but she didn't think it was a natural one since the energy formed too quickly. The clouds appeared to be boiling above them, churning up wind. Sparks of lightning crackled across the sky. This storm had been made with magic.

The elementals were coming.

21

THE HEXERS DESCENDED INTO THE clearing. Three gleaming hover bikes pulled up next to the cottage. Vivi didn't know how they had found her—a scrying spell, perhaps—but currently, she didn't care. Sabine was alive, and reinforcements had arrived. The Hexers were not known for subtlety or handholding; they were known for quick and decisive action against a threat. The time for talk or negotiations was over. Hexer Finn jumped off his bike and threw his helmet to the ground. Finn's two Hexer companions dismounted their bikes and immediately flanked out around Paul.

The young wizard had no idea what he was in for. Vivi almost smiled.

"The bracelet!" she yelled, holding up her wrist, hoping Finn would understand

LAUREN QUICK

Paul was wearing the magical power source. Getting the bracelet off his wrist was key to a fair fight and was the best chance they had at bringing him down.

Finn and the muscle-bound Hexer named Adam moved left and right, while Hannah came up the middle. Holding a wooden staff in front of him, Adam took a defensive position, preparing for magical combat. A milky blue film covered Hannah's eyes. She moved forward as if in a focused trance, her jaw set in tight concentration. Pale scars crisscrossed the witch's arms. Her left wrist was ringed with black rubber bracelets and she carried a staff of wood with a thin sharp metal tip. She was pulling the air with her staff, shifting and moving the wind. Dark storm clouds billowed across the sky the color of slate. A ball of electricity sparked in her right hand.

Hannah was the true elemental. *She* was controlling the storm. No wonder Finn was so curious about elemental magic. It wasn't for him, but to help his sister.

Paul stood firm. His gaze shifted between the three Hexers, finally settling on the one in control—Hannah. He raised his right arm, pulled it back, and then thrust it forward. The levitation magic he had stolen from Sabine was literally at his fingertips. Taken completely by surprise with Paul's magical skills, Hannah's face slackened and her entire body flew backwards as she was thrown against her hover bike. A flare of anger crossing his face, Finn rushed the young wizard, wand raised, to defend his sister while the other Hexer turned back to help Hannah.

Vivi wisely decided this was not her fight. She would just get in the way, and more importantly, the Hexers' arrival provided the perfect opportunity and cover for her to find Sabine. She crouched low and followed a perimeter of trees over to the cottage. Paul wasn't keeping her in a rabbit hole, so she had to be inside. She made her way to the side of the house, getting clear of the oncoming battle, and inched to the door. But when she grabbed the handle and tried to push it open, a shock stung her fingers.

"Ouch!" She jerked her hand back. Paul had a security ward in place. Vivi opened up her senses, and she discovered the ward surrounding the entire cottage was a magical protective dome. If she wanted to get inside, she would have to figure out a way to deactivate it. She leaned against the door and ran through a list of security wards. She had studied wards prior to opening The Potion Garden, deciding on the best security magic to protect her store, so she had a decent knowledge of the different types.

The magical ward securing the cottage wasn't advanced. Paul probably didn't suspect anyone would find him out here. Deactivating a ward was kind of like picking a lock, but with magical phrases. Hoping to get lucky, Vivi started with a few basic counter spells, but the ward held firm, not surprisingly. Next, she focused on the ward, sensing the magical phrases, understanding twists and turns of the ward's lock. She uttered another string of deactivation spells using connective dome wards, but none worked. Because the spell zapped her, she assumed he added a warning spell to the dome ward, which was basically like stringing spells together like beads on a necklace. She wiped sweat from her brow and kept experimenting with additional strings.

Suddenly, a burst of magic erupted above Vivi's head as a deflected spell hit the cottage and sparks and bits of debris rained down on her. Vivi dove for cover as the fight around her intensified. A spell spooled from Finn's lips. He pointed his wand at Paul, unleashing a series of stunning pulses, but the young wizard was too quick and constructed a protective bubble to deflect Finn's magic. He grimaced when Finn's spell ricocheted off the surface, dropped his shield, and flicked his fingers, causing a fallen log to fly into Finn's stomach and throw him to the ground with sickening force.

"Finn!" Vivi yelled, but he held up his hand, motioning her to stay back.

Finn's distraction had given the other two Hexers time to regroup. Hannah was back on her feet. She motioned with her fingers as if the wind were an instrument that only she could play. The air shifted violently. Vivi pressed her back against the house and kneeled down to avoid being carried away by the strong current. The gusting wind caused Paul to stumble, but he held his ground. He reached both hands out, sending leaves, stones, and debris shooting toward Hannah in a storm of projectiles. Hannah rotated her staff in widening circles and caught the debris in a gyre of force, thrusting Paul's magic back toward him.

The wind slapped at Vivi's exposed skin. Fat raindrops fell from the sky. Thunder erupted. Between Paul's new kinetic force and Hannah's elemental power, Vivi wasn't sure whose magic would break first. She shivered as a jagged bolt of lightning shot from the blackened mass of clouds that hovered above them and exploded into the ground, creating a huge crater right in front of Paul's feet. His protective bubble collapsed. He cursed and scrambled for cover behind a small grove of bushes.

Within seconds, Paul emerged from his hiding place and stood with his hands outstretched, face twisted in defiance. He slashed his arms back and forth. The effect was immediate. Rain and debris went swirling in all directions. Adam wove a magical net and swooped up as much debris as he could. Hannah and Finn tried to deflect the rest with protective wards and shields, but rocks ricocheted from all directions, hitting them, making dull, thudding sounds.

Vivi's pulse pounded. Getting the ward down was more important than ever. After going through another series of spells, she heard a small popping sound and reached out her hand. Clasping the doorknob, she pushed the door open. Relief flooded over her as she stepped inside.

Paul's tiny cottage was the same one from her vision. The cottage had a high-pitched ceiling with a sleeping loft. The main room contained a chair, sofa, and stone fireplace. There was a small kitchen and a wooden table and chairs. Nothing jumped out at her. The surfaces were clean, practically sterile, lacking all personality.

The door to the basement was off the kitchen. Once opened, it revealed a flight of wooden stairs that led down into the dank cellar. Her pulse quickened. "Illuminus," she said and her ring glowed, lighting her descent.

Vivi carefully navigated the soft rotting boards. At the bottom, she realized that the basement had been transformed into a laboratory. A few dim illuma lights barely lit the room. A stench of sulfur and burnt wood filled her nose. She coughed into her hand and kept going. One work surface was covered in copper cauldrons, glass beakers, and stone pedestals for heating brews. Paul had extensive laboratory equipment and medical devices. Rolls of parchment littered the floor. Stacks of inky pages crowded a desk with ink bottles and quills. He also had the makings of a potion shop, Vivi realized, as she inspected the dozens of ingredients. Unfortunately, he also had jars of blood salt, black ash, and shards of glass and bone locked in a metal cage—all the evidence they needed to lock him away for a very long time.

From the looks of it, the desperate wizard had spent long hours in this lab, developing his magical invention turned weapon. She spun and scanned the room. A thick black drape, almost invisible in the darkness, hung like a shroud, concealing a corner of the room. Her heart pounded, rising in her throat. She pulled the curtain back. Her ring cast a hazy light in the dark corner.

Vivi sunk to her knees when she saw Sabine curled up on the floor, still as a stone. She crawled forward, but stopped up short when she saw a circle of black ash, blood salt, and broken glass that ringed the witch's body. A thick silver collar hung around her blistered neck and a mass of tangled hair covered her face. Her eyes were closed. Her wrists were burned raw. She was trapped in a circle of toxic black magic. A horrible realization washed over Vivi—without a wand, she had no easy way to break the circle. She reached her hand out and felt a pulse of energy encasing the witch. The circle thrummed. It was sealed. Sabine was trapped.

Vivi was so close. She leaned in and called her name, but the witch didn't answer, didn't move. Vivi's voice choked in her throat. She stood and paced the room. The collar was killing her. She couldn't let her die when she was so close to setting her free. The image of Sabine's death haunted her. She had to break the circle. But how?

She hurried over to Paul's workstation. There had to be something she could use. She grabbed a spell book off the shelf and thumbed through the musty pages. Maybe she could find the spell Paul used to cast the circle. Frustrated, she flipped through the pages, but nothing jumped out at her.

Her mind raced. She stared at Paul's collection of herbs and ingredients—potion-making supplies. "Potions aren't weapons!" she yelled in frustration. "Isn't that what you said, Paul? They won't hurt you." It was all she knew, conjurer of the kettle. A potion wouldn't bring down a circle. She racked her brain, but she couldn't think of any potions strong enough. Even the best potions couldn't fight black magic.

But what about the worst potion? Her heart raced as a memory of her academy days flashed through her head. Vivi wasn't blessed with the *persuasion* of potion making. She had to study really hard at the academy, and she often brewed up many disasters in the school laboratory. Her greatest failure was her junior-year final when she tried to make a cherry-flavored love potion that she envisioned would cause a spark of attraction. Unfortunately, something went terribly wrong with the formula, and the potion exploded in her professor's face when he popped the cork, covering him in a bright red, cherry mess and singeing off his eyebrows, beard, and nose hair.

The howls of laughter were deafening. Vivi had been mortified. Her classmates called it the *cherry bomb* for months. But with a few adjustments, she might just take that failed potion recipe and blow a hole in Paul's black magic cage.

She grabbed a copper kettle and dove into the shelf, digging through the supplies. She had never worked so fast in her life. She lit the burner, measured, sifted, and poured the ingredients into the kettle. Luckily, the potion was not a complex recipe, and Paul had all the basic ingredients. All she needed to do was up the ratios and hope it worked. She stirred the mixture as it began to boil. Under normal circumstances, she would let the potion cook for a few hours, but she didn't have time. A few minutes of boiling were all it was going to get. She found a small jar, poured the bright red liquid inside, and shoved a cork in the opening.

A swirl of smoke coiled inside of the bottle. The glass started to heat up immediately, forcing Vivi to hold the bottle with a rag. No time to wait. It was her only chance. All the potion had to do was disrupt the circle, not smash through it completely—kind of like a little cherry firecracker. She didn't want to hurt Sabine, and the potion wasn't strong enough to injure her, just break the magic seal. Honestly, in her condition, a shock might do the witch some good.

Vivi backed up as far as she could and cocked her arm, sending the bottle flying at the circle. The glass shattered and sparks exploded. Red smoke filled the basement. Vivi covered her face and ran into the chaos. The circle was down. The potion had worked.

Vivi dropped to the ground and gently held Sabine's hand. It felt like she was holding a fragile bird in her palm. She was so thin, covered in dirt, her hair hanging in greasy tangles. Her neck was raw and blistered and a thick silver collar rested on her collarbone.

She wasn't moving. A terrible feeling washed over Vivi. "No!" Her voice caught in her throat. "Please. Can you hear me?" Vivi cupped the witch's face in her hands. "Wake up," she begged, and brushed the tangled hair out of her eyes. Refusing to accept Sabine's death, she stroked her cheek and whispered a basic healing spell. *Please, be enough. Wake up.*

The witch's arm flinched. She stirred. "You're alive!" Vivi said. Tears sprang to her eyes. "I'm here. You're safe now."

"Get this off," Sabine mumbled through her dry, cracked lips. She groaned and pulled at the metal collar.

Vivi tried to unhook the metal clasp, but it was sealed shut. She mumbled a few unbinding spells. Within seconds, she slid the bolt into the lock and the collar broke open. Sabine was near collapse. Vivi practically had to carry the frail witch up the stairs from the lab before helping her to the sofa to rest while she checked outside. Vivi knew the fight between Paul and the Hexers wasn't over. Wind and debris lashed the windowpanes and shook the small cottage.

Adam was lying flat on the ground. His leather coat was shredded. Spells flew from his wand and were easily deflected or reversed by Paul. Even Finn, who was pinned down behind his hover bike, was having trouble. His sleeve was ripped completely off, and a bloody gash ran down his arm. Hannah was perched on a tree limb, her face smeared with dirt. Vivi couldn't tell if the young elemental had climbed up into the tree or been blown there.

Paul was overpowering the Hexers with sheer kinetic destruction. Finn threw spell after spell from his wand and Paul deflected each one, using his own magic against him, bouncing spells back in his face. He was barely breaking a sweat and looked mostly unharmed, as if the more he fought, the stronger he grew.

Hannah leapt to the ground and threw her head back and yelled the most complex magical spell Vivi had ever heard. A snapping sensation filled the air. Crackling followed. A string of lightning jumped from one cloud to the next. The energy was building all around them. The hair on Vivi's arm rose.

The magical power Hannah generated intensified. The air was electric. Paul must have felt it, too, because he focused on the elemental.

Her skin was so white it was practically glowing. Her muscles trembled as she pulled more power down from the sky. Electric currents created a jagged net of energy hovering above them. She sliced her hand through the air and lightning struck, shooting from her fingertips, sending thin electric charges directly at Paul, smashing into his protective ward, shattering his defenses, and hurling him backwards. Encouraged by her success, Hannah intensified the magical attacks on Paul. He staggered, taking multiple hits, recovered momentarily, and took two additional bursts before dropping to the ground.

His wounded body lay in a heap. He had stopped throwing up wards, stopped deflecting the spells. What was he doing? His head rose, and he crawled to his feet, a devious leer on his face. He pulled a second bracelet from a pocket inside of his jacket. The silver cuff glowed hot as an ember, loaded with magic. He had the additional siphon on him the whole time. He slipped it onto his wrist and thunder roared. Paul could control the elements. Rain and wind lashed out under his command. His outstretched arms trembled with power. Hannah's eyes went wide.

Paul had taken the hit on purpose and used the cuff to siphon Hannah's power. Somehow he had created a siphon that didn't need to be worn by the witch, but could absorb the magic directly, and now he struck back, shooting a beam of pure electric energy at her in a powerful surge. Throwing up a ward seconds before impact, she screamed and fell to her knees, the impact too great. She absorbed the hit. Her body trembled, and she struggled to regain her footing. Sweat-soaked and breathing heavily, she pulled elemental energy down from the sky, but Vivi sensed the power she pulled down was too great. The force rippled across her skin in a wave of crackling heat.

Body shaking, Hannah threw all she had at Paul, but this time he was ready for her, and he deflected the magic. She took a hit from the recoil, the kickback exploding into her. Red blood spread down her arms as one of her scars opened up. Vivi gasped, realizing the witch's scars had come from using her own magic. Hannah opened her mouth to scream, but this time she just collapsed to the ground. Her body went limp, her eyes closed. A pool of blood formed around her. The stench of smoke filled the air. Vivi's stomach clenched. She couldn't tell if the young witch was alive or dead.

Finn called out to his wounded sister, but she didn't respond. He dove for the satchel attached to his bike and pulled something out. At first Vivi thought it was a medical kit, but then she saw the wooden box—the elemental spheres.

Finn turned a wild gaze on Paul.

"You'll pay for hurting her." Finn clasped the box in his hand.

"Collect up your dead and wounded and go," Paul said. "Think of it as mercy."

Finn's gaze swept over his broken and

battered sister. His brow was creased with dirt and sweat. Rage filled his face. Vivi knew he would never surrender to Paul. Not now, not ever. It wasn't the Hexer's way.

"You're pathetic," Finn taunted Paul. "I'm done fighting a wizard with no magic who has to maim other witches and steal their power to use for himself. You need to be exterminated." Finn held out the box and lifted the lid. The elemental spheres swirled inside of the velvet-lined box.

Paul's face went blank. "Are you insane? You can't use those." For the first time, Vivi saw real fear in him. For a second, she considered letting Finn take him down, sphere or no sphere, but she knew, it was wrong. It would destroy everything.

Finn pulled a dazzling red fireball from the box and set the rest at his feet.

"No!" Paul screamed. He glared at Vivi. "He's mad."

Vivi raced out into the open toward the Hexer. She couldn't let him use the powerful magic. It was volatile even in the most careful hands, and in that moment Finn was not in a careful mindset. Anger rose off him like steam off a boiling cauldron.

"Listen to me, Finn! You can't use the spheres!" Vivi shouted. "They're too dangerous!"

A vengeful shadow was cast across his

face. There was darkness in his eyes she hadn't seen before. He held up the sphere, tossing it up and down in his palm. Finn wasn't listening. Paul saw the look, too, and for a second he appeared as if he might run.

Vivi tried to reason with the Hexer. "You could take out the whole meadow and Willow Realm. Are you prepared to destroy the entire woods with that thing?"

"Powerful magic is going around. Looks like anyone can use it, so who cares if I can't control it? Who cares if other people get hurt? I've got a job to do, and I have to use any means necessary."

"No one should have that much power," Vivi said. Her muscles trembled. Sweat trickled down her back. Her gaze darted between Finn and Paul. They had so much raw power and magic between them, literally at their fingertips. This fight would not end well.

"If you use that thing, this whole forest goes up in flames," Paul said, his eyes wide. Even he realized that his kinetic power was not enough to stop an elemental sphere.

Vivi's whole world was at risk—the woods, the meadow, even Willow Realm would be in the fireball's path. Paul was right. Finn wasn't an elemental; he didn't know how to control the blast of heat and destruction that existed in that tiny ball of fire. That was why the elemental spheres had been outlawed. In the wrong hands, even with the best intentions, too much power was lethal.

Vivi tried again. "Arrest him. Hold him accountable for what he's done. Just not like this," she implored him. "This fight doesn't have to happen. We can call a truce." It was all Vivi could think to do. Both men had to agree to lay down their weapons. The thought of negotiating with a swine like Paul made her sick, but they had to get Sabine out of danger and out of the forest without torching the place. She saw little choice. As long as Paul was wearing the bracelet, he had power to negotiate, and getting close enough to rip the cuff off his skinny wrist was futile, unless she wanted to get crushed or flung into a tree.

Finn grunted. "That's not enough. I want him to surrender or I will toast him like a marshmallow."

"I'm not going to a Hexer cell. I walk away from this." Paul twisted the silver cuff on his wrist. His eyes darted around nervously, searching for a way out.

Vivi knew that Finn would never agree to let him go. His team was down and Paul was the one to blame. He had killed one witch and wounded at least three others. He would be locked up in a Hexer jail cell for a long time. Somehow she had to get Paul to believe he could still get out of this.

"Take the bracelet off," Finn said. "And

then we'll talk."

"You're joking. This cuff is my lifeline." Paul's hand went to the silver band on his wrist. "It stays on. You give the elemental sphere to the Mayhem witch, and I ride out of here on a bike. That's my deal."

"Then there's no deal." Finn smirked, a flicker of finality in his eyes, and Vivi knew she had lost any hope of a truce. He held the swirling red sphere up in the air. "You need to pay. The wizard fries."

Finn threw the elemental ball into the air and the sphere erupted in an arch of fire that danced across the sky. The air went dry and warm. Vivi's skin flushed with heat as if she had just opened an oven and peered inside. There was movement on the ground behind Finn. Suddenly, Hannah stirred to life, leapt to her feet with her wand in hand, and caught the fire, pulling it, directing the flame.

Tendrils of orange fire were spinning at her command, weaving into a fiery net that grew in a widening arch around the clearing. She controlled the power that had been contained in the sphere like a master.

Finn dove at Vivi and dragged her back to the porch out of harm's way. "You didn't think I was that crazy, did you?" He gave her a gruff smile.

"Yes!" Vivi blurted. "Next time give me a heads-up." Her shoulders slumped. It had been a trap. Finn and Hannah had set Paul up. Finn had never intended to use the power. Hannah had not gone down; she had been waiting on the ground, crouched like a lioness, waiting for her prey to relax before she pounced.

Relieved, Vivi wished she had known Finn's intentions with the spheres, but she was just happy that Hannah was all right. And from the look of things, she was more than all right; she was a magical prodigy. She moved the flames toward Paul, bringing the net of glowing strands closer. She surrounded him in a magical web of fire and trapped him inside. He spun in a circle, desperate for a way out, but the magic was tight.

"This is how it feels to be caged, jerk," Hannah said, and the flames jumped higher. Her brow was pinched. Her eyes squinted as she concentrated and anchored the flaming circle to the ground.

Paul cowered, crouching behind the fire that caged him.

After securing Paul, Hannah waved her partners in to arrest their prisoner.

22

MORE HOVER BIKES DESCENDED, AND within minutes the woods were crawling with police. Lance and Juniper approached, along with a team of healers and a transport. Vivi waved them over, filled them in on the situation, and then stayed with Sabine until a healer unit attended to her.

Though weak, the witch was eager to tell her story.

Sabine's *persuasion* of levitation had come on in her late teens and was a complete shock. She had assumed that her *persuasion* would only cause trouble, so she kept it hidden. She worked in Golden Bears Bank as a teller and never dreamed of displaying her power. She and Paul met by chance at a *Spellbinders* party thrown by the swanky Ex Libris bookshop in Stargazer City. Both were fans of the novels and began spending time together.

Sabine had confided in Paul, told him all about her strange and powerful *persuasion*. She had no idea he was hungry for a *persuasion* of his own. She thought he would understand and even sympathize with her strange power, since he lived with a minor *persuasion* all his life, but she was very wrong. Paul was not sympathetic to her new surge in magical power; he was jealous. He cultivated a friendship with her, only to turn on her once his plan was in action, drawing her to his cottage in the woods and holding her in the basement, slowly and painfully siphoning her power from her.

Sabine was taken to the healer's ward, as was Hannah. Both would need time to recover from their interaction with Paul, but had survived the worst of it. After the two witches were safely transported out of the woods, Vivi made her way over to talk with Finn. Additional Hexer teams crowded the area, took Paul into custody, and worked with Lance to process the crime scene.

"You need to trust me more. I'm not totally stupid," Finn said to Vivi.

"I had no idea what you were going to do with those spheres." Vivi felt a pang of guilt. He was right; she hadn't trusted him, not entirely, especially after discovering he got the elemental devices from the Darklander.

"I only found out recently that Hannah was your sister and an elemental. You're a wizard with many secrets."

"You're right about that. I'm protective of my sister. Always have been," he said, shrugging it off and motioning to the cottage. "I'm glad we found your missing witch. Your visions saved her life."

Vivi swelled with pride. "Me too." There was a nagging question she wanted to ask him. "Why was the Hex Division so involved in this case? It had to be more than the spheres."

He sighed and sat on the edge of the porch. Vivi joined him and waited silently until he replied. "I guess you could say it was personal and professional. I was hoping the bracelet Paul had invented would work. I still do. Even though he used them to steal magic, they do have a purpose. I want to help my sister control her power. It's just too much for her sometimes."

"The scars?" Vivi asked. She winced, remembering seeing Hannah's wounds open up when she was pulling down the electrical current from the clouds. Her magic was dangerous, painful, but also truly awe-inspiring. "It has to be hard on her."

"My sister suffers for her *persuasion*. She has so much power, literally, at her fingertips, but the magic is brutal. The elements are cruel, especially to the witches who try to control them." He bowed his head, hands in lap.

Vivi gave him a reassuring pat on his shoulder. "She's very talented, but the magic cutting through her like that must be taking its toll."

"I can't get her to stop using her *persuasion*. It's her life. She can't deny it. The bracelet could help her siphon off some of the power so she doesn't end up killing herself."

"Maybe there's still a way to use them." Vivi thought of Dr. Fowler and Dax and wondered if they could help develop the bracelet to be used safely for witches with too much magic to help them control it. "I'll see what I can do."

One of the other Hexers brought Finn a wooden box and set it next to him on the porch. Vivi recognized it immediately as the same one that held the elemental spheres. She raised an inquisitive eyebrow at him.

"Don't worry. The elemental sphere has been returned to its case and is going into the vault at the Witch Council headquarters. No one is ever going to use them again."

"Good. That's where they belong."

The next couple of days had Vivi running all over Everland. One of her first stops, after making sure everything was going smoothly at The Potion Garden, was to the healer's ward to visit Clarissa and Sabine. Both witches were showing remarkable signs of recovery. Due to her actions in the lab, Miranda was given community service and issued a public apology to Vivi, vindicating her in the press, so Vivi decided not to press additional charges against the witch. To their credit, when the Mender twins found out what was *really* going on with the bracelet, they personally paid the witches a visit, providing their healing expertise. In time, the witches would make a full recovery. Hannah's wounds were also healing, but her scars would remain. Both she and Sabine were recovering in rooms next to each other and had struck up a friendship based on their unusual *persuasions* and seemed to be a good support system for each other.

Vivi's next stop was Mender Corp, and this time she even had an appointment. Using her connections with both Finn and Lance, Vivi took a selection of Paul's magical bracelets to Dr. Fowler's lab. The Hex Division confiscated the ones the company was using to sell *persuasions*, since the magic had been developed from criminal practices, but it was agreed upon with the Healers' Guild's approval that Dr. Fowler would be allowed to research the cuff and see if he could design a model to help witches like Hannah control their power.

Vivi had high hopes and so did the doctor. Always the entrepreneur, Dax was more than agreeable, since he negotiated the rights to sell the product if Dr. Fowler was successful, providing a portion of the profits went to charities to help witches to use magic safely.

Within a few weeks, life returned to normal in the little village of Willow Realm. After putting in a busy day at her shop, Vivi carried a take-out container from Nocturnes up to her apartment. The leaves had all fallen from the trees as old man winter stirred from his sleep, ready to send them a wintery blast. She put her food on a plate and curled up on the sofa, too tired to sit at the table like a civilized witch.

Rumor cawed from his perch. He ruffled his feathers, shifted on his claws. Her familiar was restless. She knew the feeling.

"Sorry, guy. You can fend for yourself. This dinner is all mine."

There was something scratching at the window, tapping on the glass. Vivi set her plate on the coffee table. The apartment was too high up for an average prowler to break in. Senses alert, Vivi lunged at the window, but was too late as the latch gave way and the window heaved open. The Darklander's leathery familiar screeched. Its huge wings were too big to gracefully make it through the opening, but its claws dug into the wood frame.

The hideous beast screeched and hissed. She backtracked toward the shelf where she kept some emergency potions and grabbed a trusty silver bottle while Rumor dive-bombed the relentless creature, cawing madly.

Vivi uncorked the bottle. A pale vapor rose from the rim. She blew the smoke toward the creature and whispered a spell. The potion was a new knockout enchantment she was working on and was part sleeping potion and part freezing spell. After the past few weeks, she had a feeling the new potion would come in handy. The smoky vapor rolled over the creature's rubbery skin like a fog and within seconds a loud thud came from the back garden. The familiar was gone. Vivi peered tentatively out the window. The beast was out cold, snoozing in the herb garden.

"Keep an eye on him, will you, Rumor?" Her valiant raven gave a caw and settled on a tree branch above the familiar.

"Is this how you always greet your guests?" The deep voice came from behind her, causing her to jump. Vivi had heard the voice before when she'd been scrying.

The Darklander stood in her living room.

"Only when they try to climb uninvited into my window." Grabbing a sweater off a chair, Vivi tried to remain nonchalant, even though fear pulsed through every muscle in her body. His scarred face was impossible to ignore.

With his magic, he could use a glamor to hide the red fleshy ridges and puckered skin that covered one side, but he wore his scars proudly along with a well-cut suit. He seemed taller in person and his chest broader, making her feel very small standing next to him.

An intimidating smirk curled up his lip. "That's why I used the door."

"Yet I didn't hear a knock." She raised a brow and sat on the arm of an overstuffed chair. Her gaze drifted to the stairs, but there was no way she'd make it out safely if she tried to run.

"I like surprises." He noticed her plate and took a seat opposite her. "So sorry to interrupt your dinner."

"Why are you here?" Hopefully, he was not seeking a little payback.

"To pay you a visit. Turnabout is fair play. I have decided that you and I shall form a friendship, call it a mutual alliance."

Alliance? Was he serious? That was the last thing Vivi wanted. She couldn't imagine what he was up to. It must have shown on her face, because the Darklander chuckled. "Why?" she asked. Her mouth was dry.

"Because you're on the verge of owning your power. You possess a strong *persuasion* and an even stronger presence." He leaned back in his chair, and the scent of amber wafted off of him.

"My *persuasion* is none of your business."
She crossed her arms in front of her.

He ignored the comment and continued,
"You haven't shown signs of the madness
caused by your *persuasion* that so many
others of your kind have succumbed to. Have
you ever wondered why you were able to
control your magic for so long?"

She narrowed her eyes. "I denied it."

"Yes, and denial is a way of controlling it.
You kept it in check for over a decade. A sign
of true power."

She sensed his real motives. "I'm not about
to let you or anyone else control me or take
my power. I've had enough of witches trying
to take what isn't theirs. Got it?"

His gaze was unnerving. "I'm not so petty
and crass that I would stoop to such levels. I
make deals. I'm a businessman."

"I'm not doing business with a wizard of the
black arts." She steadied her voice. She didn't
want to argue with him; she just wanted him
to leave her in peace.

"Oh, don't be so sure." He stood.

"No, I'm sure. Very sure."

Before she could stop him, he darted up
and took her hand in his. She couldn't move.
Not a muscle. Talk about a freezing spell.
All she could do was stare face to face with
the most feared wizard in Everland, who had
suddenly taken a liking to her.

"You have no idea how powerful you and your sisters are. The Mayhems are legendary, but more importantly, they will play a role in what is to come." His voice was liquid warmth rolling over her.

"What's coming?" Vivi whispered.

"Everland is changing. The barrier between worlds is weakening."

"That's impossible." Vivi remembered his minions with their horns and ancient-looking tattoos. The Darklander wanted the old ways to return. He hated living in a world solely of witches, but the old ways were dangerous. Witches were safe now in Everland. Never again would they live among other supernatural beings. Never.

"You will be an oracle. You will see our future, and when you do, I want you to know that I will be here. I will be ready to assist you." He put a Y-shaped piece of wood in her hand. "This is where we will meet."

"The tree where the victim was found." Her stomach lurched.

"You saw the tree because I wanted you to see it. And you were right. Nothing happens in my woods without my knowing about it." His gaze was intense, all- encompassing.

"You knew what Paul was doing and yet you stood by and did nothing." He repulsed her. What kind of wizard sat back and watched such misery? The Darklander. That was why he'd been banished to the Dire Woods in the first place, because he let bad things happen, nurtured them, encouraged a dark vine to grow in their world.

"I simply stayed out of the way and let law enforcement do its job," he reasoned.

"And what about Hexer Finn and the elemental spheres? Where did you get them?" she countered, not letting him slip through the knotted conversation.

"Like I said, I'm a businessman. I deal in magical artifacts. Remember that. Know that you can always contact me for anything you might need."

Vivi inwardly cringed. She would never need his help. Ever. And even if she did, she would never ask. She had her sisters, her neighbors, Pepper, the sheriff, and even the Hex Division. She would go to all of them before she ever went to the Darklander. He was trying to flatter her with the oracle remark. Oracles were long gone from the witching world. They went the way of old magic and hadn't been seen for centuries.

"Just get out." Vivi was too tired to play games, and she didn't want to fight with him tonight. "My dinner's getting cold."

"As you wish," he said. "I'll go pick up my familiar from your garden."

Vivi dropped to her knees on the carpet. The Darklander was gone as quickly as he had come, leaving her alone. He had easily gotten through her wards. She had been foolish to spy on him. No one does so and gets away with it, and now she had drawn his attention. She shuddered. That was the last thing she needed.

VIVI STOOD IN THE FRONT of her shop and gazed out the window, sipping a hot cup of pumpkin latte. Lance Gardener gave her a wave as he walked by on his daily morning trek to Nocturnes. She definitely planned on seeing more of him in the coming months. The time for daydreaming about the handsome sheriff was over. Her cheeks warmed, and it wasn't from the coffee. A smile spread across her face.

Honora, Clover, Vivi, and Pepper were hanging out in The Potion Garden having a full-scale brewing party. Two cauldrons were bubbling on the stove, and the counter was crowded with crushed herbs and glass bottles filled with new creations. Plus, they'd brewed up a dozen potions to replace the stock Paul had destroyed.

"I'm going to make a climbing potion," Vivi said, strolling back to see what her sisters were up to. "I want to have a way to get out of holes or wells or deep ditches." She set down her drink and pointed at her sisters with a wooden spoon. "Being in that rabbit hole was scary."

"As long as it's not a flying potion," Honora said. "I've had enough of amateurs taking to the air. I don't care what Dax says about *persuasions*, not all of them should be used by everyone."

"Flying potions don't work," Pepper said. "I've tried and tried. All I ever ended up doing was hovering a few feet off the ground and then toppling over. I could never get it right. I guess some magic is just too hard to master with a spell or a potion." She lined up a row of potion bottles she was unpacking from a crate. Vivi had discovered a new artisan glassblower she was trying out so she could expand on the idea for wearable potion vials.

"I need a creativity potion," Clover said, cupping her chin in her hand as she leaned her elbow on the counter. "The last *Spellbinder* novel put me into a real slump."

Pepper's eyes went wide. "You aren't struggling with the next novel, are you? You can't end the series. I'll do anything to help you." She raced over to the bookshelf and started sifting through her collection of spell books. "I'll brew you up a potion myself. If a creative spark is what you need, then that's what you'll have."

The three sisters cackled warmly as they watched Pepper flipping madly through the pages, head bent over her arsenal of books, searching for a spell. "I'll take all the creative magical help I can get," Clover said. "I should have thought of this a long time ago."

"You don't need a potion to bring on the magic." Honora ruffled Clover's hair as she stood in the doorway, keeping an eye on the front for any customers. But the joyous expression on her face quickly soured when a bell jingled and Scarlet Card pushed open the front door with her hip, bringing a big gust of autumn air and a trail of leaves into the store with her. At the sound of the bell, Vivi came out of the back room.

Scarlet's long hair was pinned up under a knit cap, and she wore a red velvet top and black leather pants. One of the girls who Vivi had seen at Scarlet's shop was with her, and they both sauntered through the aisles admiring the potions.

Joining her sister in the front of the store, Honora made a low sound somewhere between a growl and a grunt into Vivi's ear. Vivi gave Honora a nudge as she made her way from behind the counter. "Hey, Scarlet," she said. "Come to pick out a potion? I still owe you for helping me with my *persuasion*."

"Yep, thought I'd see if you had anything new." Scarlet perused the aisles, picking up potion bottles and reading the spell descriptions. "But we're not done working on your *persuasion*, remember?"

"I remember, and I promise to attend meetings." Vivi made a cross sign over her heart. She had promised her sisters and herself that she would continue to develop her *persuasion*, and Scarlet had invited her to a divination club's monthly meeting and support group. She would need all the help she could get now that she was committed to becoming a registered seer.

Vivi could feel Honora staring holes into her back. Her sister balanced a big copper bowl on her hip as she stirred a freshly brewed concoction.

"Anything special you have in mind?" Vivi asked. She really wanted to give Scarlet something worthy of all the time the witch had put into helping her with her *persuasion*.

"Well, the girls and I have been working a lot of long hours and late nights. The harvest time and All Hallows' Eve are the busiest time of year for us, so we're looking for something to perk us up during late midnight sessions."

"Hmm." Vivi twisted up her mouth in concentration. "How about a peppermint 'snap out of it' potion? It is a quick jolt to change your state of mind. I use it when I'm in a bad mood, but it would work well if you're sleepy." Vivi handed Scarlet a round bottle that swirled with red liquid. "I also have a clear-headedness potion. It's good for those groggy days." Vivi climbed a wooden stepladder to retrieve a bottle.

"How about a 'mind your own business' potion or a 'you aren't welcome here' potion? Do you have one of those?" Honora asked snarkily, whipping the spoon around the bowl so hard Vivi thought she was going to spill half the mixture on the floor. Her sister held tightly to her grudges, but Vivi was prepared. She had anticipated the inevitable run-in between Honora and Scarlet, and she and Pepper had done a little preventive potion making on their own.

The fight between the two witches had gone on for too long. Vivi had had enough. Good friends were too hard to come by, and everyone deserved at least one second chance. Not even Dax was worth this kind of tension, especially since neither one of them was dating him anymore. Honora had come to the same rapid conclusion she had the last time she and Dax dated—his top priority was work and always would be. Their recent reunion had ended with a cordial but frosty goodbye.

Vivi gave her sister an annoyed glance. "Stop insulting the customers."

Scarlet smiled and put her arm around Vivi. "It's nice to see that at least one of you is a mature professional."

"Actually, I have a special gift for the two of you," Vivi said.

Honora and Scarlet both scoffed in unison. Some things never changed. Vivi nodded to Pepper, who with a big grin pulled a wooden box from behind the counter and handed it to her boss.

"Why do I get the feeling we aren't going to like what is in that box?" Honora asked, resting her bowl on the counter and peering over Vivi's shoulder.

"Just wait and see. You might like it." Vivi raised the lid, revealing a sparkling fuchsia potion bottle with a silver stopper.

"Gorgeous," Scarlet said with an appreciative grin. "You've got this packaging and marketing thing down."

"I hate to tell you this, Vivi, but there's only one bottle." Honora shrugged. "I don't need a present as much as she does, so you can let her have it."

Scarlet arched her brow, looking like a villainess out of a fairy tale. "No way. I'm not going to take it if she doesn't."

"Both of you are going to take it. The potion is meant to be shared." Vivi grinned.

"A shared potion? Is that new?" Honora tentatively reached into the box, lifted the bottle from its velvet bed, and examined the contents. Held up to the light, the potion sparkled, sending a cascade of glittering reflections across the room.

"Actually, the potion is brand new. Pepper and I collaborated on it. We wanted to create something special to remind witches of their past and the people who mattered to them."

"We call it 'the good old days.' The potion triggers the memories of the witches who drink from the bottle. It lets them relive special moments, bringing back the good feelings they once had." Pepper smiled. "That was the hard part. We didn't want to dredge up the bad stuff, just the happy memories."

"You two could really use it." Vivi closed the box. "Time to mend some fences. Stop fighting and give it a try."

Honora shook her head and sighed. "It's a nice try. I get where you're coming from, but it's not going to happen. It's too late."

"I knew we should have gone with the 'stubborn old goat' potion," Vivi said. "It makes the drinker turn into a hairy-chinned, tin-can-munching goat."

"You're kidding, right?" Pepper asked.

"Come on. Try it." Why did her sister have to be so stubborn? "You know potions don't last forever. It's just a little nudge in the right direction. Who knows? It might not even work."

Clover popped her head in from the back room. "I'll try that potion. It sounds great."

But it was too late. In a flash, Scarlet reached over and grabbed the bottle right out of Honora's hand, popped the silver stopper, and took a swig. "I'm not scared or stubborn." She held the bottle out to Honora. "And I'm not ashamed to admit that I miss you." Her eyes welled with tears, but she quickly got her bearings and wiped them away.

Honora paused for a few seconds, seeming to consider her options, until taking the bottle from Scarlet and gulping down some potion.

Within a few minutes the mortal enemies were giggling like two Haven Academy freshmen. They were smiling, talking, and sharing stories. Vivi even caught them hugging and cackling at each other's jokes.

"Job well done," Clover said to Vivi and Pepper as they continued to brew up more batches of potions.

"Just like old times," Vivi said. "There will always be darkness in the world. We were born knowing there would be mayhem, but the one thing I also know is I've always got my sisters, and that's what matters."

"To sisters," Clover said, holding up her cup.

"To the Mayhem sisters," Pepper said.

"To all our witchy sisters," Vivi said, and then spoke the Everland creed, "A coven of one."

AFTERWORD

THANK YOU FOR PURCHASING THIS novel. I really appreciate it. If you enjoyed it, please leave a review. Also, if you're interested, check out my facebook page for the latest news on the Mayhem sisters.

ACKNOWLEDGEMENTS

SPECIAL THANKS TO FRIEND AND editor extraordinaire Elizabeth Buck for all her help. I couldn't have done this without her. And thanks to Claudette Cruz for her editing services.

ABOUT THE AUTHOR

SINCE SHE WAS A LITTLE girl, Lauren Quick has been a believer in the unbelievable. She loves all things fantasy from fables and fairy tales to high fantasy and urban paranormal and everything in between, especially if witches are involved. "The more magic, the better" is her motto, and if a mystery is involved, then she's all in. She lives in Maryland with her familiar cat that has so far shown no magical tendencies, but there's always hope.

ALSO BY THIS AUTHOR

THE MAYHEM SISTERS
FLY BY MIDNIGHT, BOOK 2

Made in the USA
Lexington, KY
09 May 2014